# The

# Moments

by

# NICOLE PYLAND

# The Moments

Bailey Sayers has a decision to make. That decision will impact her entire life. If she says something, she risks embarrassment and her heart. If she doesn't say something, she may never know if Jenna Cabot feels the same way about her.

In Path I, Bailey risks it all and asks Jenna out on a date on their high school graduation day.

In Path II, Bailey does not ask Jenna out on a date on their high school graduation day.

What follows in both paths is Bailey and Jenna's story. It's the most important moments that make up their lives together and apart. It's the story of how they were always drawn together and always would be. It's the ups and the downs, the perfect moments and the difficult ones. It's the tears and the laughter. And it's the drive to make forever possible with the love of your life no matter the circumstances.

---

To contact the author or for any additional information, visit: **https://nicolepyland.com**

# BY THE AUTHOR

## Stand-alone books:

- The Fire
- The Moments
- The Disappeared
- Reality Check
- Love Forged

## Chicago Series:

- Introduction – Fresh Start
- Book #1 – The Best Lines
- Book #2 – Just Tell Her
- Book #3 – Love Walked into The Lantern
- Series Finale – What Happened After

## San Francisco Series:

- Book #1 – Checking the Right Box
- Book #2 – Macon's Heart
- Book #3 – This Above All
- Series Finale – What Happened After

## Tahoe Series:

- Book #1 – Keep Tahoe Blue
- Book #2 – Time of Day
- Book #3 – The Perfect View
- Book #4 – Begin Again
- Series Finale – What Happened After

## Celebrities Series:

- Book #1 – No After You
- Book #2 – All the Love Songs
- Book #3 – Midnight Tradition
- Book #4 – The Path Forward
- Series Finale – What Happened After

## Sports Series:

- Book #1 – Always More
- Book #2 – A Shot at Gold
- Book #3 – The Unexpected Dream
- Book #4 – Finding a Keeper

# CONTENTS

# PROLOGUE

If your life could be defined by one moment, what would it be? Would it be that perfect job offer you took that started your career off right? Would it be that blind date you reluctantly agreed to where you met the love of your life? Maybe that moment was much earlier in your life. Maybe it happened when you were a young child and you walked in on your parents in a screaming match. Maybe that was the first time you realized they weren't superheroes or people who loved one another unconditionally. Maybe that moment made you shy away from marriage later on in your life. Maybe it was something smaller than all those things. Maybe the one moment that changed your life was that field trip you went on to a museum in seventh grade where you felt right at home. Maybe that simple field trip led you to a career in paleontology or art history.

Moments add up. Sometimes, we live in them. We stop to make a mental note that this is something we'll want to remember forever. Maybe it's as we're standing at the top of a mountain we just climbed. Maybe we bring that cool, fresh air into our lungs and smile as we think about what we've just accomplished. Maybe it's the moment you land on home plate after hitting your first home run. Maybe it's the moment you become a parent for the first time and you hold the baby in your arms.

Sometimes, we live in the moments, but most of the time – we don't. We let them go. We don't think about how one moment could change the trajectory of our entire lives. We don't think about how if we said yes or no to something, how it could move us down one path instead of another.

There are so many moments in our lives. There went one just now. You just lived a moment. Did you stop to think about what happens next? Have you ever wondered if you had one moment in your life back to change, what that moment might be? Would you really change it? Would you be too scared to take that chance? What if you could know how it would all work out ahead of time? Would you take the chance then? If that were possible, would any of us?

# PATH I: SHE ASKED HER

# CHAPTER 1: IT HAPPENED ON GRADUATION DAY

It was strange to Bailey how she'd been waiting for this moment for so long and yet, now that she was in it, living it, she wasn't sure she was ready for it to be over. The gown was red and uncomfortable. What did they make graduation gowns out of anyway? Did they search for the scratchiest material on the planet? Who decided on the damn cardboard hats that make everyone look ridiculous? Why were the hats and tassels necessary to indicate that someone has graduated high school?

Those were the ridiculous questions Bailey thought about as she sat in a white wooden chair and listened to the principal of her school drone on and on about potential, opportunities, and how they'd all spread their wings and fly. The weather was perfect, save the high humidity, which was causing Bailey's overly processed hair to frizz. Her mother had insisted she help Bailey that morning even though Bailey had planned to wear her hair down. Her mother wanted it down, of course, but she wanted it styled and with product so that it fell just the right way. She had forced Bailey to try on that damn cardboard hat at least ten times while moving her hair this way and that. That part about graduating and moving away from home Bailey would not miss.

It was clear to her she wasn't exactly what her mother had hoped for in her only daughter. Bailey wasn't the top student. She wasn't the class president or even a treasurer. Hell, she wasn't even an athlete. She was average. Maybe a little more than average, but not by much. She wasn't sure if others were asked, if they'd say she was pretty or hot. She didn't feel like she was those things, but she didn't feel like she was exactly an ogre, either. She did know though that she was no Jenna Cabot.

God, Jenna Cabot. Bailey turned her head to the side and leaned forward in her seat to take in Jenna. She had done that every five minutes or so since she'd first spotted Jenna in the long line of graduates about to embark on that new phase in their lives. Jenna wasn't perfect – Bailey understood that objectively – but, sometimes, when Jenna was next to her, Bailey thought Jenna might be the closest person to perfect she had ever met. She hadn't met many people, but even if she had, Jenna would still be high on that list.

Jenna Cabot wasn't someone Bailey likely would have spent any time with over the years. They had gone to the same grade school but had been in different classes until sixth grade. By then, they'd each had their own group of friends and only spoke when working on group projects or shared homework assignments. When high school began, though, everyone was assigned lockers. The freshmen had their own freshman hallway with bright red lockers lining both walls. Everyone had assumed assignments would be alphabetical, but when Bailey Sayers arrived that morning, stared down at the piece of paper that indicated the combination to the school-provided lock, and turned the lock to the first number, she smelled the most intoxicating scent she had ever smelled before. She had lifted her head then, forgetting the lock in her hand, and realized that Jenna Cabot was going through the same motions at the locker right next to her own.

"Hey, Bailey," Jenna had greeted.

"Hi," Bailey had replied as she continued to take in the aroma of something fruity she couldn't identify.

"Excited for the school year?"

"Sure," Bailey had agreed because Jenna was smiling at her and she didn't know what to do.

"What do you have first period?" Jenna had asked.

"What?"

Jenna had laughed then and replied, "Your first-period class?"

"Oh, algebra."

"That sucks, starting your day off with math. Who wants that?" Jenna had unlocked her locker then.

"Right," Bailey had answered as she returned her attention to her own lock.

Bailey actually liked math alright. She didn't think she would pursue a career in anything math-related, but she didn't mind algebra. She had done well in their eighth-grade pre-algebra class, and she would probably do okay in algebra.

"I suck at math," Jenna had continued.

Bailey had zoned out there for a minute. Jenna was still talking to her. She should pay attention probably.

"Yeah?" Bailey had asked as she pulled open the locker door. "I'm not bad at it, actually."

"I have algebra for third period. Maybe you could help me sometime?" Jenna had suggested as she began loading books, notebooks, and other supplies into her locker. "How cool is it that we have lockers now?" she had added enthusiastically.

"I'll help you," Bailey had said. "Whenever. I mean, if you need it."

'Smooth, Sayers. Real smooth', Bailey had thought as she dumped her items unceremoniously into her locker. She looked over and noticed Jenna was placing everything on the top shelf first. It looked so organized. Then, she pulled out a mirror that stuck to the side of the door. Bailey hadn't bought a locker mirror. Should she have bought a locker mirror? I mean, this was high school. That was a necessity now, right?

"Cool." Jenna had smiled at her again. "I'm pretty good with history, if you ever need help there."

"Yeah, I hate history," Bailey had lied. She had no real opinion on history. "I have that sixth period."

"Me too," Jenna had said. "Let's sit next to each other."

"Okay," Bailey had agreed instantly.

That had been one of those *moments*. It had formed the next four years of Bailey's life. It was one of the first moments she really considered she might be different than most girls. When she watched Jenna finish up at her locker, Bailey took in Jenna's long, dark hair that the girl had pulled back into a ponytail and braided for the first day of school. Her eyes were between brown and green. Bailey honestly didn't know what to call that exact color. She called it *beautiful* in her mind, and that was what clued her in. Jenna wasn't just pretty, she was *beautiful*. Later, Bailey would call her *hot* to herself when Jenna wore a short skirt to school. Jenna was *gorgeous* when she was elected homecoming queen their junior year, and she was *sexy* when she showed up to a party Bailey happened to go to, wearing a tank top and tight jeans, dancing with a few of her friends.

Yeah, Bailey knew back then – on the first day of school – she wasn't like most girls. As she stared at Jenna Cabot, she realized this might be the last time she ever saw her longtime crush. Their lockers had been next to one another for four years. Jenna had helped Bailey with history, while Bailey had helped Jenna with her various math classes. They had sat next to one another in at least two classes every year, though they had never been best friends. Jenna had her own group of people she hung out with outside of class. Bailey had her best friend, and that was enough for her. She had wished a million times that she could tell Jenna how she felt about her, but Jenna was off limits. She had gotten a boyfriend halfway through freshman year, and they had remained together until the second quarter of sophomore year, but Jenna wasn't single long. She had started dating a junior on the lacrosse team during Christmas break. They had been together until senior year. By the time they'd broken up, though, Jenna had decided to remain single until she left for college. She would be going away for school. *'There is no point in starting something new,'* she had told Bailey. Bailey had agreed because she hated having to watch Jenna date boys. Jenna would get a good-morning kiss from her boyfriends, or even a see-you-later kiss or a hug between classes, and they would walk around the halls holding hands – all of it hurt Bailey. Each time she saw Jenna with someone, it was like a piece of her heart chipped off and away.

Jenna would be going to school in Michigan while Bailey would be staying somewhat local by comparison and going to a university about two hours from home. Bailey also knew Jenna was going to South America for the summer. She had applied for and had been accepted into a program that worked with Habitat for Humanity. She was going to spend time building a school for an impoverished village. When Jenna had told her about that, Bailey fell a little more in love with her. She also cried later that night because she knew then that she would never see Jenna again. She just had this feeling that once they graduated, it would be over. She'd never again stand next to Jenna at their lockers, talking about homework or the upcoming dance. Jenna would never again try to help Bailey find a date by pointing at the guys that walked past them down the hall and asking if Bailey liked them. Bailey didn't like any boys like that. She'd also not liked any other girls like that, though. For four years, her heart had belonged to Jenna Cabot. Now, she would have to find a way to move on and, maybe one day, she would be able to give it to someone else.

The principal wrapped his speech. The valedictorian and salutatorian followed in quick succession. This whole time, Bailey watched Jenna. Bailey always watched Jenna.

She watched her in class when Jenna wasn't looking. She watched her hair fall down over her face when they were leaning over their textbooks, sitting cross-legged in the hallway before classes. She loved watching Jenna. It was probably her favorite hobby in the world, and today would be the last day she'd get to watch Jenna like this.

Bailey lined up when it was time. She received her diploma and shook hands with the various members of the faculty on the stage as required. That was a *moment.* She should remember that moment more than any other today. She turned toward the camera aimed at center stage, held the diploma in one hand and the principal's hand in the other, and smiled as the flash engulfed her vision. When it cleared, her eyes went to Jenna again. Jenna was already seated. She smiled up at Bailey with that thousand-watt smile she had. Bailey knew then that she had to tell her.

After the ceremony, Bailey took a million pictures with her parents. Sometimes, it really sucked being an only child; she was the focal point of their lives. She loved her parents, but she was so over this whole graduation thing. After the final shot of her with her grandparents – both in and out of the graduation gown – Bailey had to go join the line of fellow graduates to return the rented property. The cardboard hats were theirs to keep, but the gowns had to be returned. She handed over her gown to a woman who checked her name off a list, and turned just in time to see Jenna wrapping up her own family photo shoot.

Did it get hotter outside? It felt like it got hotter outside. Bailey was wearing a light-blue sundress that her mother had insisted upon. She always felt awkward in dresses, like everyone knew she didn't belong in one. Luckily, she had convinced her mother she'd fall flat on her face on that stage if she wore heels. Her mother had acquiesced and allowed ballet flats. Jenna was wearing a strapless dress. It was a deep plum. She had matching nail polish, and her dark hair was down, framing her face perfectly. Her eyes stood out even from twenty feet away due to the color of that dress. Bailey waited until Jenna was on her way to meet a group of her friends. They'd already ditched their parents and were waiting over in the parking lot by their cars.

Bailey knew there was sweat forming on her forehead, under her arms, and in other uncomfortable places as well. She had managed to steal her mother's bottle of water from the ceremony and chugged it down before tossing it in the trash can on the lawn. She wished it was something stronger than water, but she couldn't exactly take a shot while the principal and vice-principal were stacking chairs right behind her.

"Hey, Jenna," she half-yelled across the lawn while walking briskly to meet her before Jenna could join her friends.

"Hey, Bail." Jenna had taken to that expression by the second week of freshman year. It was their thing. Only Jenna could call her Bail, and only Jenna could use those two words together. "You do all the pics with the fam?" she asked, abbreviating the words as was her custom.

"I did. They're going home. I'm going to meet them there."

"Cool. Will you be at my open house tomorrow?"

"That's the plan," Bailey replied as she stood a foot in front of her.

"Awesome. I guess I'll see you then," Jenna said.

"Hey, Jen?"

"Yeah?" Jenna asked just as she was about to walk off.

"When do you leave for your trip?"

"Tuesday."

"And today is Saturday," Bailey said more to herself.

"You earned that diploma, huh, Bail," Jenna joked with her.

"Are you doing anything tomorrow?"

"Um, my open house. I just asked if you were coming," Jenna replied, looking a bit confused.

"Right. I mean after that. Are you doing anything after that? Or Monday?"

"I don't think so. Why?"

"Do you want to maybe go out?" Bailey asked as the lump in her throat grew three sizes.

"You want to hang out? Sure. We can do that." Jenna stared at her quizzically. "Monday would be better. It's not for sure, but Brandon, Jarrod, Liz, and I might go to a movie. Do you want to come if we do?"

Bailey let out a deep breath, stood her ground, and met Jenna's gaze. God, those eyes were beautiful, and she still hadn't figured out their actual color.

"No, I don't want to do that. I was thinking it would be just you and me."

"Oh, okay," Jenna replied. "You can come over to my house tomorrow night. I'll probably just be cleaning up from the party. We can go to my room and watch TV or something."

"I'm asking you out, Jenna." Bailey gulped. "I'm asking you out on a date. I would like to pick you up at your house and take you somewhere."

"A date?" Jenna's eyes grew big. "Like, *a* date?"

"Yes, like a date." Bailey laughed because Jenna was adorable sometimes.

"Like, you want to date me? Like, go on a date with me?"

"Yes."

"But I'm a–"

"Girl, yes."

"And you're a girl," Jenna stated the obvious.

"Yes."

"Bail, I'm not... I mean, I date boys." She paused. "Do you date girls? Is that why you never went to the dances with any of the guys I tried to hook you up with?"

"I've never dated anyone, Jen; boys or girls. But I want to date you. I mean, I'd like to go on *a* date with you."

"Oh, Bail, I'm not–"

"No, I get it. It's cool. Just forget I said anything."

"Bailey, I don't want to forget about it. Should we talk about this, though?" Jenna asked her with pity in her tone.

"No, it's totally cool. We're all good." Bailey waved her off. "I'm good. You're good. We're good."

"You said that twice," Jenna pointed out. "Let me go tell my friends to go on without me, and we'll talk at the bleachers or something."

"No, Jen. I have to go anyway. My mom needs me home," Bailey lied. "I'll just see you around." She paused. "Or I guess I won't. You'll be gone."

"Not until Tuesday. Bail, if–"

"I should go," Bailey interrupted her. "Have fun on your trip. Be safe and everything."

"I will. Thanks," Jenna replied. "Have a good summer, Bail."

"Right," Bailey replied, turned around, and walked off, wondering how she'd ever have a good summer now.

# CHAPTER 2: MESSAGES

What Bailey did with her time over the next few weeks, she couldn't remember. She was sure she talked to her future campus roommate on the phone a few times to set things up for their freshman year, and she was pretty certain her mother bothered her to pick out new clothes, new bedding for the tiny twin she'd be sleeping in, and to pick out her first semester classes online. Bailey did a few of those things, skipped some others, and got a part-time job working at a store in the mall to pass the time. She also wanted to save up money for when she'd be on her own. She had worked every school break and every summer since she'd been able to. She didn't have much saved up, but it would be enough to get her through the school year with her parents helping out.

It was three weeks after graduation when Bailey 'woke up' for the first time since the moment she had so stupidly asked Jenna Cabot out. What the hell had she been thinking? They'd been friends, but not good friends. They rarely spent time outside of school together. What had gotten into Bailey that day that made her think Jenna would be interested in dating her; dating any girl for that matter? It must have been that graduation day nostalgia that made mere acquaintances hug one another and say they'll talk soon when they won't see one another again.

But three weeks after that mistake, Bailey was lying on her bed, scrolling through her fairly bare Facebook feed on her phone, when her email notification chimed. Thinking it was her future roommate, emailing her some of the details they'd discussed sharing, she moved to the app to click it open. What she saw made her squint her eyes closed for a second because she had to be going crazy. Jenna was somewhere in South America, building a school for poor kids. She wouldn't be emailing her. Bailey read the email silently to herself.

To: baileys@brownehigh.net
From: jennac@brownehigh.net
Subject: Hi

*Hey, Bail,*

*Listen, I wanted to say I'm sorry for how I handled things at graduation. I didn't know what to say, I guess. I still don't exactly know what to say. I guess I wanted you to know that I don't care. It doesn't bother me. I don't know if that's the right thing to say, either. God, I'm bad at this. I hope I'm making you laugh right now because I am rambling on like an idiot. I think you're used to that from me, though. Anyway, I don't have my phone here, and we only get email access every few weeks since we have to drive into the city to get it. I hope you get this. This whole place is basically a shack, so maybe it won't even send. Maybe, when I get back, we can hang out and talk. I don't leave until mid-August. I don't know when you're leaving for school or even if you want to see me, but if you do, just let me know. See you soon, hopefully.*

*Jen*

Bailey read and reread the email at least ten times on her phone before opening her laptop and rereading it on their old, school email server another ten times. She realized then that she only had Jenna's high school email address, and Jenna only had her Browne High School email address. Bailey only had Jenna's school email since she hadn't had the need for any other. She wrote and rewrote her response before, just over three hours later, she sent it.

She stared at her computer then as if Jenna would instantly reply. Unfortunately, she'd have to wait for at least a few weeks, according to Jenna's email. So, she turned on the TV and tried to distract herself with terrible reality television. She knew it wouldn't go anywhere. Jenna told her she was straight, and Bailey understood that. But while she had her best friend, Samantha, she didn't have any other friends. She wasn't sure if, now that she'd told Jenna about how she felt in a roundabout way, they'd be able to get back any of what they used to have. She would sure try, though.

To: baileys@brownehigh.net
From: jennac@brownehigh.net
Re: Hi

*Hey, Bail,*

*I'm sorry it takes so long for me to reply. I kind of hate being so detached from everything right when everyone is getting ready to go off to school. I like what I'm doing here. It's exciting to be helping people like this. The kids are helping us build their school. Think about that. They have to build their own school. Isn't that crazy? Our school is huge and has been there for a million years. This place is three rooms. You probably don't care about that, but I'm rambling again. They told us we can come into the city by bus every Sunday now. So, I'll get your reply then and respond right away. It's kind of weird being here on my own. None of my friends came. I guess I didn't think about that when I signed up. It's good practice for the fall, I guess. None of them are going to school with me either. So, what are you doing? Still working at the mall? Can I ask you another question? It's kind of personal, and I don't want to type it if you don't want to talk about this stuff. It's about what happened at graduation. Anyway, I have to get going. Will you let me know?*

*Jen*

Bailey was happy that this time she at least knew when she'd get a response. She didn't have to hurry to reply. She could take her time. She didn't, though. She typed, read, and reread her response before she clicked send. Then, she just had to wait a week until Jenna would reply. Jenna had been gone for four weeks now. It had been four long weeks for Bailey, and she missed her terribly. She missed Jenna every summer, but this time, it was worse. This time, they wouldn't be going back to school to open their adjacent lockers.

To: baileys@brownehigh.net
From: jennac@brownehigh.net
Re: Hi

*Hey, Bail,*

*So, my question is probably obvious. I don't even know if I should ask it. And if you were in front of me, or if we were on the phone, I probably wouldn't. I guess that makes me a little bit of a coward, huh? When did you know? I guess that's my question. When did you know that you liked me like that? When did you know that you like girls? I know you said it was just me, but does that mean you're gay or bisexual? Is it okay to ask that? If not, it's totally okay for you not to answer.*

*Jen*

Bailey replied instantly. This time, she didn't reread her response. She just trusted it.

To: jennac@brownehigh.net
From: baileys@brownehigh.net
Re: Hi

*Jen,*

*I don't know which question to answer first, but I'll try to answer all of them. When did I know I liked girls? I didn't know I liked girls until I met you, honestly. I think it happened at the same time. I didn't always know I liked you or anything. Once we got to Browne, though, it was like something changed in me. You were suddenly someone I thought of that way. I didn't know what it meant back then. Even at graduation, I didn't know. I just knew that I liked you. It wasn't about girls or boys. It was you, Jen. You've probably only ever seen me in the periphery of your life. I'm that girl that helped you do your calculus homework or lent you a pen when you needed one, but you've never been that to me. You were always so nice to me, even though we never really hung out. You're smart – except for math, obviously – but in everything else. You're beautiful. God, Jen! You're so beautiful. I can't believe I finally get to tell you that. I never had the guts to say it, but it's the truth. And can you tell me something? What's the color of your damn eyes? Are they green? Are they brown? Are they something in-between? I've been staring at them for years, and I still don't know. I didn't know at graduation, but I know now. I still haven't told anyone, so I'd appreciate it if you didn't say anything. I don't think there's anyone I know that you'd tell, but still. I haven't even told Sam yet. So, congrats! You're the first one to know that I am gay. This email is really long. I'm sure you have better things to do than read this. Have fun on the rest of your trip.*

*Bail*

Bailey couldn't put off getting ready for school any longer. Her mom took her to several stores to find her presentable clothing to wear to college, and she insisted that Bailey not wear sweatpants and t-shirts to every class. Bailey agreed, knowing that once she was in her dorm, her mom wouldn't know what she wore to class. Her future roommate was from Seattle, and she would be arriving at the dorm around the same time as Bailey. She would be bringing the microwave, and Bailey was in charge of the TV. She worked five shifts at the mall and deposited her check. Then, the email came.

To: baileys@brownehigh.net
From: jennac@brownehigh.net
Re: Hi

*Hey, Bail,*

*My eyes are hazel. Sometimes, they look brown. Sometimes, they look green. If you would have asked me that, I could have told you years ago. You've never been on the periphery of my life, Bail. If I did something to make you think that, I'm sorry. You're one of my closest friends. I know we didn't hang out a lot. You never seemed interested in going to the games, the dances, or participating in school stuff. My life kind of revolved around that stuff. You always seemed cool just hanging out with Sam after school. I watched you walk off with her like a hundred times. I guess I always kind of thought I was on the periphery of your life. Weird, huh? Also, how cool are we that we're using words like "periphery" now? College girls! Listen, I'll be back in two weeks. Do you maybe want to hang out? I don't know when you're leaving for school. I can't remember if you told me. I'll have a month before I have to go. Just let me know.*

*Jen*

Bailey did let her know. She sent Jen another email telling her that she would be in town until mid-August. They sent several more emails to one another before it was time for Jenna to come home. Bailey had gotten smarter with time. On Sundays, she knew Jenna's email would likely come in around nine in the morning. She'd wake up before that, turn on her computer, and wait for the sound. Once the email came in, she would read it and reply as quickly as possible. The first time, she didn't know if it would work. Moments later, though, Jenna's reply came. They were able to get in an exchange of five or six emails before Jenna had to sign off. Bailey loved Sundays now.

They talked about everything, or at least as much as they could in the thirty or so minutes Jenna was online. They couldn't video chat. Where Jenna was, there was no webcam. They *could* instant message one another, and on the last Sunday prior to Jenna coming home, they actually had a good enough connection for it to work.

JennaC: My flight gets in late. Are you sure?

BailS: I'm sure. Are you sure your parents won't mind?

JennaC: My brother has a soccer tournament for the weekend. They're going to be out of town. I was just going to get someone else to pick me up or take an Uber.

BailS: I'll come get you.

JennaC: Okay. Thanks, Bail.

BailS: Jen, can I say I can't wait to see you, and it won't be awkward?

JennaC: Yes.

BailS: Just yes?

JennaC: Yes, you can say that, and it won't be awkward.

BailS: Are you sure?

JennaC: I can't wait to see you, too, Bails. You know you're the only person I've talked to since I've been here, right? Besides my parents, obviously.

BailS: Really?

JennaC: Bails, I miss you. Is that okay to say? Can we talk when I get back?

BailS: I am picking you up at the airport.

JennaC: You know what I mean.

BailS: If it's about what happened at graduation, you don't have to worry about that, Jen. I can push that stuff aside, and we can go back to how things used to be. It's cool.

JennaC: Can you really do that? Just push it aside like that?

Bailey went to type her response, but before she could, she saw Jenna's next message.

JennaC: Because I can't.

# CHAPTER 3: EXPLORING

Bailey had spent the past several days wishing Jenna had gone on a trip to a country that had a strong Wi-Fi connection or at least decent cell service. The moment Jenna's last message came through, they had lost their connection. Bailey had actually smacked her laptop in a fruitless attempt to get Jenna back online. The morning Jenna was set to return came way too slowly for Bailey, but it did come. She knew Jenna's flight information and was at the airport a full hour early. She had never picked someone up at the airport before, so she didn't exactly know how it would work. She also didn't know what they'd do when Jenna got off the plane. Would they hug? Would they high-five? Maybe they would just kind of stand there awkwardly for a few minutes until they went to baggage claim to get Jenna's luggage.

She also wasn't sure if she should wait in the car in short-term parking or if she should go in. After thirty minutes of playing on her phone, checking on Jenna's flight arrival time in between, and turning the air conditioning on full blast to try to prevent herself from sweating through her clothes from nervousness, Bailey finally went inside the terminal. When she arrived, she saw three men with flowers. Should she have brought Jenna flowers? No, they weren't dating. They were friends. Did friends bring other friends flowers when they picked them up at the airport? Probably not, she reasoned. She wiped her hands on her jeans repeatedly, went to the bathroom, bought two bottles of water – because Jenna might be thirsty when she got off the plane – and stared at the arrivals screen until she saw that Jenna's flight had arrived.

An interminable amount of time later, Bailey saw her. Jenna was at the top of the escalator, making her way down, with a giant backpack on her shoulders. Jenna hadn't seen Bailey yet, which meant Bailey could stare at her for a moment. Jenna looked tired but still unbelievably beautiful. Her hair was pulled into two braids that rested on her shoulders and looked a bit mussed. Her eyes were still that same shade of brown and green.

"Hazel," Bailey said to herself in a whisper.

Jenna's hazel eyes finally connected to Bailey's, and her face lit up instantly. Her smile went wide. Bailey couldn't hear it, but she could swear Jenna was laughing lightly. Her hazel eyes also seemed to water just a bit, but it could have been because she was exhausted. It couldn't possibly be that Jenna was *that* happy to see Bailey.

"Hey, Bail," Jenna greeted the moment she was three feet in front of Bailey.

Bailey could only smile at both, Jenna actually being in front of her *and* the way Jenna always greeted her. Jenna lowered her backpack to the ground and reached out for her the moment it was on the floor. She pulled Bailey into her body and hugged her hard. She hugged her like she *had* missed her *that* much. Bailey didn't know what to do at first. Her arms remained limp at her sides until she realized she could hug her back. She had probably only ever hugged Jenna a handful of times. Now, she had an excuse to touch her. Yes, it was just as one friend picking the other up from the airport, but it felt good all the same. Her arms went around Jenna's waist. She pulled her in closer, tighter, so that their bodies were pressed together fully. Was that a gasp she heard from Jenna? Had Jenna gasped when Bailey hugged her? Bailey pulled her tighter as Jenna's arms held on to each other around her neck.

Then, they moved to touch Bailey's neck pretty intimately; like in a way no friend ever did. Her fingers grazed the soft skin of Bailey's neck. She toyed with Bailey's hair for a moment, and Bailey could have sworn she heard Jenna breathe in deeply. Was she smelling Bailey's hair? What was happening right now?

"I think your bag is on carousel five," Bailey interrupted the moment.

"Oh, right." Jenna pulled back.

Why had Bailey done that? Why had she ended the first perfect moment between the two of them? She had done it because she had to. Bailey couldn't keep touching her like that. Jenna couldn't keep touching Bailey like that. It was doing things to her, and those were the things that Bailey couldn't deal with. Jenna wasn't her girlfriend; she was her friend. She repeated that mantra to herself as they walked silently to the carousel to pick up Jenna's bags.

"Do you want to come in?" Jenna asked when they pulled up to her house. "No one's home."

"Oh, I've never actually been to your house," Bailey said and realized at the same time.

"Let's rectify that. I mean, if you're free." Jenna looked at her from the passenger's seat with such reverence in her expression; Bailey nearly allowed herself to hope that something *was* going on with Jenna.

"I'm totally free. I have to work later today, but that's not until five."

Jenna smiled and nodded before opening the door and getting out of Bailey's car. Bailey helped Jenna with her bags. They made their way to the door that Jenna unlocked. Once inside, Jenna left her bags by the door and gave Bailey the quick tour of her parents' ranch-style house. It wasn't as nice as Bailey's, but it felt somehow much more comfortable to Bailey than her own home did. Finally, they made their way to Jenna's bedroom. Bailey stood outside for a moment while Jenna made her way into her room for the first time in two months. She flopped on top of her comforter, which was a light shade of plain purple.

"Are you coming in?" she asked Bailey.

"Oh, yeah," Bailey replied with some trepidation.

She walked a few steps into the room but remained standing awkwardly. Jenna turned her head and gave her a smile.

"Bail, can we talk?"

"Sure. What about?" Bailey asked.

"About my message to you last week," Jenna replied. "Do you want to come here?"

"I should probably stay where I am." Bailey slid both hands into her back pockets.

"Why?" Jenna remained on her bed, lying flat.

"I don't know." Bailey shrugged.

"Bail, come here. Please." Jenna patted the spot on the bed next to her.

"I don't know if I should be on your bed, Jen. I mean, I'm not going to try anything or–"

"Bailey Anne Sayers! Get over here," Jenna commanded with a small laugh. Then, she stopped laughing. "Bail, did you ever think that I might want you to try something?"

Bailey's mouth went dry. Her hands grew instantly clammy, and she balled them into tight fists. This had to be the cruelest joke anyone had ever played on anyone else, right?

"Jen, are you…" Bailey finally moved to the bed, but she didn't lie down. She just sat on the edge of the bed and stared down at Jenna's beautiful face. "You knew what I meant when I said *'try something,'* right?"

"I don't know how to do this, Bail," Jenna said with a worried expression.

"Do what?"

"Tell you about this," Jenna replied. "I didn't expect to feel this way."

Okay, Bailey's heart definitely leapt out of her chest

when Jenna placed her hand tentatively on top of Bailey's and remained there while Jenna's eyes connected to her own.

"What way?" Bailey breathed out.

"I missed you, Bail." Jenna attempted to shrug while lying down. "It was strange. And I've missed you before; every summer, actually. We'd have our last day of school, and then I wouldn't see you for three months. I always thought about trying to see what you were up to and asking you to come over or hang out, but I never did. I guess I assumed you were busy or hanging out with your friends." Jenna paused and finally looked down at their connected hands. "But, this time, I knew we weren't going back to school. I wouldn't see you in three months." She again connected her eyes to Bailey's. "At graduation, I honestly didn't know what it was. I promise, if I did, I would have told you."

"What do you mean?"

"When you asked me out, and I freaked out. I said I dated boys. And I did. I mean, I do date boys. Not right now, obviously; I'm single." Jenna looked away and out the window that had a giant oak tree blocking the view of the street. "I didn't know until I left. I started thinking about those mornings when you and I would sit on the floor in front of our lockers. You'd have your textbook in your lap. I'd lean over to read something, and I'd smell your hair accidentally. There was that time I saw you at homecoming. You were with Samantha. I don't know why, but I was kind of jealous of her. You two were talking, and you must have had something on your face because she leaned in and touched it."

"An eyelash," Bailey remembered.

Jenna turned her eyes back to Bailey's and said, "I didn't realize it until I was in South America all alone. I missed you. I didn't want graduation to be the last time I saw you, but it was more than that. I guess knowing that you liked me like that, that you're…"

"Gay?" Bailey finished it for her.

"Yeah." Jenna slid her hand away from Bailey's. "It made me think more about what I wanted."

"And?"

Bailey wondered why Jenna had pulled her hand away. The contact had been exquisite. The words Jenna was dancing around were so full of promise. The air in the room seemed fresher, crispier somehow. Jenna's scent was surrounding her. The feel of the comforter beneath her clammy hands was softer now. The room was impossibly bright. Still, Bailey couldn't be all optimistic. There was a chance that Jenna was about to say something about just being friends or her needing time to figure out whatever she was feeling. She might also say she didn't want to pursue it because she would be leaving in less than a month to go away to school for four years.

"Will you lie down next to me?" Jenna asked.

Bailey nodded. Jenna slid over on her full bed, but only slightly. Bailey's body was connected to Jenna's side at nearly every possible spot as they both stared up at the ceiling. Bailey didn't know what to do, and Jenna was quiet now. Bailey didn't have words to say until Jenna told her what to do; what *she* wanted. They lay like that for several silent moments. Those moments were so full of hope, of promise, that Bailey nearly cried silent tears of joy. She finally decided she would risk embarrassing herself again.

She reached over into the nearly imperceptible space between their hands and linked her fingers with Jenna's. She heard Jenna's breath deepen and shudder slightly before it seemed to regulate itself again. Jenna didn't say anything, but she also didn't let go. Bailey decided to take another chance. She reluctantly let go of Jenna's hand but used the tips of her fingers to apply barely-there touches to Jenna's somewhat clammy palm, allowing her fingers to dance along Jenna's skin. Then, she slid the tips of her fingers up and down Jenna's forearm, and once again, Jenna didn't stop her. Bailey wanted more, but she didn't want to scare Jenna. Just the fact that she was allowing Bailey to touch her skin like this was enough for Bailey to never ask for anything else from Jenna ever again. If she went too far and Jenna wasn't ready, they might never have anything other than this.

"Jen?" Bailey asked softly.

"Yeah?"

"Is this something you want?" she asked, being purposively ambiguous.

"I don't know," Jenna replied just as softly. "It feels good," she added a second later. "What you're doing feels good."

"Do you want me to keep doing it?"

There was no response, but Jenna rolled onto her side, removing her arm from Bailey's touch. She then placed her arm under her head and faced Bailey. Bailey wasn't sure if she was supposed to turn to Jenna or if she should continue staring at the ceiling. She decided to turn to Jenna because if she could meet Jenna's gaze, it was likely she'd be able to figure out how Jenna was feeling. Jenna's eyes always gave her away. Bailey rolled and took in the beauty that was Jenna Cabot. Jenna stared into Bailey's eyes for a moment before tentatively reaching a hand out to touch her cheek. Jenna's eyes followed her fingers' movements as she grazed the skin ever so softly. Her fingertips explored Bailey's cheek, the side of her neck, her collarbone, and moved back up to Bailey's chin. Bailey was certain she would combust at any moment. Jenna's thumb ran over Bailey's bottom lip as her eyes continued to follow her own movements.

Bailey tried not to gasp, but she couldn't hold it in. Her lips parted ever so slightly, causing Jenna's eyes to flit up to her own and silently ask Bailey something. Bailey knew what the question was because she had the same one. She slid forward another inch, but it was enough for Jenna to understand. Jenna slid forward, too, while her thumb moved to Bailey's top lip and then away entirely.

Bailey's forehead connected with Jenna's. They remained there for what was likely several minutes, breathing the same air, applying gentle, hesitant touches to skin they'd yet to discover. Jenna's hand went to the back of Bailey's neck, and Bailey's hand stayed on Jenna's hip for a while before wrapping around Jenna's back and pulling her in more tightly to Bailey's body. God, this felt good. This was what she'd been missing. This was what made sense to her. Jenna Cabot being pressed up against her like this made sense to Bailey in a way that nothing else ever had. Jenna's eyes were closed. Bailey loved her eyes, but she knew now she could stare at Jenna like this for hours. She could watch her sleep or just relax into the calm that was Jenna. Before Jenna could open her eyes, though, Bailey pressed soft kisses on each eyelid. Jenna remained still, though her heavy breathing gave away her nerves. Bailey moved to kiss Jenna's forehead, her nose, and her cheeks before she pulled back, and her forehead, once again, connected to Jenna's. They fell asleep like that moments later, with Jenna's breathing going slow and steady and Bailey feeling like this was the best moment in her entire life.

# CHAPTER 4: THE FIRST DATE

Bailey had picked Jenna up at her house the following night. She hadn't brought flowers because Jenna's family was home, and they hadn't exactly discussed what their families knew or would be told. It was merely understood that this was a private thing between the two of them, at least for now. Bailey didn't mind. She only wanted to spend as much time with Jenna as possible. The more people they had to tell, the more time they'd have to spend with those people. Bailey only wanted to spend time with Jenna.

They'd gone to a restaurant that wasn't cheap but also not too expensive. Bailey figured she could spend some of her hard-earned money on a good first date for the two of them. Dinner was only somewhat awkward. Neither of them seemed to know how to act. Was it different than just going out with a friend? Should they touch more? Should they touch at all since they were in public? It was also strange because, while they'd been friends for years, they'd never actually spent any significant time together outside of school. Bailey had never looked across a table lit up by a small white candle in a bright red holder to see Jenna staring back at her, her eyes near-glowing in the light. When the check came, Bailey paid while Jenna attempted to fight her for it. They'd laughed and acknowledged out loud for the first time how awkward the whole thing was. Then, Bailey had an idea.

"I was thinking we could go to a movie now," she said. "But I don't know."

"You don't want to go?" Jenna asked and seemed

worried Bailey might be cutting their date short.

"My parents are out of town tonight," Bailey replied instead. "My mom went to visit my aunt. My dad is on shift," she added. "We could go back to my house."

"Oh," Jenna said. "And watch a movie there or something?"

"We could do whatever," Bailey answered. "But, yeah, we could watch a movie. My dad had the basement finished last year. He actually put in a game room and a small theater. It's pretty cool. Of course, he had to do that right when I'm about to move away for school." She laughed at herself. "Anyway, it might be better than going to a crowded theater. I mean, I know we know each other, but I feel like there's so much more I want to know about you, and it would be hard to do that there."

Jenna smiled at her and replied, "Okay, sure."

Bailey drove them back to her house, where she parked in their three-car garage and closed the door behind them. Then, she ushered Jenna into the lavish home she shared with her parents. Bailey had to admit that, as much as she wanted her freedom and to live on her own, she would miss the luxury of this three-story house with a game room, a movie theater, and a wet bar downstairs right outside her own bedroom. There was also a pool and a hot tub out back that she guessed didn't come standard with on-campus housing.

"Bail, this place is amazing," Jenna said the moment they made their way downstairs.

"It's pretty cool, yeah." Bailey shrugged. "We used to live in a smaller place when my dad was just starting his medical practice. It was nice, but once his practice blew up, he and my mom bought this place."

"He's on shift tonight?" Jenna asked.

"He works at a hospital, too. He takes shifts in the ER sometimes," Bailey explained. "He's on for twenty-four hours at a time when he does that."

"And your mom is gone, too?"

"Yeah, my aunt just had surgery, so she's there helping my uncle take care of her until at least the end of the week," Bailey answered. "Do you want something to drink? There's alcohol, if you want something."

"Are you drinking?"

"Water," Bailey said. "I'm not really a drinker."

"Me neither," Jenna replied. "I have, obviously, but I don't. I mean, I don't want to tonight."

"Water? Soda? Something else?"

"Just water is fine," Jenna replied.

They stood awkwardly in the middle of the basement game room for a moment before Bailey went to the fridge and pulled out two bottles of water. She returned to find Jenna standing in the same spot with her hands clasped together in front of her. Bailey nodded toward the room off to the right. Jenna followed her inside the dark room. Bailey turned on the lights, and Jenna gasped.

"I know. It's a lot," Bailey laughed. "My dad went a little overboard."

"There's a freaking popcorn machine in here!" Jenna exclaimed before making her way over to the bright-red full-sized popcorn machine.

"Do you want me to make some?"

"Obviously." Jenna turned back with her bright smile.

Bailey taught Jenna how to make the popcorn and turned the machine on. It took several minutes for the popcorn to begin popping. By then, they'd picked out a movie and sat down in one of the two loveseats that also reclined. Bailey started the movie, grabbed a bowl of popcorn for them to share, and turned off the lights. They settled in, and for the next thirty minutes or so, they remained mostly silent, sharing accidental touches over the popcorn bowl, but nothing more. Once the popcorn was gone, Jenna moved the bowl to the table in front of them and moved back into Bailey. She pressed her side to Bailey's and placed her head on Bailey's shoulder. Bailey didn't move for the next hour. She was afraid if she did, Jenna would move, and she did not want Jenna to move.

"Hey, Bail?"

"Yeah?"

"I'm having a good time."

"Me too."

When the movie ended, Bailey realized she would have to take Jenna home soon. Their date was about to end, and she hadn't even held hands with Jenna yet. They hadn't really talked about what any of this meant, or the fact that they'd both be leaving for their respective colleges in just a few weeks. Why hadn't she had the courage to say something to Jenna sooner? They could have had years together instead of weeks.

"Do you want to watch another one?" Jenna asked as she lifted her head. Bailey's eyes grew big. "Or not? I can just go home if–"

"No, I do. I want to watch another one. I wasn't sure you would. I thought you'd want to go home."

"I don't," Jenna replied.

Her face was so close, and the room was so dark; Bailey could still make out Jenna's face, but nothing beyond it. She wanted to kiss Jenna. She had wanted to kiss her for years, but now, she actually could. Bailey could just lean in and kiss Jenna, and Jenna would likely kiss her back. They were on a date, after all.

"Then, we can put one on," Bailey said. "Whatever you want is fine."

"Can we maybe watch it in your room?" Jenna asked.

"Oh. Yeah," Bailey said, surprised. "Sure, it's just through there." She pointed in the dark as if Jenna could see her. "Let me just turn everything off."

A few minutes later, Bailey walked Jenna into her bedroom that she, thankfully, had cleaned that morning. She hadn't expected Jenna to come over. Her mom, prior to leaving, had instructed her to take care of it. Bailey's room was larger than Jenna's, but it came stocked with the same basic furniture. She had a full-sized bed, one bedside table, a dresser, a makeup table Bailey never used that her mother had bought her, and a TV her father had mounted to the wall. Her closet was a small, walk-in one, and she had her own bathroom that had a door from her room and one from the hall.

"This is awesome, Bail."

"I used to have a room upstairs, down the hall from my parents. When my dad decided to do all this down here, I asked if I could move my room. That way, when I come home from school, I'll have a little more privacy and stuff. This past year, it's been pretty awesome. It's basically like having my own apartment."

"But your mom still does your laundry and cooks?" Jenna smiled at her.

"No way." Bailey laughed. "My mom orders in a lot, and I've done my own laundry for the past three years. Once I was able to get a job, she told me I was able to do my own laundry as well."

"My mom would probably do your laundry if you ask. I mean, if you ever need to borrow her," Jenna said with a smile.

"Do you want to lie down?" Bailey asked and motioned to the bed.

"Can we maybe just talk and not watch the movie?" Jenna asked as she moved to Bailey's bed and stationed herself sitting up, leaning against the pillows.

"We can do that. I guess we have a lot to talk about."

Bailey moved to the bed and mimicked Jenna's posture. She tried not to freak out at the thought that Jenna was in her bed. Jenna Cabot was sitting next to her on *her* bed. Jenna turned to her and took Bailey's hand at the same time.

"This feels good," she said after a moment. "It's different, but it's good."

"Yeah," Bailey agreed. "Is it something you want to continue doing?" Bailey asked.

"What happens when I go to Michigan, Bail?"

"You're assuming you won't be sick of me by then," Bailey tried to joke.

"Bail…"

"Sorry." Bailey squeezed Jenna's hand. "I don't know, Jenna. I never thought *this* would happen. And I definitely wasn't planning for what would happen if you did like me back and we had to go away to school. It hurt too much to do that."

"Why?"

"Because it was something I would never have. I didn't want to think of it."

"But we're here now," Jenna added. "I'm in your room. We're on a date."

"I know. I still can't believe that." Bailey laughed lightly.

Jenna moved to lie down, encouraging Bailey to lie down with her. They faced one another and, within moments, resumed their light touches from the previous day. Silently, they explored without taking things too far in any direction. Bailey's hand skirted under Jenna's shirt, but just barely, to glide her fingers over Jenna's hipbones. Jenna's hands did the same to Bailey as if following Bailey's lead. Several minutes later, Bailey was up on one elbow, staring down at Jenna while sliding her fingers across Jenna's face, her throat, and down back to her hip where she rested her hand there. Jenna stared up at her before she closed her eyes as if to take in the sensations even more. Bailey slid her hand up an inch or two higher, and after receiving no objection, she moved her hand across the flat plain of Jenna's stomach and rested it just below Jenna's breast. Jenna gasped. Bailey immediately went to pull back, but Jenna's hand pressed into her own, and it pressed hard enough to let Bailey know that Jenna didn't want her to move her hand away. Jenna's eyes finally opened, and she looked up at Bailey.

"Can I stay tonight?" Jenna asked.

"Yes," Bailey answered without hesitation.

Jenna's eyes closed again. Her hand released Bailey's and moved back to her side. Bailey remained in her position. She stared down at Jenna's soft skin and found a freckle just below her right eye. She kissed it gently while her hand slid a little further north. Jenna's breath was coming in short bursts as Bailey cupped her breast over her bra. Bailey gasped nearly at the same time. She was touching Jenna's breast, and she didn't know what to do now. She hadn't planned what she would do after this. Hell, Bailey hadn't planned on doing this until Jenna clasped her hand and asked her if she could stay. When Bailey gave Jenna's breast a light squeeze, Jenna responded by fluttering her eyes for a moment before closing them again. Bailey repeated the action, all while staring down at Jenna's face, attempting to memorize it in this new way. She could feel then as Jenna's nipple hardened beneath her touch. For some reason, in that moment and that moment alone, this all felt very real. She was touching Jenna intimately enough to feel the hardness of her nipple beneath her own palm.

She squeezed Jenna's breast repeatedly, lavishing attention on it before her thumb skated over that nipple, moving back and forth as Jenna's eyes shot open. Her body squirmed slightly with Bailey's touches, and Bailey loved it. She loved *her*. In a way, Bailey knew she always had, but she had never touched Jenna before; she had never felt Jenna's reactions to those touches. And now that she had, Bailey knew she loved her. Jenna's hand moved to Bailey's neck, and she pulled Bailey down to her. Their faces were only separated by an inch. Jenna licked her lips, and that was all Bailey could take before she leaned down and captured them with her own.

This wasn't Jenna's first kiss; Bailey knew that. It was Jenna's first kiss with a girl, though, and Bailey loved that. Jenna probably didn't know that this was Bailey's first real kiss. That one, haphazard peck with Jesse Simmons during a game of spin the bottle at a party when she was twelve, didn't count. She'd never wanted to kiss anyone else. It had always been Jenna. Now, Jenna's lips were moving against her own. They were soft and warm, and they wanted her. They wanted Bailey. Jenna's lips parted slightly, and it was just enough for Bailey to pull Jenna's lower lip into her mouth. She repeated that when Jenna let out the softest moan. Bailey's hand continued to grasp, squeeze, and toy with Jenna's breast, while Jenna's hand played in Bailey's hair.

When Jenna's tongue moved inside Bailey's mouth, Bailey nearly lost it. She didn't know, at first, what to do with her own tongue, so she just let Jenna take the lead. And Jenna didn't seem to mind. She explored and flicked before massaging. Then, her tongue was gone, but her lips were more insistent. They moved faster against Bailey's now. Bailey's hand seemed to desire the same rhythm, but it also wanted skin. It sought the softness of Jenna's breast on its own and slid under the cup of Jenna's bra. Again, Jenna didn't protest. Bailey wondered then if she was dreaming. Maybe she'd wake up in a few seconds, and if that were so, she would enjoy every single one she had. She stroked Jenna's nipple freely now. Jenna's hips even lifted ever so slightly off the bed. Bailey had never experienced sensations like this before.

She was hot. Her skin was boiling at Jenna's insistent touches. Jenna's free hand was now under Bailey's shirt as well, stroking the small of her back. The hand in her hair was coaxing Bailey further down into her. Just as Bailey's lips connected with Jenna's neck for the first time, Jenna's hand had managed to unclasp Bailey's bra. Bailey stopped kissing her neck for a moment as Jenna's hand moved unencumbered over the skin of Bailey's back. This was happening. Jenna was touching her just on her back, and Bailey thought she might have the first orgasm of her life just at Jenna's fingertips stroking down and around to her hips.

Bailey moved her hand to Jenna's other breast, wrestling the cup of the bra away. Jenna's hand moved up and under her shirt to do the same thing to Bailey's. When Jenna touched her there for the first time, Bailey nearly burst. The space between her legs was throbbing now, painfully so. She was wet, and her jeans felt tighter than they had when she had put them on earlier. Bailey's hips moved a little against the side of Jenna's thigh as Jenna's fingers played with her nipple and Bailey's hand squeezed Jenna's breast.

"Bails…" Jenna muttered as Bailey sucked on her earlobe.

"Should I stop?" Bailey asked on instinct.

"No," Jenna replied through a gasp. "I want you to take your shirt off."

"You do?" Bailey asked and kissed just below Jenna's earlobe.

"Yes."

"Jen, are you sure?" Bailey whispered into Jenna's ear. She couldn't believe she was this close to the girl she had only ever dreamed about experiencing this with. "We don't have to do anything."

Jenna didn't reply. She removed her hand from Bailey's breast, and Bailey worried she'd said something wrong for a moment, but Jenna used both hands to lift at Bailey's shirt. Bailey then lifted herself to allow it to be removed, and Jenna starred at her. Bailey's breasts were covered by an unclasped bra that Jenna lifted up and away. Then, she just stared again through darkened eyes, flushed cheeks, and swollen lips.

"Bails…"

Again, Jenna's face showed complete reverence for what she was seeing. She was still lying flat on her back with her shirt mussed from Bailey's hand. Her eyes were wide. Her hazel eyes had turned nearly complete brown, and they were glued to Bailey's chest. After a moment, she reached her hand out so tentatively, Bailey wondered if she would ever actually touch her. Despite the fact that Jenna had just had her hand there, this seemed different. She first touched between Bailey's breasts, and her hand rested there for several moments. Bailey watched her as Jenna stared at her own hand.

"Jen?"

"I can feel your heart, Bails," Jenna said finally.

She moved both of her hands to cover Bailey's breasts and just held them there for a long moment. Then, she started squeezing them softly before applying more pressure. Bailey felt her nipples harden instantly, and Jenna must have had as well because she began playing with them experimentally to see how Bailey would react. At this point, Bailey could barely contain herself. Her eyes closed tightly on their own as Jenna continued her caresses. Then, Jenna's right hand slid down her exposed abdomen and, without hesitation, popped open the button on Bailey's jeans.

"Oh," Bailey muttered.

Jenna sat up then and kissed Bailey. She pulled back only for a moment, removed her own shirt, and took care of her bra before she pulled Bailey back down to her. It all happened so fast; Bailey wasn't exactly sure what was happening. Her lips were back on Jenna's, but this time, Jenna had pulled her on top of herself. Bailey was *on top* of Jenna Cabot. Jenna's arms were back around her neck. Their breasts were pressed together. God, this was right. Bailey's hand instinctively moved to Jenna's breast again. She loved the feel of it, the weight of it in her hand. She lifted herself enough to squeeze it again, to toy with the hard nipple, and then to slide her hand down to Jenna's jeans. She kept it there for a moment, just over the button, giving Jenna a chance to object. When she didn't, Bailey unbuttoned the jeans and pulled down at the zipper. She pulled down at her own zipper next and lifted up into a kneeling position to stare down at Jenna.

Jenna's breathing was shallow. Her skin was flushed.

Her chest was heaving, and she was gorgeous. Bailey leaned down and finally did what she had been wanting to do all along. She took a nipple into her mouth and allowed her tongue to play. Jenna's hips bucked once. Bailey's free hand played with Jenna's other breast. She switched breasts, ensuring each got the same attention, before she kissed down Jenna's stomach. She swirled her tongue around Jenna's belly button like she had seen in a movie once and went lower still.

"Bail?"

"Yeah?" Bailey's eyes met Jenna's questioningly.

"This is our first date," Jenna said with a smile.

Bailey wasn't sure what she was trying to say with that comment. Should they stop? Should they talk more before they do this very big, important thing with one another? Bailey was a virgin, but she had no idea if Jenna was. They'd never talked about that in their friendship. Either way, it would be Jenna's first time with another girl. For both of them, this was a major step. They should probably talk more about what was happening between them, where they were going, or if this would be it with them because they'd be separating in a few short weeks. Maybe that was what this was. Maybe, to Jenna, this was their hello and their goodbye.

Bailey waited for Jenna to take the lead again, but it appeared Jenna wanted her to take things from here. Bailey placed a gentle hand on Jenna's abdomen just above the now unbuttoned jeans, and Jenna continued watching her but said nothing. Bailey moved both hands to the belt loops of Jenna's jeans, moved herself back, and tugged them off and down Jenna's body. Jenna lifted herself up to allow them to be removed.

Bailey stood at the end of the bed now. Jenna was wearing pink bikinis. Was this a dream? This had to be a dream. On top of that, she was wet. Jenna was wet. Bailey could see it: Jenna was turned on. She was turned on by her. Bailey stripped off her own jeans, leaving herself only in the white boy shorts she never thought Jenna Cabot would see. When she went to move back on top of Jenna, Jenna motioned for her to stop. Bailey grew terrified then. They'd gone too far; Jenna didn't want this.

"Take those off, too," Jenna told her and pointed at Bailey's underwear.

Bailey reached down and did as she was told. She stood in front of Jenna, and she was naked. Jenna was nearly naked, too. No, Jenna was naked *now*. Jenna had removed her own underwear, tossed them to the floor, and was now completely naked in Bailey's bed. Bailey took one moment to take in Jenna's body before she climbed back on top of her.

Their first time together was rushed. Neither of them knew what they were doing. They touched one another hurriedly, like they'd only have this moment together. When Bailey touched Jenna for the first time, she nearly collapsed on top of her. She still could not believe this was happening. Her fingers slid through Jenna's most intimate folds and entered her. She was inside the girl beneath her. That girl was writhing beneath her, and it was because of what Bailey was doing. When Jenna came, Bailey couldn't believe the sight. Her fingers played against Jenna's clit then until she realized Jenna was coming again. When Jenna's tremors finally subsided, Bailey pressed her entire form to Jenna's. She remained there until Jenna called her name softly. Then, Bailey lifted herself up. She met Jenna's hooded eyes and kissed her until Jenna rolled them over and touched Bailey in all the ways she had dreamed about being touched.

# CHAPTER 5: THE DISTANCE

"Hey, Bail," Jenna greeted.

"It's so good to see your face," Bailey replied to her girlfriend.

"I know. I miss you. I can't wait for this weekend," Jenna replied while smiling through Bailey's laptop screen.

"Me neither. Three months is far too long to go without seeing you. How did I do that when I used to get through the summer without you?"

"Well, we weren't together then, and we weren't having sex." Jenna wiggled her eyebrows at her.

"Really?"

"What? We only just started having sex, and then we went off to school." Jenna moved closer to the screen, and Bailey loved her eyes when she looked at her like this. "I miss you," Jenna added.

"I know. I miss you, too. I miss us."

"I can't believe we only have four days, though."

"We'll just have to make the most of it, I guess," Bailey suggested.

Bailey had a girlfriend, and her girlfriend was Jenna Cabot. They were in love. Well, Bailey was in love. She knew that much. She loved Jenna with her whole heart. They'd been together for close to four months. Three of those months had been spent in different states, though. As many phone calls, FaceTime chats, text messages, and everything else they had exchanged, they still hadn't said those words to one another. Bailey knew she wanted to say it; she just wanted to say it in person. This was her fall break for school. She would be flying to Michigan to see her girlfriend and would be staying in Jenna's dorm for three nights before she had to fly back. Jenna's fall break was the following week, and she would be flying back home to spend time with her family. Bailey also planned to drive home as soon as her last class on Thursday was over in order to spend the whole weekend with her girlfriend.

There were just two problems with their plans. In Michigan, Jenna had a roommate who would be there. And back home, their parents had no idea they were a couple. Bailey had already told her parents that she and Jenna would likely have at least one or two nights where they'd share the basement apartment. They didn't know they were a couple, and that was fine with Bailey for now.

When Bailey arrived at the airport, Jenna engulfed her in a hug. Bailey took in her scent and the sounds of Jenna's breathing in her ear. She also felt Jenna's skin with her fingertips and held on to her for dear life. When they finally pulled back, Jenna didn't even bother to look around to see if anyone was watching; she leaned in and kissed Bailey first hard on the lips and then more softly. Bailey's hands were around Jenna's neck. She tasted her mouth, the warmth and the familiarity of it. She missed Jenna's kisses. There was something so perfect about the way Jenna kissed her.

"You're here," Jenna said as she pressed her forehead to Bailey's.

"I'm here," Bailey replied and kissed her again.

"Good. Let's get out of here." Jenna pulled on Bailey's roller bag. "My roommate is giving us the room for the night, and I want to make the most of it."

Bailey laughed as Jenna took her hand with her free one and pulled her swiftly out of the airport toward the bus that would take them back to campus. When they arrived, Jenna helped Bailey carry her stuff and unlocked her door. What they found in the room was a very much present roommate named Mandy.

"Mandy, this is my girlfriend, Bailey. Bails, this is Mandy," Jenna introduced and closed the door behind them.

"Hey," Bailey greeted.

Mandy was sitting at her desk with headphones in her ears that she then removed.

"Oh, hey." She stood to shake Bailey's hand and then returned to her chair. "I promise, I'll be out of your hair in, like, five minutes. I just have to finish this paper," she said quickly.

"No rush," Bailey said, and Jenna glared at her like she was the craziest person in the world.

Bailey smiled at her and laughed silently inside. Those days of thinking Jenna would never want to be with her were long gone now.

*\*\**

"Twin beds suck," Bailey said as they snuggled up in Jenna's bed.

"Or, they're awesome because you have to basically sleep on top of me," Jenna replied as she kissed Bailey's neck.

"That too," Bailey said back. "Are we going to sleep naked, Jen?"

"We probably shouldn't. I don't know when Mandy's coming back. She was nice enough to crash in someone else's room for the night, but she has class tomorrow. I don't know if she'll come back before that or not."

"I guess we should get dressed then," Bailey stated and attempted to sit up, only she was promptly pulled back down. "Jen!" she exclaimed while laughing.

"Bails, I haven't had you like this in three months. I don't know if I can kick Mandy out of her own room for the next two nights. Can we just stay like this a little longer? It's only midnight."

"We can stay like this as long as you want," Bailey replied. "I happen to love you naked; I have a very hot girlfriend."

"You love me naked?" Jenna laughed as Bailey stared down at her.

"No, I love you all the time," Bailey replied confidently. "I love you, Jen,"

"I love you, too," Jenna replied. "Finally," she added.

"What?" Bailey asked with a smile.

"I've wanted to tell you that forever." Jenna kissed Bailey's lips and attempted to roll them over.

"Really?" Bailey asked once she was safely under Jenna's warm body.

"Bail, you always act like it's crazy that I want to be with you."

"Because it is."

"Why?" Jenna asked. "What is it that makes you think someone wouldn't fall in love with you?"

"Not someone, Jen. It's crazy to me that *you* did."

"Bails, I am in love with you. I think I have been since before graduation. Even when I was dating my boyfriends, I spent every morning with you. I loved that time together. You always smelled like you'd just gotten out of the shower."

"I did?"

"Yes, it was so nice." Jenna smiled at her. "You were always making me laugh and not making me feel like an idiot when I didn't know the answer to some stupid math problem. Back when you asked me out, I reacted poorly because I hadn't expected it. When I was gone for those eight long weeks, though, I just felt wrong. And I didn't feel right again until I saw you."

"It felt right when I held you in the airport and when we went back to your place," Bailey replied.

"It always feels right with us." Jenna kissed her

gently. "I love you, Bails." Jenna's hand moved to Bailey's center, which she cupped, and then she used her hand to spread Bailey's legs. "There's something I'd like to do to show you how much, but it's something we haven't done."

"What?" Bailey asked as Jenna lightly stroked the hairs just above her clit.

"I want to taste you, Bails."

Bailey's tired eyes went wide with that declaration. While they'd had three weeks to explore one another at home, their parents were typically somewhat nearby, and there was no lock in the world, in Bailey's opinion, that could take away the fear of being caught by one's parents having sex in their childhood home. They'd had a few sleepovers, and they'd had sex on several occasions, but it had been rushed nearly every time with the possibility of getting caught. Even tonight, they'd rushed their first time together in months. They had touched one another lightly and then firmly, and they had kissed and licked every part of one another's body with the exception of one. Bailey had wanted to do it right away, but they'd gone so fast together, she kept thinking and worrying that any one thing might make Jenna pull back or away. Little did she know, Jenna was the one catapulting them forward with nearly every step of their relationship.

When Jenna's mouth met Bailey's center for the first time, it was with a very hesitant lick that just grazed the hairs between Bailey's legs. It was also very awkward. The twin bed offered no real easy position for this type of activity. Bailey could turn and hang her legs over the side of the bed, but then Jenna would be kneeling on the hard, tile floor. Jenna didn't seem to mind basically having her ass in the air and her legs folded beneath her because, at the end of the bed, her desk blocked the possibility of stretching them out. When Jenna licked a little harder, but still with hesitation, Bailey thought about telling her it was okay to stop. She thought about how she might taste to Jenna and worried that Jenna didn't like it. And if that was the case, they just wouldn't do this part. They could do everything else, but Jenna wouldn't have to do this again if she didn't want to.

Oh, fuck. Jenna's mouth was now sucking her clit into her mouth, and Bailey stiffened instantly when she realized just how good that felt. Jenna was sucking on her clit. Her tongue was flicking it back and forth and licking her, too. Bailey's hands were in fists at her sides as she spread her legs farther to allow Jenna to settle more into her. It didn't take long. It never did with Jenna. Bailey came into Jenna's mouth with just a few hard strokes to her clit, letting out Jenna's name with her breath. Jenna stayed down there for a little bit longer, licking and applying gentle kisses, while Bailey couldn't move from both the pleasure and the shock of it all.

"I liked that," Jenna answered the unasked question as she moved back up Bailey's body. "We're doing that again later."

She kissed Bailey's lips then, and as Bailey tasted herself on Jenna's lips, she knew she wanted to do the same to Jenna. And she wanted it now. After another haphazard roll, Jenna was now under her, and Bailey slid down her body and tasted Jenna's desire for her for the first time.

\*\*\*

"It's funny. I don't remember you girls spending any time together while you were in school. Now, I feel like I never see Samantha, and Jenna's here all the time," Bailey's mom said while they were eating breakfast.

"Mom!" Bailey exclaimed before she took a drink of her orange juice. "She's sitting right here."

"I didn't say it was a bad thing," Bailey's mom offered in response and finished her coffee. "You're staying over again tonight?" she addressed Jenna.

"If that's okay," Jenna spoke softly.

"Oh, of course," Bailey's mother replied somewhat passive-aggressively.

Bailey knew her mother was upset Bailey had spent her own fall break in Michigan with Jenna. The woman had already complained about how she had wanted her only daughter to come home instead of flying all the way to Michigan when she'd be seeing Jenna the following week. Bailey had used her own hard-earned money to pay for her flight, and she wanted to spend every chance she got with Jenna. School breaks were few and far between when there was a long-distance relationship involved. The way it was now, they wouldn't see one another for another two months. And that would be on Thanksgiving when Bailey would have her family obligations, and so would Jenna. They would have very little time together as is, and Jenna had already told Bailey seeing one another for Christmas would be difficult since her family went to Colorado for one week that time of year every year, and then the rest of her break would be spent going to other family parties. Bailey's family also visited her grandparents for several days during that time. All that left them with only one or two nights together. Then, the next break was spring break, and that wasn't until March.

"Mom, we're going to go out tonight, so we won't be here for dinner."

"I was going to make that pork roast you like."

Bailey rolled her eyes in Jenna's direction so that her mother wouldn't see. What her mother really meant was that she was going to take the pre-made pork roast dish and heat it up around dinnertime; no real cooking would be involved.

"I'm sorry. We already have plans."

"Are you going to see Samantha while you're on break?" her mother asked.

"Sam's not on break right now. She's at school in Florida, and I probably won't see her until Thanksgiving."

"Oh, I see." Her mother stood with her dirty plate

and coffee mug to take it to the sink.

"What are you doing today?" Bailey asked her.

"I'll be here. I assumed my daughter would want to spend some time with her parents on her school break."

"Mom, I was literally home for the weekend three weeks ago."

"Bails," Jenna muttered and gave her a stare that told Bailey to leave her mother alone.

"Jen and I are going to be out most of the day, but maybe you and I can spend some time together tomorrow. We could go shopping," Bailey said, giving in, knowing how much her mom was dying to take her shopping to buy her yet more clothes.

"Great. It's a date."

Several minutes later, they were in Bailey's car, driving to Jenna's house. With Bailey's mother at home, she knew they would get no privacy or downtime. Jenna's parents and younger brother were out of the house, though, so the two of them would have several hours together before Jenna's family arrived home. Bailey planned to use it wisely.

They'd locked Jenna's bedroom door and had their hands all over one another an instant later. Now, they were lying next to one another naked, wrapped in each other. This was Bailey's happiest place on earth. Wherever Jenna was, she wanted to be there.

"And then, he asked if I was single," Jenna said.

"He did, did he?" Bailey replied with clear jealousy in her tone.

"I said no, Bails." Jenna chuckled into Bailey's shoulder.

"This is, like, the third guy that's asked you out that I know of," Bailey said.

"It happens, yeah. Like you never get asked out," Jenna replied as she lifted her head to meet Bailey's eyes. "I know my girlfriend is hot. There's no way people aren't asking you out all the time."

"No one has asked me out, Jen; not one person since I got to school."

"How is that possible? Look at you." Jenna leaned back on one elbow, pulled the sheet covering them, and marveled at Bailey's body. "I love your body. I love you as a person, obviously, but I love your body, Bails."

"I'm glad." Bailey chuckled. "I don't know. No one ever asked me out in high school, either. I must just give something off that says, 'stay away.'"

"Hey, Bail?"

"Yeah?"

"Mandy knows about us, but no one else at school knows I'm dating a woman. Is that still okay?"

It was interesting how over the course of a few months, they'd gone from calling one another *girl* to calling one another *woman*. Bailey was dating a woman now; Jenna was dating a woman. They were adults in a long-term relationship.

"As long as people know you're unavailable, it's okay." Bailey ran her hand along Jenna's face. "But can you tell me why you haven't told anyone else?"

"I don't know," Jenna began. "I told Mandy pretty much right away because I knew you and I would be talking every day, and it was just easier to tell her than to try to hide it. With my other friends at school, though, I haven't seen the point."

"In telling them you have a girlfriend that you love?"

"I guess." Jenna shrugged. "You know you're gay; I don't know that for sure yet. I feel like the moment I tell someone I have a girlfriend, they're going to assume I'm gay." She paused and met Bailey's eyes. "And there's nothing wrong with that, obviously; my girlfriend's a lesbian." Jenna winked at her. "I just don't know if *I* am. I'm not ready to answer all those questions. I don't know what mold I fit. Maybe I'm gay; maybe I'm bisexual. Maybe I'm something else entirely."

"You don't have to know yet. Technically, you don't

ever have to know. I love you, Jen, and I don't care what your label is or even if you have one. I just want you to be with me," Bailey offered while stroking her cheek.

"Thank you," Jenna replied. "You're so good at taking the pressure off me sometimes. You used to do that in school, too."

"I did? What, with homework?"

"No, when I'd be nervous about something, you would notice it. Like that time they were announcing the homecoming court over the loudspeaker, and we were standing at the lockers: they read off three names, and there was only one spot left. You just leaned over and told me they were saving the best for last."

"That's right." Bailey smiled. "You thought they'd leave you off the list; you were crazy. You were always going to be homecoming queen, Jen."

"I love you, Bails. I know I don't know what I am yet, but I know I want you. Okay?"

"That's enough for me," Bailey replied.

*** 

Spring break was not something Bailey was looking forward to. With the exception of seeing Jenna for the first time in three months, there was nothing exciting to her about going to Miami with Samantha. Bailey and Sam hadn't talked much since they'd both gone away to school, and since Sam was going to school in Florida, she had invited Bailey to stay with her on campus for spring break so that they could catch up. Bailey still hadn't told her best friend that she had been in a relationship with Jenna Cabot for about eight months. She didn't want to break her best friend's heart, and she did want to see Sam, so she asked if it was okay to invite Jenna along. Samantha lived in an off-campus apartment with two roommates. Both of those roommates were going elsewhere for their break, and Sam had offered Bailey and Jenna their rooms.

"Are you planning to tell her while we're here?" Jenna asked in the car on the way to Sam's apartment.

"I don't know. I hardly talk to her these days. I've just been so busy with school, and you're busy with school and pledging these days; what little time I have leftover, I want to spend talking to you. I hate that I only see you every few months."

"Me too, Bail." Jenna leaned over and rested her head on Bailey's shoulder. "But we have a whole week together now."

"With Sam," Bailey added, "who barely knows you and who has no idea we're dating."

"If she did, do you think she would have invited me to come along? I'm worried I'm interrupting your time with your best friend."

"I want to see her, but, Jen, I freaking miss you, like, all the time." Bailey kissed Jenna's forehead and squeezed the hand she was holding. "This distance thing is hard. First semester, it wasn't as bad. The time difference can make things challenging, but now we're both studying more. I also have a few friends there now, and you have your friends at school. Plus, your pledging takes up a lot of your nights."

"I know. I'm sorry. It's just the pledging, though. Once I'm in the sorority, it'll calm down, I promise. It's my mom's sorority. It's important to her that I join."

"I get it. I want you to have what you want. I just miss you."

"I miss you, too. You know that, right?" Jenna lifted her head and looked at her.

"I know."

When they arrived at Sam's shortly after, Samantha greeted Bailey with a giant hug and an excited smile. She greeted Jenna with a handshake and an awkward glance that told Bailey she still wasn't exactly sure what Jenna was doing there. Bailey didn't know what to do. She didn't want to make things awkward by telling Sam now that they were actually a couple, but she also didn't like lying to her friend.

"I'm glad you're here. My friend Taylor told me about a party tonight. It's off-campus, and they won't card. I thought you could get settled in, and we could head over there," Sam said.

"Actually, I don't know about Jenna, but I am wiped. It's a long flight to get here. And then, I had to wait at the airport for Jenna's flight to get in. The ride from the airport was over an hour. I kind of want to just take a shower and maybe call it a night. I thought we could start the fun tomorrow," Bailey said, meaning every word.

"Oh, okay." Sam was obviously disappointed. "That's fine."

"You can totally go, though. I'm sure we'll be okay here on our own. I'll probably be asleep within the hour," Bailey replied.

She wasn't trying to get Sam out of her own apartment, she told herself. She just didn't want Sam to miss out on a party she wanted to go to just because she and Jenna didn't want to go. Of course, she wanted Jenna all to herself, too, though. The guilt washed over her as soon as Sam lowered her head to the floor before raising it back up to her.

"I'm already dressed and ready; I should at least make an appearance. My friends are expecting us. I'll tell them you guys were too tired. Maybe you can meet them tomorrow," she said.

"Of course, Sammy." Bailey smiled at her.

Ten minutes later, Bailey's things were in one bedroom, and Jenna's things were in another. Samantha had just left the apartment to join the party. Bailey and Jenna were in the shower together.

"I feel kind of bad," Jenna said. "I *am* exhausted, but I know we're not going to be asleep in an hour."

"Oh, yeah?" Bailey asked her as she wrapped her arms around Jenna's waist and pulled her closer.

"I don't plan on letting you sleep at all during this trip. We're on spring break; we're supposed to exhaust ourselves by having fun." Jenna's arms were around Bailey's neck. She leaned in and kissed the spot under Bailey's earlobe. "I plan to have a lot of fun with you," she whispered.

"I can't wait," Bailey said and pressed Jenna to the back wall of the shower.

Bailey meant it: she really couldn't wait. She hadn't been with Jenna like this since Christmas break. She wanted Jenna, but she also needed her right now. When she finally touched Jenna between her legs, Bailey could feel how much Jenna needed her, too. She coaxed a slow orgasm out of her girlfriend with deliberate stroking fingers. Now that they'd been together for so long, she knew exactly where to touch Jenna to make her feel good.

Jenna didn't return the favor in the shower. Her plan was to take her time with Bailey in bed. The only problem with that was, as soon as they exited the bathroom, with towels barely attached to their bodies and their mouths attached to each other, they ran into a very confused and surprised Samantha, who had returned when she'd realized she had left her phone on the sofa.

"Sam!"

"Bailey?" Samantha looked at both of them as they clung to their towels and moved about five feet apart at the same time. "Jenna?"

"Hey, Sam." Jenna gave an awkward wave.

"Were you two just–" Sam pointed at the bathroom they'd just exited.

"Yeah, we were," Bailey said. "Jen, would you maybe give us a minute?"

"Of course. I'll go get dressed."

Bailey hated hearing Jenna utter those words. Jenna moved into the room with her stuff and closed the door, leaving Bailey and Samantha standing in the small living room.

"So, you two aren't just friends, are you?" Sam flopped onto the sofa, staring off at the space behind Bailey.

"No, we're not."

"For how long?"

"About eight months," Bailey replied.

"Eight months? What the hell, Bailey?" Sam met her eyes. "I talk to you all the time. You've never said anything about this."

"We don't talk all the time anymore, Sammy. Before arranging this trip, we didn't speak for over a month. And before that, it was probably longer. I don't even know if you've declared a major yet or who your new friends are," Bailey said as she wrapped the white towel more securely about her body.

"I try calling you all the time. You always seem busy. I guess I know why now. You've been in a relationship for eight months."

"I've called you, too, Sam. You've made a lot of new friends here and have different priorities now," Bailey replied.

"Different priorities?"

"You go out almost every night, from what I see online. You're always out at parties or with a different guy. I'm not judging or complaining; I want you to do what you want."

"Well, you certainly are," Sam shot back. "Did you two just have sex in my shower?"

"Sam, when Jenna and I started dating, we didn't tell anyone. We still haven't told anyone. The only person that knows is her roommate because I stayed with Jenna once. Our parents don't even know yet. They just think we suddenly became really good friends." Bailey sat on the sofa but left some space between them. "I love her, Sam. I've loved Jenna for almost five years now. I've wanted to be with her since we first got to Browne. Nothing happened until she got back from her trip last summer.

When it did, though, it was perfect. We've been doing long-distance, and it's been really hard. I've been trying to keep up with school, my friends, and my family. I'm trying to run for student government next year to get more involved, and I'm also trying to find any excuse to see my girlfriend when she's just as busy and lives a thousand miles away." Bailey paused. "When you invited me here, I wanted to see you. I do miss you, Sam. I just also needed to see Jenna. I haven't seen her in three months. The flights are just too expensive. I don't have enough saved up to see her more, and neither does she. Our parents helped us with spring break because they wanted us to have fun. Plus, my mom loves you; she wanted me to spend more time with you."

Sam brightened at that and replied, "So, are you two both lesbians?"

"I'm gay, yes. Jenna doesn't know what label best applies. It doesn't matter to me. I just love her." Bailey smiled. "She makes me happy, Sammy. Since we can't see one another often, we talk every single day. We call to say goodnight whenever we can. If not, she records her voice for me so I can hear it just before I fall asleep. She even sends me handwritten letters sometimes so that I can get something in the mail. She's amazing. I was kind of hoping you two would get to know one another on this trip. My plan was to tell you after you spent some time with her and, hopefully, told me you liked her."

"I guess I'm third-wheeling it this week, huh?"

"No, Sammy. You're not a third wheel. I promise, this isn't just about Jenna. I wanted to see you."

"Then, be honest with me."

"Okay."

"Did you two just have sex in my shower?"

"I'll clean it for you tomorrow," Bailey offered with an embarrassed shrug. "Now, can I go get dressed?"

"Yes." Sam stood. "I'm going to the party. That'll give you two some time to be all over one another. Just make sure you clean the sheets before the roommates get back."

\*\*\*

"Bails, I said no. What more do you want from me?" Jenna asked as they walked back to Samantha's from a party.

"Nothing. I guess I want nothing. Never mind." Bailey folded her arms over her chest.

"Bails, please… Just talk to me." Jenna moved in front of her and stopped their progress. "You're obviously upset."

"Two guys were flirting with you like crazy, and you did nothing, Jen."

"That's right. I *did* nothing. I didn't flirt back, and when one of them asked me to go to an upstairs room with him, I said no. I said no, Bailey. You were standing right there. You know I didn't do anything wrong and that I'd never cheat on you. I love you." Jenna took both of Bailey's hands in her own.

"Why didn't you tell them we were together?"

"Because they're two strangers I will never see again. What does it matter if they know I'm with you or not?"

"I get you not wanting our parents to know yet, Jen. I just don't understand why we can't go to these places together. Sam knows now, and she doesn't care if her friends know about us. Half the girls in that place were making out with other girls. Does it bother you that you're with me? That I'm not a guy?"

"What? Bailey, no." Jenna placed both hands on Bailey's cheeks and stared into her eyes. "I'm a private person; I always have been. I don't tell my friends about my sex life or the lack thereof before I met you. I wouldn't have told most people who I was dating back in high school, but I had no choice, really. That place was rumor city. And when you go to school with someone you're dating, it's kind of hard to hide it."

"Hold on." Bailey stopped her. "You just said something… Can you back up?"

"To what?"

"Lack thereof before you met me?"

"Huh?" Jenna had obviously enjoyed a few too many drinks tonight because she wasn't as quick as she normally was.

"You said, '*your sex life or the lack thereof before you met me.*'"

"Oh, yeah. What about it?"

"Jen, I never asked." Bailey grabbed Jenna's hands and lowered them away from her face in order to hold them between her own. "I really didn't want to know."

"Know about what?"

"I assumed you'd had sex before me. I knew you dated. I didn't ask because the thought of anyone else touching you made me want to vomit. It still does."

"Bails, you are the only person I have ever had sex with." Jenna smiled at her and gave her that same reverent stare. "You were my first. I thought you knew."

"I didn't."

"I'm sorry. I should have told you." Jenna pressed her forehead to Bailey's. "If you need me to walk back to that lame party and tell those guys that I'm with you, that you're the only one who gets to touch me like that, I will. I'll do it right now if it means we're okay."

"No," Bailey began. "Sam's still there. Right now, I want you to take me to her apartment. I need you, Jen."

"Let's go." Jenna kissed her briefly.

***

"I miss my girlfriend. I feel like that's all I say these days," Jenna told Bailey through her laptop. "We were supposed to have the whole summer together, Bails."

"Jen, what did you want me to do? I couldn't turn

down this internship. It's what I want to do with my life once I'm out of school. They picked me, and I'm only going to be a sophomore."

"I know. I'm happy for you, Bailey. But it's the end of July. I go back to school in two weeks, and I've seen you all of two days this summer."

"I can't help that the internship is in Portland. And it's unpaid, Jen; I don't have any income. I can't just fly back and forth to see you. If I asked my parents to pay for stuff, they'd want me to spend that time with them instead."

"Bailey, it's our first anniversary. We've been together for one year, and you're not here to celebrate it with me."

"Jen, I love you. I wish I could be there, but I can't get away. I can't pass up this opportunity, just like you couldn't pass up joining the sorority and spending, like, twenty hours a week doing pledge activities so you could get initiated. We were supposed to have a week before my internship started, but you had to stay there for some sister-bonding experience."

"I didn't have a choice, Bails. It was a Big Sis – Little Sis event."

"I don't have a choice, either."

"When am I going to see you? Fall break?"

"I can try to come home a night early."

"Great. One night." Jenna rolled her eyes at Bailey through the screen. "My last night at home; my parents want to take my brother and I out to dinner. We'd have, like, three hours together if we were lucky, and we'd probably just spend all that time having sex since we're not going to be doing that anytime soon."

"You don't want to have sex with me?" Bailey asked.

"Of course, I want to have sex with you, Bailey," Jenna half-yelled. "I love you. I love having sex with you. Sometimes, it's all I fucking think about. But I don't want to see you for a few hours just so that we can have sex before I have to get on a plane and go back to school."

"Okay. Okay. I'm sorry. Jen, I'm sorry."

"I know you are." Jenna lowered her head, and Bailey missed her eyes immediately. Even when Jenna was angry with her, she always loved Jenna's eyes. "I'm sorry. I know this isn't your fault or your choice. I just really hoped we'd have this night together," Jenna added.

"Me too," Bailey agreed.

"This was the night of our first date, Bails. We had our first time together a year ago today. I woke up next to you, and I knew I wanted to be with you no matter how terrified I was."

"I will make this up to you, I promise."

"Just come to Michigan for fall break, please."

"I'll see if I can borrow some money from my parents. I'll get a job at school or something so that I can have money to come see you."

"You can't do that; you need the time to study."

"I *need* to see my girlfriend," Bailey replied.

"Tell me about it, Bails."

"I just got my class schedule. I don't have classes on Wednesdays, so I can book a flight for Tuesday afternoon and spend Wednesday through Sunday with you."

"In October," Jenna added.

"I know," Bailey replied, defeated.

\*\*\*

"You realize you've been here for two days, and we haven't had sex, right?" Bailey asked.

Since Bailey had made the previous trip to see Jenna, it had been Jenna's turn to stay in Bailey's new, off-campus apartment. They were supposed to have a fun four days together before Jenna went back to school, and so far, it hadn't exactly been a lot of fun. Their sophomore years were turning out to be busier than their freshman years. Bailey had more friends; Jenna had more friends. Bailey had been elected class vice-president; Jenna was in a sorority. They had spent a lot of time in bed just sleeping to try to catch up on what they missed when in school, and the majority of the rest of their time was spent doing schoolwork or just sitting quietly, watching TV.

"Is that my fault?" Jenna asked and seemed to genuinely wonder if she were the reason they'd yet to be together in that way.

"I'm not saying that."

"It didn't seem like you wanted to. You didn't even pick me up at the airport."

"I couldn't, Jen. I had a student council meeting." Bailey turned to her on the bed.

"I know. Doesn't it feel like things have changed?" Jenna rolled to face her. "We couldn't wait to see each other before. I literally ran to you in the airport, made out with you in public, and the moment we were alone, we had to be all over one another."

"I remember," Bailey replied mournfully. "I miss that."

"When did we lose it, Bails?" Jenna asked with concern in her tone. "We've spent two days together, and we've hardly even touched. You kissed me hello when I got here, and we've kissed good morning and good night. It's like we've forgotten how to be us."

"Because we never get to be us," Bailey surmised. "We spend more time apart than together. We don't really know how to be us because we never get the chance."

Jenna slid closer to her, placing her hand on Bailey's cheek.

"I love you," she said.

"I love you."

"I want us back, Bailey." Jenna moved on top of Bailey and stared down into her eyes. "I want you to want me how you used to. I want to want you like I used to."

"Me too," Bailey replied.

Jenna rolled her hips down into Bailey, and Bailey knew, no matter what may be wrong in their relationship, she would always be turned on by this woman. Jenna's lips met Bailey's for their first *real* kiss in over four months. They stayed like that for a long time, enjoying one another in a way they had so few opportunities to experience. When Jenna finally slid a hand under Bailey's shirt to cup her breast, Bailey knew she couldn't wait any longer. She took Jenna's free hand and tried to push it down, begging Jenna to touch her.

"Not yet," Jenna told her. "I want everything tonight. I want slow. I want all of you, and I want you to have all of me."

And they did. Jenna kissed every part of Bailey's skin as Bailey luxuriated in the touches. Jenna's mouth brought her to a remarkable orgasm while Jenna's fingers were buried inside her. She made Bailey come again and again after that before Bailey was allowed to touch her. Bailey touched Jenna in every possible way to make Jenna breathe out her name in that sexy way she always did. She tasted her, touched her, and loved her. She gave Jenna everything she had, because something she kept trying to dismiss, told her this would be the last time they'd touch one another like this.

***

"I love you, you know? This doesn't change that," Jenna said through sobs.

"I know," Bailey replied through her silent tears. "I don't want this, Jen. I love you."

"I know. But we tried. Bailey, we tried. It's too hard."

"What if I don't do the internship again this summer? I don't have to do it. They asked me back, but I can turn them down." Bailey wiped at her eyes as she tried to take in Jenna through her laptop screen. "We'd have three months together."

"Bails, it's not enough. Even if we have the whole summer together, we still have two years of school to get through. Besides, I can't ask you to give up that internship; that's not fair."

"I don't care," Bailey replied. "I'll call them right now and cancel. They can give it to someone else. Jenna, you're what I want."

"Hey, Bail?"

"Don't," Bailey said seriously. "Don't do that."

"You'll always be my first love. No matter what happens, you will always be my first in every way," Jenna said softly. "I thought we'd at least make it two years," she added after a moment.

"I don't want two years, Jen. I want forever."

"Maybe someday, we can find our way back to one another."

# CHAPTER 6: JUNIOR YEAR

"How is it that we're both finally twenty-one, but we're not going anywhere for spring break this year?" Samantha asked on the sofa in Bailey's basement.

"You didn't have to come here, Sam. I feel like I ruined your spring break," Bailey replied. "I've been in a funk lately. I don't mean to bring you down with me."

"Please, you've been in a funk since you and Jenna broke up. It's been over a year, Bailey," she said as she turned to face her. "Do you want to talk about it? You never talk about it."

"No. Like you said, it's been over a year. Closer to a year and a half, I guess." Bailey let out a deep sigh. "I haven't even seen her since. Every time I come home, I drive by her parents' house to see if she's there. I don't even know what I'd say to her if I actually saw her."

"Bailey, you have to move on. Jenna probably has."

"Do you know that?" Bailey turned to her, suddenly interested.

"What? No," Sam replied. "I guess I can assume. You don't still follow her on Instagram or Facebook? I think she's on Snapchat, too."

"We're not Facebook friends anymore. I had to delete her after we broke up. And I don't really pay attention to Instagram. I don't have Twitter, and I never followed her on Snapchat. She didn't have it when we were together. I only followed her Facebook updates for about a month after it happened. I guess I wondered if there was someone else. It seemed like that was better than we couldn't make it work. When I didn't see anything, I removed her. I realized I couldn't see her pictures with other people. I'd wonder if every single person in them was her *new* person. Was she taking them home later? Had they already had sex? Were they a couple? Did she tell them she loved them, too? Has she already forgotten me because she has them? I couldn't keep going on like that."

"Oh, Bails. She really did a number on you, didn't she?"

"I thought she was the one, Sam." Bailey's tears formed in her eyes. "God, I haven't cried over her in a long time. Sorry," Bailey said as she wiped her eyes.

"She's in town for spring break, Bails." Samantha placed a hand on Bailey's shoulder. "I do follow her on all forms of social media. I guess you could say I've been keeping an eye on her for you."

"You have?"

"You haven't been the same since you two broke up. I didn't do anything; I just paid attention to her updates. Her relationship status says 'single.' As far as I can tell, it hasn't changed since the two of you ended."

"She's here?"

"She's back home, yeah. Her mom is sick, Bailey. She was just diagnosed with breast cancer."

"What?" Bailey sat upright. "When?"

"Like a month ago. She's in treatment and everything, according to Jenna's posts, but I don't know anything other than that."

"I didn't know."

"And I didn't know if I should tell you. I still think you need to move on from her, but I know how important she was to you. Maybe you should think about reaching out just to get some closure," Sam suggested.

***

When Bailey parked her car on the street outside Jenna's house, she didn't plan to go inside. She planned on sitting there for a few minutes and driving off, as she'd done about five times since Sam told her Jenna was home. Bailey shouldn't be here, she knew that. Jenna wasn't her girlfriend. Hell, Jenna wasn't even her friend anymore. They hadn't spoken since they'd broken up. They hadn't even done the thing where they give borrowed items back to their original owner. Jenna still had at least two of Bailey's sweaters, a pair of Bailey's fuzzy socks that Jenna once borrowed to keep her feet warm, and probably a handful of other things. Bailey still had a few of Jenna's things as well.

"Bails?" Jenna asked when she opened the front door.

"Hey, Jen," Bailey replied with a gulp.

Jenna looked tired but still crazy beautiful. Her dark hair was pulled back, and her bright eyes were less bright than normal, but still the perfect shade of hazel. She was wearing a pink t-shirt and a pair of gray shorts. Jenna looked surprised to see Bailey at first, but then her lips turned up and into a beautiful smile.

"Do you want to come in?" she asked.

"Is that okay?"

"Yeah, I'm alone in here," she replied. "We can talk, if you want."

"Okay."

Bailey took a few steps inside the house, and Jenna closed the door behind them.

"You look good, Bails."

Bailey turned around to see Jenna leaning back against the door with her arms behind her back, staring at her.

"You do too," Bailey complimented. "You always do, though."

"It's been a while." Jenna's smile had turned into a near-smirk.

That smirk had been Bailey's undoing a hundred times before; Jenna had to know what she was doing. Bailey had told her on numerous occasions that she found that smirk sexy.

Bailey held her hands in tight fists to try to prevent herself from launching at Jenna. This was the first time she'd seen Jenna where she didn't greet her with a kiss or a hug. She wanted to press her body against Jenna's. She missed her touch. She also hadn't been with anyone since her last time with Jenna. She was twenty-one years old, and she'd had exactly one girlfriend and one sexual partner. Jenna had been the one Bailey had planned to grow old with.

"It has, yes." Bailey watched Jenna's eyes rake over her body and stop at where Bailey's fists were still clenched.

"Can I ask you something?" Jenna's eyes moved back up Bailey's body.

"Sure."

"Are you dating anyone?" she asked after a moment.

"No," Bailey replied instantly. "You?"

Jenna shook her head, and the smirk widened. Bailey knew she had come over here for closure. She had also come over to find out how Jenna was doing, with her mother getting sick. Now that she was looking at Jenna's long legs and adorably small bare feet along with her exposed collarbone and breasts not covered by a bra – which meant Jenna's hardening nipples were showing through the pink of the shirt – Bailey knew she couldn't just get closure today.

Jenna gave her an almost imperceptible nod, and Bailey moved to her then. Her arms were lifting at Jenna's shirt while her lips found Jenna's mouth. Jenna kissed her back hard while her hands went to Bailey's jeans. She unbuttoned and unzipped them in one fluid motion. Bailey pulled Jenna's shirt over her head, and just like that, Jenna's breasts were bared to her for the first time in so very long. Bailey grasped one of them in her hand and tweaked a nipple in the way she knew Jenna liked. Jenna's head went back hard against the door. Bailey stopped her movements and looked at her. Jenna's eyes were closed. She looked like she needed Bailey more than Bailey needed her, and Bailey decided to give her what she needed. She slid her hand into Jenna's shorts and touched her, leaning into Jenna's body and kissing her neck softly as she stroked her.

"Oh, yes," Jenna whispered out. "I missed you," she added.

Bailey stopped kissing her then. Her hand stopped moving, and she leaned back to stare into Jenna's confused eyes.

"We can't do this," Bailey muttered against Jenna's lips.

"What? Why? We're *already* doing this." Jenna's eyes showed disappointment. "Bailey, your hand is literally in my pants. Your fingers are on my clit right now. Why–"

Bailey removed her hand, now wet with Jenna's arousal, and then looked down at her jeans and buttoned them back up hastily.

"I haven't seen you since we broke up, Jen. This isn't right," Bailey insisted. "I shouldn't have come here. I just heard about your mom and that you were home. I thought–"

"You came here because you heard about my mom?" Jenna asked as she bent down to pick up her shirt. She threw it back on. "That's why you stopped by my house for the first time in over a year?"

"No, I've stopped by your house about a hundred times. You just weren't here when I did."

"What?" Jenna started walking down the hallway and toward the living room.

"Jenna, you dumped me." Bailey followed her. "I still

loved you. What was I supposed to do? I couldn't stand to follow you online on the off-chance you might meet someone new, and I'd have to see how happy you were with them. I'd drive here whenever I came home from school. Sometimes, I'd drive right by. Other times, I'd park and just sit there and wonder where it all went wrong."

"You sat outside my house?" Jenna asked as she stood in front of the sofa they used to share when Bailey visited.

"It's creepy. I know." Bailey shook her head at herself. "I missed you, Jen. It hurt me that we couldn't find a way to make it work. And I know things were hard, but-"

"Things weren't just hard, Bailey. Things were terrible. I loved someone more than anything, but I could never see her. We were nineteen, Bailey. Life got in the way, but that didn't mean I didn't love you or that I didn't want to make it work. I did. And I tried. I tried so hard to make it okay, but it wasn't okay for me. Once we both got so busy with school, we stopped talking, Bails. We checked in every night when we could, but we stopped *really* talking. We stopped planning our breaks together, stopped talking about our future after school, and we stopped trying to learn more about one another. We had check-ins, Bails; we didn't have a relationship near the end. So, I did try. I tried so hard. I think you did, too. I didn't want to be nineteen years old and have a girlfriend I had check-ins with and never actually got to see. I wanted to be a normal college student, Bailey."

"Were you? Have you been?" Bailey asked as she crossed her arms over the chest. "Have you been a normal college student since we broke up?"

"I flunked advanced calculus; that's pretty normal behavior for a college student. I got a D in statistics the semester we broke up; I got drunk every weekend for a month after we broke up; I spent a lot of nights on the floor of my bedroom then because I couldn't make it all the way to my bed. One of my sorority sisters had to hold my hair for me at least ten times. I'm a full semester behind in school because I ended up on academic probation, and I'm no longer an active sister because of that. I had to move out of the house for junior year, and I'm in a crappy off-campus apartment because it's all I can afford. I have a part-time job now because I need money since my mom got diagnosed, and my parents need money for whatever insurance doesn't cover. I eat ramen almost every night." She paused to let out a breath. "I guess the only thing that separates me from being a normal college student is the fact that I'm home for spring break instead of partying it up in Daytona or Myrtle Beach. I'm home because my mom just started chemo, and I wanted to spend as much time with her as I could. I had to scrape together what money I could and take the cheapest possible flight with two layovers to get here. And I had no one to talk to about any of this because I have no friends at school, and the one person I used to tell everything to doesn't talk to me anymore." Jenna paused and looked away from Bailey's eyes. "So, if that's a normal college student, then I guess I am one."

"Jen–" Bailey took several steps toward Jenna and wrapped her arms around her.

This was how they should have started when Bailey showed up today; they should have hugged like this. Bailey's arms pulled Jenna's waist tighter to her while Jenna's arms wrapped around her neck and did the same. Jenna's face was against her neck. Then, the tears started to fall, and Jenna's sobs began slowly before they picked up. Bailey held her tightly as Jenna wobbled against her. She managed to get them both to the sofa, where Jenna fell into her lap. Her face was still buried against Bailey's neck. Bailey just let her cry. She rubbed her back and whispered soothing words until Jenna's sobs finally slowed before silencing altogether.

They stayed that way for several minutes. Bailey hated to admit it, but this was the best moment she'd had in such a long time. She knew Jenna was in pain, but she was holding her; Bailey had Jenna in her lap. She was holding on to Jenna for dear life, and she loved it.

"Hey, Bail?" Jenna mumbled against Bailey's throat before kissing her there.

Bailey closed her eyes at both, the way Jenna said her name and the touch of Jenna's lips.

"Yeah?"

"Can we talk more?"

"We can talk about whatever you want," Bailey replied.

"Can we do it after?" Jenna asked as she kissed the same spot again. "I need you, Bails."

Jenna's hand moved to Bailey's cheek. She slid her thumb along Bailey's bottom lip and pulled it down momentarily before her hand slid down the front of Bailey's neck. It landed between her breasts and stilled.

"We shouldn't, Jen. We–"

"I know, but I've missed you. I've missed how you hold me like this, how you calm me down so easily, how you just let me be me, and how you touch me. No one touches anyone how you touch me, Bailey Sayers."

"Have you been…" Bailey took a deep breath as Jenna kissed her again. "With–"

"No one else," Jenna whispered in her ear. "As much as I tried to be a normal college student and find someone that made me feel how you do, I couldn't even come close. I haven't been with anyone else, Bails."

Bailey turned her face to Jenna and kissed her. They kissed slowly this time, reveling in how it still felt so familiar to kiss one another this way while also feeling so brand new. Bailey's hand went to Jenna's cheek, and she cupped it before running her hand back around Jenna's neck to pull her in closer. Then, she removed the rubber band from Jenna's hair to allow it to flow freely, and she ran her hand into it and felt how soft it was as it moved through her fingers.

Jenna's hand moved down to Bailey's hip as she turned more into Bailey's lap. Not being able to find a comfortable position that would allow her to remove Bailey's shirt, she moved to straddle her instead. Jenna's hands lifted her own shirt first. Then, they moved to Bailey's and pulled it up and over Bailey's head. Bailey reached behind her own back to unclasp and remove her bra. Then, Jenna stood. She stared down at Bailey for a moment; her eyes were showing just how much she wanted this. Jenna pulled her shorts and underwear down at the same time, and she was now naked in front of Bailey for the first time in so long. Bailey wanted to memorize her all over again. She leaned forward, pulled on Jenna's hands, and moved Jenna into her. She wrapped her arms around Jenna's back, pressed her face to Jenna's stomach, and breathed her in.

"Do you remember when we used to talk about putting a baby in there one day?" Jenna asked softly.

"Yes," Bailey replied and kissed Jenna's stomach. "Jen, I remember everything."

Bailey's lips lowered to the curls between Jenna's thighs. She kissed them just barely. Jenna gasped, and her legs wobbled slightly. Bailey resisted the urge to smirk. Jenna's hands were in Bailey's hair as Bailey's lips moved slowly over her body. They took a nipple into her mouth and sucked. Bailey's hand slid between Jenna's legs. She cupped her before sliding one finger into Jenna's still wet folds. Jenna groaned at the movement and fell into Bailey's lap. Bailey just continued sucking while she slid two fingers inside her ex-girlfriend. Her palm pressed to Jenna's clit while she supported the woman with her free hand on the small of Jenna's back. Jenna rocked into her slowly at first before she moved faster and faster still. Bailey's lips moved to the other nipple before her tongue poked out, and she licked Jenna's neck. Jenna's hands gripped Bailey's face and kissed her hard as she began the road toward climax. Bailey curled her fingers, thrust them up inside

Jenna, and watched the woman unravel above her as she came with Bailey's name on her tongue. Jenna collapsed on top of her, breathing hard. Bailey let her lie there for long moments before she encouraged Jenna to move and lie down on the sofa. Bailey climbed on top of her, undid her own jeans, and slid Jenna's hand inside.

"You're so wet," Jenna whispered.

Her fingers delved into Bailey's wetness, and moved them purposively against Bailey's ready clit. Bailey rocked her hips down into Jenna and allowed Jenna to bring her to orgasm. As her final tremors subsided, she leaned down and kissed Jenna softly, sweetly, until Jenna removed her hand. When Bailey stood, Jenna looked concerned, as if she worried Bailey might leave. Bailey knelt in front of the sofa then, turned Jenna to her, and kissed her thighs.

"I'm going to touch you like this now, okay?" Bailey asked her as her lips moved closer to Jenna's center.

"Yes."

"Then, we're going to get dressed, go up to your room, lie down, and you're going to tell me everything. Okay?"

"Okay."

\*\*\*

"Spring break wasn't enough, Jen. I miss you," Bailey said to Jenna's voicemail. "Will you please call me back? We need to talk about this."

It was late April now. Bailey and Jenna had spent much of spring break together. They'd talked a lot, spent time exploring one another again in Bailey's basement bedroom, and they had made an agreement that they'd talk more after they both went back to school. It had been two weeks. Bailey had called several times and left countless messages. She'd even emailed Jenna a novella about how much she wanted it to work this time. They weren't together. Sure, they'd agreed to talk and see if it might be possible to try again, but they weren't a couple. Bailey had hope, initially. But that hope was dwindling with every unreturned message.

By the end of the school year, Bailey had no hope left. Jenna had made her decision: it would be over between them. Bailey would have no choice now; she'd have to move on. So, she did. She went home for the summer but made no attempt to drive by Jenna's house. She'd heard from Samantha, who still stalked Jenna on social media, that Jenna had remained at school to take summer courses. Her mother was still sick but in treatment. That was all Bailey knew, and that would have to be enough.

When Bailey's senior year started, she made an effort for the first time. She joined the university's LGBTQ group, continued as the senior class vice-president, and started dating. The first three women she went out with were all wrong for her; she knew that. Nothing with them went past the first date. Then, there was one woman who made it to a third date. But when Bailey talked to her about her future plans, it didn't seem like their visions were in line. By the time her final semester in college started, Bailey had nearly given up entirely. She was fully prepared to end her college experience, go find a job, and try to find love again later. Then, she met Alyson.

# CHAPTER 7: THE JOB

"I get that this is important, Bails, but we've hardly had an hour to ourselves since you took this job," Alyson told her.

"I know, babe. I'm sorry. This convention is a big deal. It's only once a year, and they asked me to go. I've been there for six months, and they chose me," Bailey replied as she rolled her suitcase toward the front door of the apartment. "This is my chance to maybe get a promotion. We could use that money to go on that vacation we keep talking about."

"I don't want a vacation, Bailey. God, you just show up and say you need some stuff you left at my place so that you can go on a week-long work trip. I haven't seen you since last Saturday. We went grocery shopping. That's the last date we went on, Bailey: grocery shopping," Alyson said and moved to the front door to open it. "We haven't been a real couple since you took that job. Just go on your work trip, get your promotion, and call it what it is."

"Aly, I'm sorry. What do you want me to say? I can't not go, but when I get back, we can–"

"What? Talk about the vacation you know we'll never take? Bailey, we haven't had sex in over three weeks. Did you even realize that?"

"I've–"

"You've been busy and so tired; I know. You say that every time. I'm just over hearing it."

"So, we're breaking up, Aly? You don't want to try to work through this? I'm twenty-four years old. I don't have a choice; I have to work harder than everyone else to prove myself, to get these kinds of chances."

"I should have known. I shouldn't have started something with someone who was still in school. This is my fault. We're in different places, Bailey."

"You're three years older than me, Aly. That didn't seem to bother you then."

"You weren't gone all the time." Alyson opened the door. "You're going to miss your flight."

"I'll take a later one. Let's just talk, Aly. We've been together for almost two years."

"We haven't been together for the past six months, Bailey. It just took me this long to actually say something."

"So, it's just over?" Bailey asked.

"You can pick up the rest of your stuff when you get back. We can figure everything out then."

Bailey didn't bother trying to change Alyson's mind. If there was one thing she'd learned over the course of their relationship, there was no changing Aly's mind once it was set. The only thing Bailey could do was leave. When she came back, they could talk. Maybe Aly would take some time and rethink it. Maybe Bailey could talk to her boss about working fewer hours. It wasn't exactly what she wanted, but she never thought she'd lose her relationship over work.

When she arrived at the hotel to check in, she received her welcome packet for the convention along with her room key. She wheeled her bag into the elevator and pressed the button for the third floor. She had also texted Alyson twice already to let her know she had arrived safely, but Alyson had only replied that Bailey shouldn't text her this stuff anymore. They weren't a couple; she didn't need to know where Bailey was now. Bailey gulped that response down as the elevator took her to her floor.

Just as she pressed her key card to the reader and heard the beep, Bailey turned to see another person doing the same thing to their room down the hall.

"Hey, Bail."

\*\*\*

"Jen? What are you doing here?"

"I have a work convention. What are you doing here?" Jenna walked toward her, leaving her roller behind by her door.

"Me too." Bailey held up the welcome packet that had her company's name and logo plastered all over it.

"You work…" Jenna pointed at it. "Where?"

"Same place I went to school, Jen. You?"

"New Mexico."

"You live in New Mexico?" Bailey asked as she turned toward the woman walking toward her. "How long?"

"I got the job about a year ago, and I moved there for it," Jenna explained.

"I didn't know," Bailey replied.

"I didn't know you worked here, too."

"How would you? It's not like you ever bothered to call me back."

Jenna stared at the floor for a moment before lifting her eyes to meet Bailey's.

"My mom died, Bails." Jenna shrugged. "After you and I…" She stopped herself and looked away again. "I didn't call you back, that's true, but I didn't know what to say to you, Bailey. Nothing had changed; we still had school to get back to. My mom was still sick. I was still miserable without you, but I couldn't be with you, either. I should've had the courage to tell you that, and I didn't. I'm sorry. But then, my mom got really sick. We had to send her to a hospital that specialized in cases like hers. It was out of state. I spent the whole summer at school trying to get caught up from all my terrible grades. I didn't go back home until fall break, when it was too late. The treatments weren't working. We lost her around Thanksgiving."

"Jen, I'm sorry. I didn't know."

"I didn't exactly advertise it," Jenna replied.

"Come inside. We should talk more," Bailey said.

"I can't. I have a meeting with my team in ten minutes. I just came up to drop my stuff."

"But you're here all week, right?" Bailey asked.

"I leave Saturday morning," Jenna replied. "You?"

"Same." Bailey smiled.

Jenna smiled back and looked behind her toward her door before returning her glance to Bailey.

"We should grab dinner."

"Tonight?"

"I can't tonight," Jenna said. "Tomorrow?"

"I have a drinks thing. Night after?"

"I think I'm free. I have a meeting until six, but I can do seven."

"Seven, it is."

"Good. It'll be nice to catch up," Jenna said.

"I still can't believe you're here," Bailey replied as she shook her head in disbelief.

"I can't believe *you're* here. Let's talk at dinner. I'll make a reservation," Jenna offered. "I have to get going."

\*\*\*

"This has happened twice before," Bailey began. "Aly broke up with me right after I graduated. We'd only been together for about a month. Then, a few weeks later, she called, we talked, and we've been together ever since."

"And the second time?" Jenna asked before she sipped her wine.

"The second time was when Aly had gotten a job just out of law school that was a lot more than she'd bargained for. She was working eighty hours a week. And, you know what? I never said anything about missing her or wanting her to work less. I knew it was important to her. I knew she had no choice. Now that things are finally good for me at work, she's being such a hypocrite."

"I'm sorry, Bails." Jenna rested her hand on top of

the small table they shared. "That sucks."

"Well, it's over now, I guess."

"And you're okay with that?" Jenna asked.

Bailey stared at her. She thought of the girl she'd touched for the first time and the woman she'd touched for the last time while in her parents' living room. Jenna looked older now. She was still dressed in her convention clothes. She was wearing a business suit, and Bailey was wearing a business suit. They were business suit people now. But they were still also just Jenna and Bailey.

"I don't know, honestly," Bailey replied. "I thought we were okay. It kind of blindsided me that we aren't." She considered for a moment and added, "Weren't. I guess it's past tense now."

"I am sorry, Bails." Jenna finished her wine, but her eyes remained glued to Bailey's.

"What about you?"

"What about me?"

"Love?" Bailey asked and gulped as she awaited the response she both wanted and didn't want at the same time.

"Oh, I dated someone for about six months, and we ended about three or four months ago. Before that, there were dates, but nothing too serious. I wasn't ready after I lost my mom."

"The person you dated, were they–"

"It was a guy, Bailey. I had a few dates before him. Some were with women; a few were with men. But the long-term relationship was with a guy."

"Got it," Bailey replied.

Their eyes were still connected. Bailey could always feel so unbelievably close to Jenna just by looking at her eyes. No matter what changed between them, Jenna's eyes would always guide her back to her.

"We should probably turn in soon. It's getting late, and we have that all-company meeting tomorrow morning in the main hall," Jenna suggested.

"Right," Bailey agreed.

They made their way up to their floor and to their doors.

"I'll save you a seat tomorrow," Jenna said.

"I'll see you then. Good night, Jen."

The following morning, Bailey and Jenna sat in the main hall and listened to a few speeches. There was a brief HR meeting where they reviewed sexual harassment, and Bailey wondered for a moment what would happen if HR could read her thoughts because Jenna's legs looked amazingly soft and smooth under her black pencil skirt. Then, Bailey thought about how she *should* be thinking about Aly and not Jenna. Aly had only just broken up with her; Jenna had left her years ago with not so much as a returned message.

Lunch was a buffet. She and Jenna had to separate in order to have meetings with their respective teams. Jenna was in a completely different department, in a totally different office, but somehow, they had ended up at the same company, and now – at the same convention. At the end of the long day, Bailey had a meeting with her boss along with three other people she worked with regularly. She had kissed-up within reason, had a couple of drinks, and left the meeting feeling great about her prospects for that promotion. When she knocked on the door a little after eleven, Jenna opened it, and without saying a word, invited her into her room.

"My dad's doing well. He's hanging in there, at least. He sold the house a few months ago."

"He did?" Bailey asked.

They were lying on Jenna's bed, and both of them faced the ceiling. They weren't touching at all, but Bailey could feel Jenna everywhere.

"He's on his own now. My brother got married last year, actually, and he lives in New York."

"Wow! Things change, I guess."

"I guess they do." Jenna turned her face toward

Bailey. "Do you think you'll get back together with Alyson?"

"I doubt it. She seems pretty much done with me." Bailey turned her body to Jenna's. "I didn't even fight with her about it, Jen. She's done this or something like this to me three times now, and she's definitely a hypocrite, but I didn't even fight with her this time. I guess I tried for a minute, but then I just left. It was over, and I just left."

"Did you love her?" Jenna turned her body toward her.

"I did in the beginning, yes. Aly and I were together longer than you and I were." Bailey watched Jenna nod and lower her eyes. "Aly's not you, though, Jen. No one was ever you."

"He wasn't you, either, Bails," Jenna replied and reached out to touch Bailey's cheek softly. "No one has ever been you."

"Jen, this is a bad idea." Bailey placed her hand on top of Jenna's but didn't move it from her face. "We've been here before."

"I know." Jenna sighed. "Look, we have one more night here, right?" She met Bailey's eyes. "Can you stay here tonight? We can keep talking, and then tomorrow night, after the convention wraps, we can go out."

"Out?"

"On a real date, Bails."

"A real date?" Bailey lifted an eyebrow. "Jen, we don't even know each other anymore."

"*We* will *always* know each other." Jenna's hand moved to cover Bailey's heart. "We can just see how it goes."

"Then, you'll go back to New Mexico, and I'll go home. What's the point, Jen?"

"The point is we can't *not*," Jenna replied. "We can't not try. There has to be a reason we are both here this week; that it has always seemed to just feel like this when we're together. There has to be a reason, Bails."

\*\*\*

The following night, Jenna took Bailey to a drive-in movie in her rental car. They ate junk food, laughed, and talked while the movie played. They moved to the back seat to get more comfortable. Jenna's head moved to Bailey's shoulder, and they remained that way, watching the movie through half-reclined chairs in front of them, until it ended. It was sweet. Jenna had planned a sweet evening for the two of them. It made Bailey remember why she'd fallen in love with her, to begin with. Then, they returned to the hotel, ordered some late-night snacks and drinks, and just curled up in bed. Bailey watched as the light flickered in Jenna's eyes. They were more green tonight than brown.

They hadn't talked about what might happen next. Bailey had stayed over the previous night, and they'd held one another, but nothing more. Tonight, Bailey wanted to touch Jenna, and it was wrong somehow. They weren't a couple. They didn't even live in the same state. Bailey had just been dumped by her girlfriend of nearly two years.

"Hey, Bail?"

"Yeah?"

"I don't think we should have sex tonight," Jenna said and kissed Bailey's neck from her position, curled against Bailey's shoulder. "I want to – I really want to – but I don't think we should."

"I think you're right. We did that once, and it didn't work out."

"The sex?" Jenna leaned up. "Our sex has *always* worked out for me." She laughed as she met Bailey's serious eyes. "Bails?"

"You didn't even call me." Bailey sat up, removing herself from Jenna's body.

"What?"

"Jen, we had sex. We talked for hours after, and we said we'd keep talking, but you never called me."

"I told you–"

"You told me about your mom, and I am sorry about that, but you still didn't call me. I think I just now realized how upset I still am about that." Bailey rose from the bed.

"Bailey, come on." Jenna held out her hand for Bailey to take.

"Jenna, I loved you. Our breakup wrecked me."

"It wrecked me, too. Do you think I wanted us to end? I loved you, Bailey. We weren't ready for what this is between us back then."

"You didn't call me back, Jen." Bailey grabbed her jacket off the desk chair. "I left you message after message. God, I held you, Jenna. I held onto you why you cried. I made love to you because you needed me. I thought we'd be okay. *You* let me believe we'd be okay."

"I thought we would, Bailey." Jenna sat up. "Then, I got back to school and realized that nothing had changed; we were still in two different places. We'd still never see one another."

"You could have called."

"No, I couldn't have. I'd already done that to you once, Bails. I had to see your face when I ended things before, and I couldn't do it again." Jenna's eyes filled with tears. "I couldn't hear the hurt in your voice again. I was a coward, Bailey. I'm sorry."

"I can't do this." Bailey moved toward the door of Jenna's room. "We're just lying to ourselves here, Jen. We're lying because we think we can suddenly figure things out, and that it'll work this time, when there's absolutely no reason why it should."

"I love you." Jenna stood. "I love you. I've always loved you."

"Jen, I should go. This isn't right. Aly just broke up with me; you live in freaking New Mexico. There's no–"

"Go, then!" Jenna motioned toward the door as she raised her voice. "If you want to leave, just leave. You're clearly still pissed at me. Fine, be pissed. You don't want me, so just go."

"Of course, I want you. I've always wanted you," Bailey fired back.

"Even when you were with Aly?"

"That's not fair." Bailey pointed at her. "You were with someone, too."

"We are better together!" Jenna yelled. "You and I are better together, Bailey Sayers. You know that."

"Then, why does it never work?" Bailey yelled back. "It never works, and I end up hurting like hell. I don't want that anymore. I don't want to hurt over you anymore, Jenna Cabot." Her tears fell in earnest. "I loved you so much; it hurt every second we weren't together. I wanted forever with you, and you let me go. I understand why, but you let me go, Jen. I waited for you. I waited so long. When I met Alyson, I almost didn't even go out with her. I really liked her, and it still felt like I belonged to you, though. I was still waiting for this woman to return to my life and tell me she wants me back. I did fall in love with Alyson. She wasn't you, but I fell in love with her. And I don't regret that. I waited for you, Jen. I waited so long. I can't do this anymore." Bailey wiped her eyes. "I'm going back to my room. We should just leave each other alone. We only hurt each other."

"Bails, that's not true," Jenna said softly as she moved to Bailey. "We don't only hurt each other. I understand that I've hurt you, and I hate myself for doing that, but we have had some good times, too. We were good together."

"We were. But that doesn't change things now."

"I know," Jenna agreed. "I know."

"Let's just call this what it is: we're ex-girlfriends who ran into one another at a convention and got a little caught up in the nostalgia of being together."

"If that's what you want," Jenna said.

"It's what I need."

# CHAPTER 8: THE GESTURE

Jenna had been trying for over six months to get Bailey to talk to her. She had called, she had texted, left voicemails, sent emails, and even handwrote a letter just like she used to. She knew Bailey was right: they still lived in two different places. Things weren't easier; they were just different.

Bailey just did something to her; she always had. When they were in high school, Jenna had thought Bailey to be one of those kids that just seemed fine where they were. Bailey never seemed to try too hard to join a particular group. She also didn't participate in a lot of activities. She had her one best friend, and that seemed to be okay for Bailey. She didn't date, but Jenna honestly hadn't thought that much about it. Bailey was always Bailey. She was so sure of herself, in Jenna's mind. Bailey was smart, kind, and funny. Jenna didn't realize it then, but as she looked back on high school, she knew she had a crush on Bailey Sayers.

When Bailey had asked her out that day, she'd been so shocked. Later that night, after Jenna had ditched her friends and retired to her bedroom, she thought about Bailey. At first, her thoughts were simple. Bailey liked her. Bailey wanted to date her. Bailey was nice. Bailey had a nice smile. Her thoughts turned less simple then. Bailey had pretty eyes. Bailey's hands were always soft. When Bailey had asked her out, Jenna's heart had fluttered. She smiled that night at the idea of Bailey kissing her lips. She didn't say anything; she just allowed herself to feel it.

When she had gotten to South America, Jenna felt so alone. She had no distractions. She worked on the school during the day and spent the night in a small dorm-like space where all the students slept in. She would just stare at the ceiling and think only of Bailey. She knew within a couple of weeks that she had to talk to her. She had no idea that, by sending one email, she would end up finding the love of her life at age eighteen.

As Jenna sat down at her desk at work, she realized she had lost her. Either Bailey was getting revenge by not talking to her this time, or she just didn't want to talk to Jenna altogether. For all Jenna knew, Bailey could have gotten back together with Alyson. Maybe things with them weren't over after all. Jenna thought about waiting until next year's convention; she would undoubtedly see Bailey then, but that was six months away. She knew she needed to do something to get Bailey's attention.

\*\*\*

"Hey, Bail," Jenna said excitedly when she picked up the phone.

"Jen, you can't keep doing this," Bailey replied.

"Doing what?"

"You sent me flowers, Jen."

"I did," she answered. "I also sent you a letter. Have you gotten that yet?"

"Jen…"

"Bailey, tell me to stop," Jenna implored as she flipped the TV to mute. "If you tell me to stop – tell me you've moved on already, or that you don't ever want to hear from me again – I'll stop."

"Jenna, we're not together."

"I know."

"Do you even want to be?" Bailey asked.

"I want us to be okay. We didn't leave things right, Bails."

"I know," Bailey said as she sighed.

"Are you still with Alyson?"

"No."

"Are you with anyone else?"

"No," Bailey repeated.

Jenna ran her hand over her face, leaned forward on her sofa, and said, "I can't get you off my mind, Sayers. I don't know what to do. I keep seeing you next to my locker and then at graduation; you looked so cute that day in your little hat." She chuckled.

"You had to wear that hat, too."

"Did I look cute?"

"You looked adorable," Bailey replied as she laughed.

Jenna laid down on her sofa, stared at her ceiling, and said, "Then, I see you in my room that day I came home from my trip. It's like I can still feel you touching me softly, giving me the space to say no if I wasn't ready."

"Jen…" Bailey breathed.

"What are you doing right now?" Jenna asked.

"Lying on my bed, reading your damn letter," Bailey replied.

"What's your favorite part?"

"Who says I have one?"

Jenna laughed and replied, "Tell me."

"Where you told me the best thing about me is that I am always myself."

"I love that about you," Jenna shared. "I can see you now."

"What do you mean?"

"Bails, I see you all the time. I can see you lying next to me on your bed that first time, kissing me; I can feel your lips on me still. You're the only person that does that to me. I'll get these little pinpricks on my skin sometimes, and it's like you're there, kissing that spot," Jenna said softly into the phone.

"Jenna, you're…"

"Turning you on?" Jenna interrupted just as softly.

"Yes," Bailey breathed. "We haven't done this in a while."

"Do you want to, now?"

"We shouldn't."

"I want to." Jenna said and licked her lips. "I already am, Bails."

"Oh, God."

Jenna's hand was between her legs. She hadn't exactly touched anything that would make her come yet, but she was searching slowly for just the right spot.

"What are you doing?" Jenna asked in a barely-there whisper.

"Trying to figure out how you can still do this to me," Bailey replied. "Jenna, this doesn't change anything."

"Tell me to stop. Tell me you don't love me, Bails. Tell me, and I'll leave you alone."

Jenna's hand stopped moving as she waited for the response. Instead of words, she heard a light rustling followed by a deep breath. She smiled and moved her fingers lightly over her clit.

"Tell me what you're doing," Bailey said in a lower register than before.

"I'm on top of you. I have my lips on your neck in that spot you like."

"Where are your hands?"

"Everywhere," Jenna said, and she heard Bailey gasp. "I miss your sounds."

"Touch me, Jen." Bailey was breathing faster now.

"My fingers are on your clit; I'm stroking you just like I'm touching myself now." Jenna's fingers hurried over her clit. She needed to come, but she also wanted this to last. "Do you want me inside?"

"Yes," Bailey gasped out. "I want your mouth, Jen."

"I'm moving down your body."

"Yes."

"I capture your clit in my mouth and suck it hard while I push my fingers inside. Are you wet for me?"

"Yes!"

"I miss how wet you get," Jenna said as she slid two of her own fingers inside herself, curled them, lifted her hips, and pulled them back out to focus on her clit. "Bails, you're so hot when you come. I love watching you."

"Make me, then."

"My tongue slides up and down as I thrust deeper. Are you ready for me to go fast?"

"Yes!"

"Are you–"

"Yes!"

"Wow," Jenna said softly, and her fingers worked frantically against her own clit as she listened to Bailey come over the phone.

Jenna came as well, shouting Bailey's name into the receiver before she slowed her strokes to enjoy the aftershocks. She waited until they were all gone before she said anything while Bailey was silent on the other end of the phone.

"Bails?" she chanced.

"I'm here," Bailey said after a moment of silence.

"What do we do?"

"I don't know, Jen. I honestly don't know."

*\*\**

"So, you basically have a long-distance relationship?" Andrea asked.

"We're not together," Jenna replied.

"But you occasionally have phone sex?"

"Andrea!"

They were at dinner after Jenna's last day at work. She'd gotten another job offer that had been too good to pass up. It would keep her in New Mexico, which wasn't where she had planned on ending up, but the job was a step up, and it came with double her current salary and better benefits. She had thought about turning it down. She had even thought about finding a position with her old company in Bailey's office, but nothing had popped up over the last six months of them doing this thing where they weren't together but they talked at least once a week. And sometimes, those talks turned into something more.

"What? That's weird, Jenna," Andrea offered.

Andrea was one of her closest friends from work. Jenna would miss Andrea the most, but at least they lived in the same city. She would see her whenever she could and, hopefully, her new job would get her going in the right direction.

"I know." Jenna shook her head at herself and finished the dessert they were sharing. "I just keep doing it."

"And so does she, apparently."

"It's always been her for me, Andy. Even though we're in two different places, she's always in the back of my mind."

"And sometimes, you're so horny, you have to make a remote booty call to your ex-girlfriend? Girl, you've got to get it together. How do you expect to meet someone you can actually fall for when you're doing this thing with her? Are you going to tell the Future Mr. or Mrs. that you occasionally fuck your ex, but it's on the phone, where there's no real touching, so it's okay?"

"I know."

"You keep saying that, but do you?" Andrea lifted a concerned eyebrow. "You never go out with us. I've offered to set you up at least three times."

"I don't want–"

"Anyone other than Bailey?"

"That's not what I was going to say." Jenna finished her water. "I have to stop it, don't I?"

"Yes, you do." Andrea gave her a concerned expression. "I'm sorry, sweetie. If you two are ever going to be happy, you need to give up this part of your relationship."

"I don't know if I can have any relationship with her without that part."

"The phone sex is that good?" Andrea lightened the mood.

Jenna laughed and replied, "Yes, it is. But that's not what I'm talking about. I don't think I can just be her friend."

"Then, you should tell her that."

"But I'm the one that started it; I'm the one that begged her to talk to me, that sent her flowers and love letters."

"Oh, my God. You're so cute, Jen." Andrea clutched her hands to her chest. "If this wasn't so dysfunctional, I'd ask to meet her just so I could see you two together."

"I'm supposed to call her tonight when I get home."

"What are you going to say?"

***

"Hey, Jen?"

"Yeah?" Jenna asked as she leaned back against the pillows on her bed.

"I was talking to Sam yesterday, and I kind of told her what we do sometimes," Bailey answered.

"The phone-sex part?"

"How we act like we're together when we're not."

"Yeah," Jenna said, not really sure why.

"She let me have it, actually." Bailey laughed. "She told me I was being stupid, that you and I weren't together for a reason, and that unless we were going to make a commitment and see it through, we should stop."

Jenna sighed and said, "She's right."

"I know," Bailey agreed.

"What do you want to do?"

"Move to New Mexico." Bailey laughed again. "But that's not right."

"No, it's not. You are happy there," Jenna stated. "And I start a new job on Monday."

"I know."

"She is right, though, Bails. Andrea said the same thing tonight, when I told her. We're just stuck in this place, you and me. We're technically free to date anyone, but we don't."

"A woman asked me out yesterday."

"What?" Jenna's eyes went wide. "What did you say?"

"See? This is the problem," Bailey began. "I can't talk about this stuff with you. It doesn't work."

"Did you want to–"

"Jenna…"

"I can't, Bailey. I can't watch you be with someone else; I can't hear about it on the phone every time we talk, and that's not fair to you."

"And I can't do that with you," Bailey returned. "What do we do now?"

"I don't think I can be your friend, Bailey. As much as I want to, I don't think I can watch you settle down with someone else."

"I get it. Every time we talk like this, I keep waiting for you to tell me you've met someone. I get stressed out before every single call because of it. I don't want that for myself."

"We should stop this then," Jenna said.

"Is this our last phone call?" Bailey asked.

"I think it has to be," Jenna replied reluctantly.

# CHAPTER 9: THE BOYFRIEND

"Happy twenty-five, Jen!" Andrea blew one of those cheap party favors.

"Thanks. How drunk are you?" Jenna asked as she laughed at her friend.

"I've had a few," Andrea replied. "It's a party, and I just broke up with my terrible boyfriend; I'm drowning my sorrows, and I prefer booze to ice cream."

Jenna's twenty-fifth birthday party was at a bar. It wasn't exactly her taste, but Andrea had planned it for her without her knowledge. She'd go with it, leave as soon as she could get out of there, and head home to watch some old movie and snack on some popcorn.

"Oh, sorry."

Jenna felt a bump from behind her and turned to see a guy with a beer in his hand. He had dark hair that looked a little lighter with the bar lighting illuminating the top of his head. His eyes were blue. His jaw was strong. And she liked the smile he just gave her.

"It's okay," Jenna replied.

"I'm Joel," the guy said as he stuck out his hand for her to shake, which she did.

"Jenna."

"Jenna and Joel," Andrea said rather loudly. "That's so cute."

"Alliteration is cute?" Joel asked as he looked at both women in turn.

"You know what alliteration is?" Jenna asked him.

"I do." He laughed.

Jenna smiled at him and took in his nice, steel-gray shirt and black slacks.

"It's her birthday; you should buy her a drink. You can also buy me a drink; I'm her best friend," Andrea interrupted.

"Andrea!"

"Happy birthday," Joel said with that wide smile still on his face.

\*\*\*

"Date number three?" Andrea asked.

"Yes, it's date number three."

"You know what happens on date number three, Jen."

"I know what *you* think happens on date number three, Andy," Jenna replied.

Andrea and Jenna had decided to become roommates after Jenna left her previous job. It allowed them both to still spend time together and save money at the same time. Jenna was hoping to be able to buy a house one day soon. She still wasn't sure where she would be buying, but she didn't want to rent for the rest of her life. She also didn't really care much for her new job but was trying to give it some time before making a decision on whether or not to stay. There was a lot of stress going on in Jenna's life right now. On top of hating her job, being roommates with Andrea – who was very messy and stayed up late most nights – and trying to get her finances in order to potentially start looking at houses somewhere, she also started dating Joel.

Joel was great, and Jenna liked him enough to continue dating him. She didn't know where things would go, but she knew she needed to move on from Bailey. They hadn't talked in over seven months. Every so often, Jenna got the urge to pick up the phone and call her. That was a lie… Every day, Jenna got the urge. Multiple times a day, she wished she could talk to Bailey. She hadn't, though. She had resisted because she knew that was what they both needed.

"You're not going to put out tonight?"

"No, Andy." Jenna laughed. "I'm not putting out tonight. I like him, but with work and everything, we've only been able to go on two dates so far. Tonight is only the third one, and I don't really feel like I know him yet."

"And you have to know someone to have sex? You must think I'm a damn slut, then," Andrea replied as she laughed at her own joke.

"You have your moments." Jenna winked at her. "I know I, personally, enjoy the random guys you bring by here. Do you just go to a state fair, let the carousel go around, pick one for tonight, and go back for more tomorrow?"

"Yes. How did you know?" Andrea joked. "Seriously, though… What's the hold-up? Am I dealing with the residual Bailey-withdrawal here? Do I need to take your phone away again?"

"That was one time, and I was drunk."

"Yes, you nearly sent that woman a text message telling her you missed her body, Jen. That was what you said, word for word; you missed her body," Andrea replied. "You're lucky you had me to stop you."

"I'm not dealing with residual Bailey issues; I'm just taking my time with him."

\*\*\*

"Hey, can we talk about something?" Joel asked her as they sat on his sofa.

"Sure," Jenna replied.

"You and Andrea, are you going to sign your lease again? It's almost up, right?"

"Yeah, next month. Why?" Jenna turned her eyes from the TV to him.

"I was going to ask you to move in here."

"With you?" Jenna turned her entire body to him then.

"No, without me, Jen. You'd move in here, but I'd move out. We'd still date, though," he joked.

"You want us to move in together?"

"We've been together for six months."

"That seems soon. Isn't that soon?" Jenna asked as she turned back to the TV, her heart racing.

They had been together for the past six months. She went back and forth from his place to her place but spent most of their time at his since he lived alone. She had also told Joel she loved him, and she did. She did love him, but she was good where they were in their relationship. She hadn't expected this from him; not once had he brought up the idea of living together. Jenna had just assumed she would sign a lease with Andrea again, and if Andrea decided to move out, Jenna would just keep the place and turn the other bedroom into a guest room or office.

"It doesn't feel soon to me. I love you. You know that." Joel ran a hand through her hair and leaned into her. "We can redecorate however you want. Plus, I know you love that hot tub out back."

"I do," Jenna replied as she laughed. "I just thought I'd buy my own place one day."

"Okay. Well, if you move in here, we can consider it temporary. It's a good starter home, and I don't mind finding a place for us that we look for together."

"You want to buy a place *with* me?" Jenna asked, her heart racing even faster.

"Sure, why not?"

"Joel, where is this coming from? We haven't talked about any of this."

"Don't you think we should?"

"Talk about buying a house together?" Her voice was much higher in pitch than it had been only moments before.

"Jen, we're in a serious relationship. These are steps people take together," he replied. "I know you've been a little resistant to talk about this stuff before."

"No, I haven't."

"Last month, I brought up your lease, then mentioned that I own this place, and you didn't say a word. You literally grabbed another piece of pizza and changed the subject. Do you not want these things with me?"

"I do. I do." Jenna put her hand on top of his. "I just wasn't expecting them tonight."

"Do you want to live with me?"

Jenna stared into his eyes, and she could see how important this was to him.

"Of course, I do. I'll talk to Andrea to see if she's okay with the short notice."

"Really?" Joel asked with a bright smile.

"Yeah, let's do it."

\*\*\*

"Jenna, can you please take the meeting for me? I need to head out," her boss said as she leaned over her cubicle wall.

"I'm actually supposed to be leaving soon. I have my anniversary dinner, remember? I told you last week, and it's on my calendar that I need to be out of here by five," Jenna replied.

"Can you be a little late?"

"No, it's my one-year anniversary with my boyfriend, Monica," she answered. "I promised him I'd be there."

"Take the meeting for me tonight. It should be done by six, and you can leave after. I need to go work on a project Laurie just assigned me."

"You said you were leaving," Jenna shot back, now frustrated.

"I'm doing it from home," Monica replied. "Just take

notes for me, and I'll get them tomorrow. I really appreciate it."

Monica didn't wait for a response. She never did. This was the third time this month alone that Jenna's boss had dropped something on her at the last minute, and it was at least the tenth time she would be late for something with her boyfriend because of this woman. Joel wouldn't be happy about her being late for their reservation, but Jenna didn't have much of a choice. God, she hated this job. She knew she needed to find a different one, and she had been looking, but there was nothing in her position available within fifty miles of Joel's house. Their house; it was *their* house now. Jenna had been living there for five months now. It was their house.

"I am so sorry," Jenna said the moment she walked through the front door. "The meeting went way over, and I couldn't get out of there."

"It's after eight, Jen." Joel took a drink of his beer.

He was sitting on the sofa with his arm stretched over the back of it and the beer in his other hand. He was still wearing his shirt and tie along with his gray pants and black shoes Jenna had picked out for him.

"It took me an hour to get home. There was an accident." She tossed her messenger bag on the floor by the sofa and sat down next to him. "I couldn't help it, Joel. I did call."

"Calling me to tell me you're late doesn't make up for being late for our one-year-anniversary dinner, Jenna."

"What was I supposed to do, Joel? She just dropped this meeting on me; I didn't have a choice."

"You told her last week that you needed to be at dinner. You should have stood up for yourself." He sipped his beer again. "I waited there for over an hour. I looked like an idiot."

"I told you not to wait for me," Jenna replied.

"I'm always waiting for you, Jen." Joel sat forward and pulled something out of his pocket. He then placed the small, black box on her thigh. "I had a whole thing planned. I should probably just wait, but I feel like you need to know why this mattered so much to me. I thought about doing this on your birthday, but you and Andrea wanted to go out instead. I had her help me pick this out. The waiters all knew about it; they had champagne chilled, ready for me. And you never showed."

"Joel…" Jenna stared down at the ring box he had presented her with.

"I'm ready for this, Jen." He turned to her. "I want everything with you. Do you want that with me?"

Jenna hated herself because, in that moment, she was looking at Joel, but she could only see Bailey's face.

# CHAPTER 10: THE CHANCE MEETING

"So, it's really over?" Andrea asked her as they sat at the airport awaiting their flight.

"I'm flying to Hawaii with my best friend instead of my ex; what do you think?" Jenna glanced in Andrea's direction.

"It's only been two weeks, though; maybe you just need to get away from Joel and from work to think things through. He's such a good guy, Jen."

"I know he is. He's amazing, but I can't marry him, Andy." Jenna turned to her in the awkward chair. "I do need this time – I need four days in Hawaii to relax and get away from my job, which I hate – but I don't need it away from Joel to realize that I want him, after all."

"He was so excited to marry you." Andrea shrugged. "You should have seen him picking out rings."

"I know, and I feel terrible. I shouldn't have let it get that far; I never should have moved in with him."

"What? Really?" Andrea sipped her iced coffee through the straw.

"I only said yes because I thought I should," Jenna offered.

"Well, that's really shitty of you."

"I know." Jenna shook her head at herself. "I did love him; I just wasn't ready for all this. When I saw the ring, Andy, I thought I was going to have a heart attack. When I opened the box and took it out, he thought I was saying yes. He went right into planning the whole damn thing. He mentioned something about a fall wedding and that his mom wanted to help plan it for us. He even said we could buy that house together right before and come home to it after the honeymoon."

"Damn. He doesn't mess around, does he?" Andrea asked.

"He deserves someone that wants to tear that box open and slide that ring on her finger. He should have a girl that wants all that stuff with him. It's just not me."

"Hell, I'd marry a man like that," Andrea joked.

"Well, he's free now."

"He's broken now, Jen." Andre laughed lightly. "I'll wait for him to get his life back together." She winked at her best friend.

"Thank you for bringing me with you. I know this is technically a work thing for you, but I really appreciate the excuse to get away."

"It'll be fun having you there." Andrea wrapped an arm around Jenna's shoulder and gave it a squeeze.

"Jenna?" The voice came from someone Jenna hadn't seen in over two years.

"Hey, Bail." Jenna gulped as she looked at her ex-girlfriend, who now stood in front of her.

"Bail?" Andrea met Bailey's eyes and looked back at Jenna. "*The* Bail?"

"What's that supposed to mean?" the woman to Bailey's right asked. "*The* Bail?"

"Nothing, babe." Bailey looked at the tall woman.

Jenna looked between them and noticed their clasped hands. She then met Bailey's eyes, and her whole world imploded.

"Andy, this is Bailey. Bailey, this is my best friend, Andrea," Jenna introduced.

Andrea removed her arm from behind Jenna, reached out, and shook Bailey's hand. Bailey took that hand back and clasped it again with the hand that belonged to the woman to her right.

"It's nice to meet you." Bailey paused and let out a deep breath Jenna could swear she could feel. "This is my girlfriend, Callie."

"Callie?" Jenna said in a whisper to herself.

"Callie, this is my friend, Jenna."

"Friend?" Andrea checked with Jenna.

"Andy, stop," Jenna gave her friend's hand a light smack. "It's nice to meet you."

"Thanks. You too. Hey, I was going to run to the bathroom. Do we have enough time?" Callie asked Bailey.

"We board in twenty; you're good. I'll meet you at the gate," Bailey replied with a smile and kissed Callie's cheek.

Callie waved at Andy and Jenna before she walked off.

"I actually need another coffee if I'm going to make it through today," Andy lied and stood. "I'll be right back."

She walked past Bailey, turned back to Jenna, and gave her best friend a big-eyed expression that Bailey couldn't see before she headed in the direction of the coffee place in the terminal.

"Well, that wasn't obvious," Jenna said sarcastically.

"She shouldn't be an actress." Bailey smiled at her. "How are you, Jen?"

"I'm good. You?"

Bailey shifted her backpack and replied, "Good."

"We're really good at this." Jenna laughed.

"Clearly," Bailey said while staring directly into Jenna's eyes.

God, Bailey had great eyes that had always been able to look right through her.

"So, Andrea?" Bailey finally spoke again.

"Best friend, like I said. Callie?"

"Girlfriend, like I said."

"How long?"

"About a year," Bailey answered.

"A year?" Jenna asked.

"Ten months, but yeah." The woman smiled a little. "Where are you headed?"

"Hawaii. We're here on a layover, just waiting for our next flight."

"Friends' vacation?" Bailey asked.

"Actually, no. Andy is going there for work, and I'm just tagging along." Jenna hesitated before adding, "I just broke up with my boyfriend, and I needed some time away."

"Oh. Sorry, Jen." Bailey's hands slid into her pocket.

"I'm not. It needed to happen. I waited a little too long."

"How long?"

"Like, he-had-a-ring too long."

"Wow," Bailey's hands moved from the front pockets to her back pockets. "Marriage, huh?"

"Not to him," Jenna offered and slid her clammy hands over her jeans. "You?"

"Oh, no. We're good for now. Callie isn't big on the whole marriage thing anyway."

"She's not? Do you not want to get married anymore?" Jenna asked.

"No, I do. I still want that one day."

"But she doesn't?" Jenna squinted at her.

"She's twenty-three. She was an intern at the office during her last semester in undergrad. We started dating when her internship was up. Now, she's a grad student. Marriage isn't exactly on her mind yet."

"Wow. Twenty-three?"

"I know. I can't explain it. She is mature for her age, though."

"We're only almost twenty-seven; we're not that much older," Jenna said.

Bailey moved swiftly to the chair next to Jenna, lowering her bag to the floor and turning to face her.

"I know. But there's such a difference between those ages, right? Like, I'm ready to buy a place, settle down, find a wife, and start popping out babies; she's ready for her advanced statistics class," she said.

Jenna laughed hard, rested her arm over the back of Bailey's chair, and said, "You *would* date someone who's good at math."

"She's terrible at it. She's failing, actually. I must have a type." Bailey winked at her.

"Right." Jenna turned her head away, pretending to look at something else.

"What happened with the ex?" Bailey asked after a moment.

"Joel? He's an amazing guy. We were together for about a year. Actually, we were together for one year exactly – I broke up with him on our anniversary, which just so happened to be the night he proposed."

"That sounds terrible," Bailey said with a light chuckle. "I thought you wanted all those things, though. The marriage, kids, house, and everything that goes along with that. I guess it's been a while since we've talked, though."

"I do. I still want all that stuff, and I'm ready for it now; I just didn't see it with him." Jenna didn't add that she had only ever seen it with Bailey. "I also hate my job and need to find a new one, but I don't know that I want to stay in New Mexico. It's a big thing."

"I heard you left a while ago. I made every effort to avoid tracking you down at work; it was too hard." Bailey met her eyes again.

"I left for a promotion, and it turned out to be a mistake. Honestly, Andrea has helped keep me together all these years."

"Not the ex-boyfriend?" Bailey lifted an eyebrow and smiled sideways at her.

"You can't smile at me like that," Jenna said and laughed as she pointed.

"Like what?"

"You know that's your sexy smile."

"It's my awkward smile," Bailey argued.

"And I find your awkwardness sexy; you know that." Jenna laughed before she stopped suddenly. "Sorry."

"For what?"

"I shouldn't have said that."

"Is it true?" Bailey asked.

"Yes."

"Then, you can say it."

Jenna leaned in ever so slightly to breathe Bailey in. She smelled so familiar. She smelled like home.

"I miss you, Bails."

"I miss you, too," Bailey replied. "Do you think we're at the point where we can try being friends again? We've both moved on."

"I don't–"

"Hey, babe. Are you ready?" Callie had returned.

"Oh, yeah." Bailey stood. "I thought you'd be at the gate."

"It's down there." Callie pointed. "Bathroom's back there; I had to walk past you two in order to get there." She squinted at Jenna for a moment before returning her eyes to her girlfriend.

"We should go," Bailey said to Jenna.

"Have a good flight," Jenna replied.

"It was good to see you, Jen."

"You too." Jenna smiled at Callie. "It was nice to meet you."

"You too," Callie replied, but Jenna was certain she didn't mean it.

*\*\**

"Where are you?" Jenna asked.

"I'm at home. You?" Bailey replied.

"Home."

"We're exciting tonight, aren't we?" Bailey laughed.

"Very."

"Is this weird? Us, talking again after all this time?" Bailey asked.

"It's never weird with you, Bails." Jenna paused. "Now, tell me about your day."

"My day? How about the past few years? You've got a lot of catching up to do, Cabot."

"Catch me up, then, Sayers."

Jenna smiled the entire time she and Bailey talked. She had waited a month after their run-in at the airport to text Bailey. She was testing the waters. When Bailey replied moments later, they had set a time to talk a week later. Jenna hadn't realized how much she had missed having this woman in her life. Just talking to Bailey for five minutes made her forget about her struggles at work, the fact that she had done such a horrible thing to Joel, and that she secretly wanted to leave New Mexico and had to figure out how to accomplish that.

"How's Callie?" Jenna asked during their second phone call a few weeks later.

"She's good."

"Good."

"Yeah," Bailey said. "Have you found anyone since Joel?"

"Oh, no. I'm not really looking, though. I've got so much to work out before I date again."

"Just like high school, huh?" Bailey asked as she chuckled.

"High school?"

"You didn't want to date anyone senior year since you'd be leaving."

"Oh, I forgot all about that. I guess that plan didn't work out well, huh?" Jenna waited for Bailey's reply, and when none came, she said, "Bails?"

"I thought it worked out pretty well," Bailey finally said.

"Oh, Bails, that's not what I meant." Jenna leaned forward on her sofa. "You know that's not what I meant."

"We shouldn't talk about this."

"Because you have a girlfriend?"

"Yes, because I'm with Callie."

"Do you love her?" Jenna risked.

"I've been with her for almost a year, Jen. We're about to move in together, I think."

"You think?" Jenna asked as she flopped to lie down on the sofa.

"We've gone back and forth over it."

"Why?"

"I don't know." Bailey sighed.

"Yes, you do."

"No, I actually don't." Bailey was growing frustrated; Jenna knew that tone well. "What are you trying to do, Jenna?"

"I'm not trying to do anything," Jenna replied.

"You didn't want me, Jen."

"What?"

"In college, you didn't want me. You broke up with me. Then, after that day at your house, you never talked to me. You wouldn't have ever picked up the phone again had we not run into each other at that convention."

"And then we saw each other at the airport, Bails. What are the odds of that? Of all the airports in the whole world – of all the flights, days, and times – we ran into each other."

"I'm with Callie, Jenna."

"Yet, you're going back and forth about moving in with her?"

"Because *she's* not ready; I am." Bailey paused. "I'm ready to move in with her, and I'm giving her time to get there."

"You want to live with her?" Jenna said softly.

"I do, Jen. I'm the one that keeps asking her."

"Oh," Jenna replied. "I guess I didn't think of it like that."

"That I would find someone else?"

"No, I knew you'd find someone else." She hesitated as tears formed in her eyes. "Bailey, you're so amazing. I knew someone would find you as amazing as I do."

"Jen, come on."

"When Joel put that ring in my lap, I turned to him, and I couldn't see him at all; I could only see your face. I knew then how much I'd screwed up. I shouldn't have gotten that far with him, but I never should have let you go."

"No, you shouldn't have," Bailey said. "We could have figured something out, Jenna. I don't know much, but I know that. Did you know that Sam had a long-distance relationship with a guy senior year of college? She was in Florida, and he was in Oregon. He then went to graduate school in California while she got a job in Texas. They're married now, Jen. They got married after years of working a long-distance relationship out."

"I get it, Bailey. I don't need a recap of how much I screwed up. For the record, though, I did want you. I have always wanted you. And I want you now. I want you right now. I have always and will always love you."

"You want me right now? Right now, right now?" Bailey asked with a hitch in her breath.

"If you were single, Bails..." Jenna placed her hand on her stomach under her shirt. "When I saw you at the airport, I couldn't believe how sexy you still were. Your hair is a little shorter and lighter. It looked so good pulled back like that."

"Jen..."

"I know." Jenna's hand slid down inside her pants. "You know how we used to do this, and I would talk you through it?"

"Jenna, I can't do this."

"Then, hang up." Jenna's hand stopped before it had even begun.

"I can't touch myself."

"Can you listen to me while you talk me through it?"

"Yes," Bailey whispered.

"What are you doing to me then, Bails?"

\*\*\*

"I know it's wrong, but I can't stop, Andy."

"You can't stop having phone sex with your ex-girlfriend from, like, a million years ago, who has an actual girlfriend?"

"It's not that part; it's all of it." Jenna rolled her eyes at herself. "I can't *not* talk to her. Even though she talks about Callie sometimes and how they're about to move in together finally, I can't stop talking to her and getting to know her again."

"She belongs to someone else, Jen."

"I know."

"No, you need to really say it; you need to say it out loud. You need to tell me that you understand that she has a girlfriend; that she's with someone, and it's not you. You two have been talking for four months now. Has she asked you once to get back together? Has she told you she still loves you? Has she mentioned that she's breaking up with her girlfriend?"

"No," Jenna grunted. "She's mine, though, Andy."

"Jenna, she's—"

"I've loved her for nearly ten years. Do you know that? Ten years, Andy. She was my first everything. I thought she would be my last, but I messed up. I wasn't willing to put the work in. I was young, and I didn't know that I'd never find anyone that makes me feel how she does. I am happy when I talk to her. We could just read the phone book back and forth to one another, and I'd be completely content, because she's the person I'm supposed to be with."

"Then, what are you going to do about it, Jen?"

"I don't think I can talk to her anymore," Jenna replied. "As much as I want to talk to her all the time, see her all the time, kiss her all the time, and–"

"Okay, I get it." Andy held up a hand to get her to stop.

"She's going to move in with someone else, isn't she?" Jenna asked so softly, she wondered if Andrea even heard her.

"I think so, sweetie." Andrea placed her hand on top of Jenna's.

"So, I have to move on again?"

"Jen, you can either move on, or you can *really* fight for her. You could show her what you didn't show her last time; make the move you didn't make then. Make sure she knows she's the only one you want. Then, you wait."

"Wait for what?"

"Wait for her to tell you if she wants you back."

# CHAPTER 11: GOING HOME AGAIN

"Welcome home, honey." Her father hugged her the moment Jenna entered the house.

"Thanks, Dad." Jenna hugged him back.

"Let me get your bags," he said and moved behind her to grab her two suitcases to bring them inside.

Jenna couldn't believe she was moving back in with her father. This had definitely not been part of her grand life plan. He'd moved only about three streets over from the house Jenna grew up in after he had been unable to stay there long after her mother's death. She understood. But as she walked into the guest room, where she would be staying indefinitely, Jenna wished she had her old, comforting room to return to after failing so miserably.

"Are you ready for dinner?" her father asked as he leaned into her doorway.

"Oh, I guess."

"I kind of assumed you'd want to eat dinner with me. I shouldn't have, huh? You're an adult; you probably have plans."

Jenna didn't want to tell him how wrong he was about that statement. She had no plans; that was the problem. She had quit her job, thinking she could find another one quickly; she just couldn't stand working there any minute longer. Her boss had gotten worse, and she had no opportunities to grow. Once Jenna had begun looking, though, she had very little response. She had started to tap into her savings, which she had been trying to steadily build up to buy a home. She hated using that money to get her through, but she also knew then that she didn't want to buy a house in New Mexico.

Jenna had tried for close to four months before she gave up. She'd called her father, who'd convinced her to return home. When she really thought about her life and what she wanted from it, Jenna knew exactly two things: she didn't want to live in New Mexico anymore, and she wanted Bailey Sayers back in her life. Not as a friend; Jenna wanted Bailey to love her again.

Their phone conversations had been sparse over the last couple of months. Their phone sex, which had really just been Bailey talking to Jenna while Jenna touched herself and wished it was Bailey's hand, had also stopped. They hadn't talked about doing it, and they hadn't talked about it while they were doing it; it just happened sometimes. They also didn't talk about it when it ended. As far as Jenna knew, Bailey was still with Callie. They stopped talking about her the moment Jenna's hands went into her own pants.

\*\*\*

"Samantha?" Jenna asked as she stood in the grocery store aisle a month later.

"Jenna?"

"Yeah, hey," Jenna greeted.

"What are you doing here? Last I heard, you were living in New Mexico."

"I just moved back, actually," she answered while moving her near-empty shopping cart off to the side in order to let another woman pass her in the aisle.

"Me too," Sam revealed. "Well, about six months ago. My husband and I were thinking about trying to get pregnant, and we wanted to raise our kids here."

"Kids? Wow, that's awesome."

"Yeah, and also good on the timing because I got pregnant. I'm at fourteen weeks now and starting to show." Samantha patted her stomach.

"Congratulations, Sam. That's amazing." Jenna meant

what she was saying, but it also hurt her to think that maybe Bailey was on the same track with Callie.

"Thanks. What about you?"

"Oh, I'm staying with my dad right now. I needed to get out of New Mexico. I've been looking for apartments to move into and a new job."

"You're staying here permanently?" Sam moved her own cart to the same side of the aisle.

"That's the plan." Jenna shrugged.

Samantha looked away for a moment before she glanced back at Jenna and met her eyes.

"Jenna, can I ask you something that is totally none of my business?"

Jenna chuckled and replied, "I guess."

"Are you single?"

"Oh, yeah. I'm not with anyone. Why? Do you have someone you want to set me up with or something?" She laughed.

"Yes, with my best friend, who's been in love with you since birth," Samantha replied.

"What?" Jenna chuckled.

"God, you two are the worst sometimes." Sam shook her head. "How long have you loved Bailey?"

"What?" Jenna repeated. "Sam, I–"

"She's back, Jenna. She lives here now. She just bought a place down the street from us, actually. She wanted to move closer to home, and she found a new job, too."

"Bailey's back home?"

"She lives ten minutes away from here."

"I didn't know. I haven't talked to her since I made the decision to come back. We kind of had to stop talking again."

"I know. She told me. Then, she told her girlfriend what you two were up to."

"She told Callie?" Jenna's heart started racing as another woman with her cart moved past them.

"She felt guilty, so she told her."

"What happened?"

"Callie wasn't exactly thrilled by the fact that her girlfriend was having long-distance sex with her ex." Sam sighed. "Bailey tried to explain that she never actually touched herself while you two were doing whatever the hell was that you did, as if that would somehow make it better."

"I know." Jenna crossed her arms over her chest. "I didn't know she told Callie about it, but I knew what we were doing was wrong; I just couldn't stop it. It takes everything in me not to call her all the time, Sam."

"Do you still love her?"

"Always," Jenna replied immediately.

"You should call her."

"She's with Callie."

"Not anymore." Sam lifted an eyebrow.

"If Callie broke up with her, I doubt–"

"Bailey broke up with her, Jen. And I'm guessing you can figure out why," Sam interrupted her.

"She ended things?" Jenna uncrossed her arms, placed her hands on her cart, and leaned over it for support.

"I think they were over before that, but she's the one that made it official. I'm sure she can fill you in at the reunion."

"Reunion?" Jenna straightened.

"Our ten-year high school reunion. Did you forget?"

"I didn't know we were having one," Jenna replied. "I've been shifting my entire life around recently. I haven't exactly been paying attention, I guess."

"It's tomorrow night, Jenna. Stupid Stephanie Doyle sent the invites via snail mail. She even got them in school colors with embossed lettering. She's the worst. Anyway, it's at the Camden Hotel. My guess is your invite didn't reach you with the move."

"Tomorrow night? Bailey's going?" Jenna asked.

"She's going *solo*. Now, can you please go tell her how you feel so she can tell you how she feels, and you two can just finally be together?"

"At this point, we've not been together for a lot longer than we ever were together. I don't even know–"

"You two have never actually moved on; you've pretended like it. And you sure did bring other people into your mess, but you've never moved beyond each other. If you're staying here, and she's staying here, what's the point in pretending like you're actually not going to try? Why pretend, Jenna? Just talk to her."

***

The music that was popular when they were in high school was terrible, Jenna decided as she heard the third pop song played by the DJ and sat off to the side at an empty table. When people had approached her, Jenna talked to them, asked how things were in their lives, and learned about their spouses, jobs, and kids. She had been doing that for over an hour. She had done that while waiting on Bailey. It was after nine now. There had been no sign of the woman, and Jenna had been looking. She had been staring at the door to the room the entire time people were talking to her. Before coming to the reunion, she had prepared a speech and had run through it while someone she'd hardly talked to in all four years of high school spoke about her dog grooming business. She'd also had exactly one drink this evening to help with her nerves before she switched to water.

When she finally saw Bailey walk in twenty minutes later, her breath disappeared. Bailey was wearing a dress, and Jenna wasn't sure she had ever seen Bailey wear a dress outside of graduation. The dress was a pale purple. Bailey had her hair pulled up into an intricate braid. She was also wearing white heels, and she looked stunning. Jenna gulped before she stood up and moved to walk over to the woman but was stopped by Samantha, who'd appeared out of nowhere.

"Don't do this unless you're in it for good this time. I cannot stand to see her get hurt over you again," Sam warned.

"Does she know I'm here tonight? Did you tell her?"

"I haven't said a word. I didn't want to risk you chickening out," Sam replied. "Just don't screw this up again."

"I won't. I can't… I'm just not right without her."

Jenna moved past Samantha without waiting for a response. She made her way toward Bailey, who had joined the line at the bar. Jenna moved behind her and leaned into her.

"Hey, Bail," she said.

Bailey didn't turn around right away, but she did stiffen and said, "I didn't know if you'd be here."

"I got here right at eight because I didn't want to chance missing you," Jenna replied.

Bailey turned around then, looked at Jenna, and said, "You look good, Cabot."

"You do too." Jenna smiled at her. "Like, really, really good."

"Thanks." Bailey hooked her thumb to the bar. "Do you need a drink?"

"I need you," Jenna said honestly.

"Jen—"

"Hear me out, Bails," Jenna interrupted.

"We've tried so many times." Bailey moved up with the line.

For some reason, the time it would take Bailey to get to the bar and order, felt like the only time Jenna had to convince Bailey to give her another chance – her last chance. She decided to take Bailey's hand in her own and hold on to it tightly.

"Can we please talk?" she implored.

The line moved up again, and Jenna was growing

desperate. She squeezed Bailey's hand and gave her a pleading glance.

"Outside," Bailey replied finally.

Jenna nodded and pulled Bailey along as they made their way out of the room and past Samantha, who first smiled and then gave Jenna another warning glare. Jenna pulled Bailey until they were in the lobby of the hotel. Then, and only then did she let Bailey's hand go.

"I got a room," Jenna stated after a moment of awkward silence.

"Jen, we're not—"

"To talk, Bails. I want to talk to you. I want to talk to you for hours. I want to tell you about how I live here now; I moved back. I want to tell you about how I'm here for good; I'm not leaving. I want to know about what's going on in your life. You're back, too. I want to know about your job and your new place. I want to know who you are now."

"You're really back?" Bailey asked.

Jenna's hands went to Bailey's hips, she pulled the woman into herself, and replied, "Ten years ago, you asked me out on a date. I blew you off because I am an idiot."

"You're not an idiot," Bailey said.

"Yes, I am. I let you go then, and I let you go in school, Bails. I let you go after my mom got sick and I couldn't deal. I let you go too many times."

"Jen—"

"I will never stop apologizing to you for that, but I don't want to ever let you go again," Jenna interrupted. "I love you, Bails. You are the love of my life. I know that now like I've known it all along. You're the one I'm supposed to be with."

"Then, why hasn't it worked before?" Bailey asked with tears in her eyes.

"We were never in the right place."

"And we suddenly are now?" Bailey asked with a lifted eyebrow.

"Suddenly? What about ten years of this seems sudden to you?"

"Fourteen," Bailey said.

"What?" Jenna pulled Bailey's hips closer to her.

"Jenna, I've loved you for fourteen years. I fell for you that first day freshman year."

"At the lockers," Jenna added. Then, she realized something. "You said you've loved me. Like, present tense. You still love me…"

"Of course, I do. Why the hell do you think I'm standing in the hotel lobby talking to you about this?"

"Come upstairs with me, Bails." Jenna squeezed Bailey's hips.

"If I go upstairs with you, we're not going to talk, Jen. You know how it works with us; we can't keep our hands off each other. You're touching me right now, and I can't–"

"We'll go for a walk then," Jenna interrupted and removed her hands from Bailey's waist. "We have a lot to talk about. As much as I'd like for us to do the other thing, I think we need to talk first this time."

\*\*\*

They walked side by side for over an hour, and they didn't touch as they walked; they were both content just being with the other person for the first time in a long time. They were animated in their body language as they described their most embarrassing moments, the jobs they had loved, the ones they'd hated, their past relationships, and everything else that had transpired since the moment they'd first started dating. And they let one another off the hook for mistakes made in the past in order to focus on the future.

Around midnight, Jenna gave Bailey her sweater. She used the chance to run her hands up and down Bailey's shoulders but didn't try for anything more. They made their way back to the hotel around one. The party was just breaking up, and their former classmates were on the street either saying their goodbyes or smoking cigarettes. Jenna and Bailey said goodbye to a few people they'd known back then. It was only then that Jenna took Bailey's hand in her own, and Bailey leaned into her.

They didn't acknowledge what they were to anyone else; they just held onto one another and withstood the curious glances from their former classmates. Jenna knew there was no way they'd ever be able to define what they were to one another with these people, and there was no need to try. Sam nodded their way as her husband helped her into their car. Then, they sped off into the night. Jenna turned to face Bailey, and, without a word, she nodded toward the hotel. Bailey smiled and nodded, too.

Once in their room, Jenna helped Bailey out of her dress. She had brought an overnight bag for herself, which she opened and pulled out her own sleep clothes and a t-shirt Bailey could wear. They just readied themselves for bed, both being exhausted. Jenna pulled Bailey into her, breathed her in, and reveled in the fact that they were together.

"Hey, Bail?" Jenna whispered.

"Yeah?" Bailey answered softly.

"This is it for me. You are *it* for me."

"Took you long enough," Bailey replied just as softly.

# CHAPTER 12: SAME TIME, SAME PLACE

Jenna rolled over in her sleep. She wiped her eyes as she tried to open them, reaching to her right just to feel an empty bed. Her eyes shot open, and she turned her head to see that Bailey wasn't next to her.

"Relax, Jen. I'm right here," Bailey said.

Jenna turned her head toward the bathroom to see Bailey coming out of it, still wearing the t-shirt and underwear from the night before. She then moved to sit on the side of the bed next to Jenna.

"Morning," Jenna said and placed her hand on top of Bailey's.

"Did you really think I wouldn't be here after last night?"

"I don't know. I think my brain might have thought it was all a dream," Jenna said.

"You're so cute sometimes." Bailey smiled down at her, and then her face turned serious again, "Jen, I want us to do things right this time."

"Me too," Jenna agreed.

Bailey stood up, and Jenna watched her as she pulled off her shirt, leaving herself bare, save the underwear. Jenna gulped as she took in Bailey's breasts for the first time in years. They still looked so perfect to her. Bailey moved until she was on top of Jenna, and from her position, she stared down into Jenna's eyes. They hadn't even kissed yet since seeing one another last night. Now,

Jenna could only think about kissing her.

"I love you," Bailey said.

"I love you, too," Jenna replied with tears welling in her eyes as Bailey kissed her.

Jenna had assumed Bailey would want to wait for this. They had talked so much the night before. Bailey had explained how she had ended things with Callie because no matter how Bailey tried not to think about Jenna, she couldn't. Jenna had mentioned that she hadn't been with anyone officially since Joel; it was just too hard. While they had caught up and made plans for their future, Jenna didn't want to hope for this; she knew it would hurt too much if it didn't happen. It was happening right now, though.

Bailey's fingers were now in her hair, toying with the loose ends. She held herself up as she kissed Jenna softly. Jenna's hands slowly roamed Bailey's back, loving how her muscles moved as Bailey kissed her. She moaned into Bailey's mouth, causing Bailey's hips to lower into her. She then spread her legs to allow Bailey to move again. It had been so long. Jenna's eyes welled with tears when Bailey's lips moved to her neck. She did her best to hold them back, but, eventually, a few escaped.

"Jen?" Bailey pulled up to look down at her. "Do you not–"

"No, I do. I really, really do." Jenna placed her arms around Bailey's neck. "I just missed you." She wiped at her eyes with one hand.

"I missed you, too," Bailey replied. "We can wait if you want."

"I don't want to wait anymore," Jenna said. "We've waited too long." She lowered Bailey down to her, leaned in, and whispered, "I need you inside me. I need to be whole again, Bails."

Bailey took her time. She kissed Jenna's skin after she removed each article of clothing that had been covering it. Once they were both bared to one another again, Bailey slid back on top of Jenna. She rubbed her center against Jenna's, allowing Jenna to feel her curls damp with her arousal. Jenna gasped as Bailey rocked her hips down into her again and again as their lips met, tongues joined, and hands grasped parts they'd been long without.

"Bails," Jenna uttered under her breath.

"Mm." Bailey sucked Jenna's nipple into her mouth.

Jenna was about to explode, and Bailey hadn't even touched her yet. Jenna rolled them over until she was on top, catching Bailey off guard.

"Let me, please." Jenna rocked her hips into Bailey now.

Bailey responded by gripping Jenna's hips and encouraging her further. When Jenna sat up, straddling Bailey, she reached between Bailey's legs. She dragged her fingers through the wetness and witnessed Bailey's back lift off the bed.

"It's only ever felt this good with you," Bailey said as Jenna filled her.

"Because it's supposed to be this way," Jenna replied as Bailey's fingers entered her as well.

They rocked together like that until Bailey writhed beneath her, near orgasm, and Jenna took in her sounds. She watched Bailey come, which then caused Jenna to come. Jenna's hips moved faster and faster as she rode out the best orgasm of her life. Before she could finish entirely, though, Bailey had rolled them over again, slid back inside her, and made Jenna come a second time. Jenna came down from her orgasm with Bailey above her, holding on to her for dear life, as if she were to let go, Jenna would run away from this.

"Jen, I love you so much."

"I know, Bails." Jenna grasped Bailey's back and tugged her closer. "I know. I'm not going anywhere. We get to have this now. You and me, we get to have this now." She rubbed the back of Bailey's neck. "I only want this with you ever again, okay?"

Bailey sobbed against her neck as Jenna tried to comfort her. After several moments, Bailey pulled back to stare down at her.

"I missed those eyes when we're like this," Bailey said through red eyes.

"They missed what they're seeing right now."

***

"You two are still good, even with all the changes recently?" Andrea asked.

"We're very good, yes," Jenna replied with a smile as she watched Bailey getting dressed after her shower.

"How does it feel to be all-in with the love of your life?"

"Like a miracle," Jenna said as Bailey came back into the bedroom and smiled at her.

"That's sappy. You're all sappy now. I don't like it."

"I can't help it," Jenna replied as Bailey knelt in front of her and rubbed her hands up and down Jenna's bare legs. "Bails." She laughed as Bailey tickled the underside of her knees.

"Are you two doing it right now?" Andrea asked.

"What? No," Jenna replied.

Bailey lifted an eyebrow at her before reaching for her own shirt to pull back up and over her head. Jenna's shirt was tossed aside as well almost immediately after, while she attempted to balance the phone call with Bailey's touches. She laughed a little more as Bailey slid her shorts off her body, followed quickly by her panties.

"So, I'll see you next month, right?" Andrea changed the subject.

"Yeah, can't wait." Jenna watched Bailey's lips touch her skin on the inside of her thigh. "Bailey," she whispered as she covered the phone with her hand. "Babe, stop it," she repeated before moving her hand out of the way. "I can't wait to see you."

"I cannot wait to *really* meet your girlfriend," Andrea offered. "I plan on grilling her to make sure she's treating you right."

"Oh, she's treating me right."

Bailey's head moved to her center. She kissed Jenna there softly before she nuzzled her, causing ripples of pleasure to shoot through Jenna.

"I should let you get back to that sex you're *not* having," Andrea said with a laugh.

They hung up the phone with Andrea chuckling lightly and Jenna barely hanging on enough to tap the screen on her phone. Then, Bailey lifted herself up to straddle her. She was naked and perfect, and Jenna loved her. They had been together now for almost a year. Jenna had found a new job and had gotten a short-term lease on an apartment nearby. They'd done it right this time; they didn't move too fast; they didn't run when it got hard. When Bailey had asked her to move in with her once Jenna's lease was up, Jenna had said yes, and they'd been living together for over five months.

Jenna couldn't be happier than she was in this moment. Bailey stared deeply into her eyes; and while there was desire there, there was also love. There was *always* love. Jenna smiled and hoped her own love for Bailey was reflected in her eyes. Then, Jenna reached over and pulled something out of the drawer of her bedside table. She placed a ring box on her own stomach and looked back into Bailey's eyes.

"Hey, Bail?" she said.

# PATH II: SHE DIDN'T ASK HER

# CHAPTER 1: IT DIDN'T HAPPEN ON GRADUATION DAY

Jenna watched from her seat as Bailey received her diploma and shook hands with the various members of the faculty on the stage, as required. Jenna had already done the same thing. She should remember that moment more than any other today. She watched Bailey turn toward the camera, aimed at center stage, hold the diploma in one hand and the principal's in the other, and smile as the flash went off. As Bailey went to walk off stage, her eyes went to Jenna. That couldn't be right... Bailey's eyes seemed to be on her, directly on her. Jenna smiled up at Bailey with the best non-nervous smile she could muster. She knew then; she didn't understand it fully, but she still knew.

After the ceremony, Jenna took a thousand pictures with her parents. Some featured her younger brother, and some were just of the three of them. Some were just Jenna standing in that ridiculous bright-red cap and gown. After the final shot of her with the whole family – both in and out of her gown – Jenna went to return the rented property. The cardboard hats were theirs to keep, but the gowns had to be returned. She handed her gown over to a woman who checked her name off a list, and turned just in time to see her friends, standing over in the parking lot by their cars, tossing their caps into the air mockingly while laughing. She looked again to see that Bailey was standing with her family. Did it get hotter outside? It felt like it got hotter outside. Bailey was wearing a light-blue sundress and ballet flats.

Jenna knew this was probably the last time she would see Bailey Sayers. After four years of friendship, they would both move onto separate colleges in different states. Bailey would likely get an amazing job just out of school that would take her somewhere exciting, and Jenna would find something, too, but this would be the end of their friendship. She'd always wished she had more courage. Every year, when the last day of school came, she knew she'd go three months without seeing Bailey. She could have picked up the phone; she could have emailed. She had Bailey's school email address since they had used it a few times to exchange homework-related emails. Jenna hadn't done either of those things, though. She watched as Bailey's father squeezed her shoulders, causing Bailey to grimace awkwardly before smiling. Jenna laughed silently at the exchange. Then, she made her way back toward her parents and brother to tell them she would see them at home later.

"Hey, Jenna," Bailey half-yelled across the lawn while walking briskly to meet her before she joined her friends.

"Hey, Bail. You do all the pics with the fam?" she asked.

"I did. They're going home. I'm going to meet them there," Bailey said.

"Cool. Will you be at my open house tomorrow?"

"That's the plan," Bailey replied as she stood a foot in front of her.

"Awesome. I guess I'll see you then," Jenna said.

"Hey, Jen?"

"Yeah?" Jenna asked just as she was about to walk off.

Bailey was so close to her now; Jenna needed to address this. Maybe she would, at her open house. Sure, there would be a lot of people around, but they could find a moment to talk privately, right? Bailey was so cute right now. Her face was all scrunched up as she appeared to be considering something. Jenna couldn't help but smile at her. What was going on with her? Why was she thinking about Bailey being cute? Why was she considering how Bailey looked so nice in that dress? She did look nice. She looked more than nice; she looked *beautiful.*

"When do you leave for your trip?"

"Tuesday," Jenna replied.

"And today is Saturday," Bailey said more to herself.

"You earned that diploma, huh, Bail," she joked with her.

"Are you doing anything tomorrow?"

"Um, my open house. I just asked if you were coming," Jenna replied.

'My open house where I plan to tell you what, exactly? That I think you're pretty? You're so smart? That I've been thinking about how much I'm going to miss you? That I'm going to miss seeing you every day? That I wished we had more time? More time for what? Why do her lips look so good right now?' Jenna thought.

"Right. I mean after that. Are you doing anything after that? Or Monday?" Bailey asked.

"I don't think so. Why?" Jenna asked back with a gulp.

Bailey looked down at the ground. When she finally lifted her eyes, they didn't meet Jenna's. She glanced over at Jenna's friends, who appeared to be lighting cigarettes and still throwing those stupid cardboard caps around. Jenna rolled her eyes internally at them.

"Nothing. Never mind." Bailey crossed her arms over her chest. "I was just curious."

Jenna's eyes went to the swell of Bailey's breasts as her arms folded under them, raising them up just slightly. She looked away only an instant later, hoping Bailey hadn't caught on. What the hell was wrong with her right now?

"Did you want to do something?" Jenna asked, hopeful.

"No, I was just thinking about how busy you must be; that's all." Bailey uncrossed her arms and hung them at her sides.

"Bails, I'm heading out. Are you riding with me?" Samantha, Bailey's best friend, approached them at just the wrong moment.

"Yeah, I'll be right there," Bailey replied to Sam.

"Hey, Jenna," Sam greeted her.

"Hi, Sam." Jenna waved back.

Sam was nice enough, but did she really have to interrupt their conversation? This could be their last conversation ever. Four years of friendship was about to end, and there was someone else standing there preventing them from saying whatever they were about to say to one another.

"I guess I'll go wait by the car," Sam said.

"Okay," Bailey replied with her eyes still on Jenna. Sam waved at Jenna and headed toward the parking lot. "I should go."

"Yeah, I have to meet my friends." Jenna hooked a thumb back to her friends. "But you'll be there tomorrow, right? At the open house?"

"Sure." Bailey nodded with a closed-lip smile.

"I'll see you tomorrow."

"Okay. Bye, Jen."

"Bye, Bails."

***

Jenna had spent the past hour telling the same story over and over again: she was going to Ecuador to help build a school, where she'd be for eight weeks, leaving her with a little over three weeks before she would be moving to Michigan. No, she hadn't picked a major yet; she planned on exploring what school had to offer first before she narrowed things down. Yes, she would pledge the sorority. No, she didn't know anyone there. No, she hadn't met her roommate yet.

Jenna had also hugged and accepted gifts and congratulations. Some of her friends had stopped by briefly before they left to go to other open houses, and others had entered right after. They'd all grabbed a soda, talked to her for a few minutes, and then migrated off on their own to grab food and talk to other people.

The one person Jenna wanted to see, though, hadn't yet made her appearance, and the open house was only scheduled to go on for another hour. Maybe Bailey had decided not to come? Jenna had noticed on the list of open houses everyone had completed that Sam's open house was today, too. Maybe she had gotten caught up? The school had hung up a flyer in the cafeteria and asked every senior to put their open house day and time on it if they were opening it up to the entire graduating class. Sam and Jenna had both done that, while Bailey hadn't; Jenna knew that because she had checked regularly. When she'd asked Bailey about it, they'd been interrupted by Jenna's friends, Laura and Stephanie. Jenna hadn't brought it up again, and Bailey hadn't invited her.

"I'm too late, aren't I?" Bailey asked after the last partygoer had just departed.

"Hey, Bail," Jenna replied as Bailey entered her backyard.

"I am so sorry, Jen. I had Sam's open house, and then she wanted to leave early to go to Justin's, which was at the same time. She has a major crush on him; don't tell her I told you. Anyway, we got stuck in traffic on the way there."

"It's okay." Jenna approached her after dropping the

trash bag she had just filled with soda cans. "Come on in."

"I shouldn't; it's over. You're cleaning up." Bailey pointed at the bag Jenna had just dropped. "Unless you'd like some help? I could pay for my absence with my cleaning services."

"Do you have any references?" Jenna asked teasingly as she crossed her arms over her chest.

"My mom, but I wouldn't ask her. She'd tell you I'm terrible at it."

"I guess you can help. I mean, you *did* show up super late to my party," Jenna joked.

"I am sorry, Jen."

"I know. It's fine. I was just worried you weren't coming," Jenna said as she picked up the trash bag.

"You were?" Bailey asked as she began helping with the dirty plates.

Jenna's parents took in a few of the food items that would need to be wrapped and stored.

"You said you'd be here, and it's not like you to not show up."

"Justin is going to Europe for the summer, and Sam wanted one last shot with him before he leaves."

"Where is Sam?"

"With Justin." Bailey tossed a few paper plates into the bag. "She got her shot, I guess. She asked me to go on without her."

"Justin's nice," Jenna said.

"They've been making eyes at each other all year. They're probably making out as we speak."

"I guess graduation does that to some people," Jenna said before she had a chance to think about it.

"What do you mean?" Bailey stood behind her now and waited for Jenna to pass her the bag to toss various items into.

"Just that they liked each other all year but didn't do anything about it; and now, suddenly, they have to act because time is running out."

Bailey stared at her for a moment before she said, "Yeah, I guess."

"Are you okay, Bails?" Jenna asked.

"Jenna, introduce your dad and me to your friend," Jenna's mom said when she made her way back outside.

It hit Jenna then that, as close as she sometimes felt to Bailey, Bailey hadn't ever been to her house. She hadn't met her parents or her brother. She also hadn't gone to football games with Jenna or been in the groups of friends she had gone to dances with. Bailey had been there every day, though. She had been there each morning, when it was just the two of them. Jenna had actually started to come to school earlier for just a few moments of Bailey-time before other students began filing into the hallway.

"Mom, this is Bailey."

"Bailey? *The* Bailey?"

"Nice to meet you," Jenna's father said as he shook her hand. "We've heard a lot about you."

"You have?" Bailey asked as she looked at Jenna.

"I told them you help me out with my homework," Jenna replied.

"Oh, right." Bailey nodded, but there was something different in her tone.

"Well, we can clean up here. Why don't you two go have some fun?" Jenna's mom suggested. "Go up to Jenna's room or go out if you want, honey."

"I can't stay long, unfortunately," Bailey replied. "I'm already late getting home. I told my parents we'd have a late dinner tonight. My grandparents are in town for graduation, and they leave tomorrow morning."

"You're leaving?" Jenna asked her.

"In, like, five minutes, probably. Sorry. I wish I could stay. My phone's been vibrating in my pocket for the last two minutes. My mom's probably wondering why I'm not home yet." Bailey paused. "I just wanted to see you before you leave."

Her parents were standing there; this was not the

private moment Jenna had wanted with Bailey to maybe mention to her that she had some new feelings that had popped up recently. She gulped at the thought of telling Bailey what she still didn't understand fully. Then, she gulped again at the thought of not telling her.

"Okay. I can walk you to your car, at least," Jenna offered.

"Sure." Bailey smiled. "It was nice meeting you," Bailey said to Jenna's parents.

As they walked to Jenna's driveway in silence, she couldn't believe this would be the last time she would see Bailey Sayers. They might run into one another if they were on school breaks at the same time, but Bailey hadn't ever hung out with the same people or at the same places. This could be it.

"Well, good night," Jenna said when they arrived at Bailey's car.

"Yeah, good night. Sorry, I was so late."

"No problem." Jenna opened the driver's side door after Bailey unlocked it. "Listen, Bails... Maybe, when I get back from Ecuador, we could talk or something."

"Oh," Bailey uttered and moved behind the door. "Yeah, sure. We could do that."

"Yeah?"

"Yeah, that would be cool." Bailey smiled at her.

"Okay. I'll let you know," Jenna said.

"Sounds good." Bailey sat in the driver's seat.

"Drive safe, Bails." She smiled widely.

*** 

Jenna pounded nails with hammers every single day for over two weeks before they were finally allowed to go into town and get internet access for about twenty minutes at a time. She thought about spending some of that time emailing Bailey, but as she typed something three times before deleting it, she just ended up emailing her parents and brother instead.

She did the same thing the following week. She enjoyed hard work, but her muscles were craving a break. She had also started playing with the local kids, who would be benefitting from that hard work. As she taught them some English, they taught her a little bit of Spanish. Each week, Jenna would stare at the outdated computer with the terrible internet connection and think about emailing Bailey. She'd stop each time when she got to the actual message, though. What would she even say to her?

"Hey, Bail. It's Jenna. I may or may not have a crush on you. Any chance you'd let me just kiss you to see if I'd like it and want to do it again?" she muttered that under her breath as another member of her group gave her a confused, lifted eyebrow.

The following week, Jenna made her way to the computer *after* the last member of her group finished up. She connected to the internet, sent her parents her typical check-in email, and, by chance, opened her Browne High School email account; something just told her she should open it today. When she saw Bailey's name, she couldn't believe it. She clicked on the email immediately and leaned in closer.

To: jennac@brownehigh.net
From: baileys@brownehigh.net
Subject: My New Plans

*Hey, Jenna,*

*I ran into your mom at the mall the other day. She mentioned you didn't bring your phone with you but that you check your email every week. I don't even know if you remember saying we should do something when you get back, but I wanted to let you know that my mom decided to try to cram in one last family vacation before I go to school. She's acting like I'm going to school in another country; I'll be two hours away. Anyway, she's making my dad take time off, and we're going on a two-week cruise. It's so stupid. I don't even want to go, but I don't have the option. Since the ship will end up in Florida, she's making us stay at our grandparents' place – which is like thirty minutes away – for a week. Your mom mentioned when you'd be getting back, and I don't think I'll be able to see you before you leave for school. I just wanted you to know. I didn't want you to think I'd forgotten. I hope you're enjoying your trip.*

*Bailey*

Jenna read it and reread it again for good measure. She had been thinking about Bailey constantly since they had parted that night. She'd imagined holding Bailey's hand at first; pictured them lying side by side. They were on a blanket in the grass, staring up at the stars. She had no idea where that vision came from. They'd never done anything close to that. She liked how it felt in her vision, though. She would turn to Bailey to take in her face, rest her head on Bailey's shoulder, and even lightly kiss her cheek.

Jenna had pictured other stuff, too, but it was always so foggy in her vision. That was likely due to the fact that she had no idea what to do with another girl, or even why she only wanted to do those things with Bailey. Jenna had tons of friends, and she had never thought about any of them that way. She had been looking forward to seeing Bailey. Now, that wouldn't be happening.

To: baileys@brownehigh.net
From: jennac@brownehigh.net
Re: My New Plans

*Hey, Bail,*

*Well, I hope you have fun on your cruise and with your grandparents. That sucks that I won't be able to see you before I go to school. Maybe we can plan something for our fall break or Thanksgiving? It would be nice to hang out then, if you're free. I don't know what your plans are. Let me know. I can only check my email once a week, but I'll have my phone when I get back.*

*Jenna*

To: jennac@brownehigh.net
From: baileys@brownehigh.net
Re: My New Plans

*Jenna,*

*My fall break is the last week of September. I have Thursday and Friday off. When's your break? My mom told me they're not paying for Wi-Fi on the ship because she wants us to bond. She thinks if my dad and I have internet, we'll stay in the room all day. She's not wrong. I won't know what kind of connection I'll have until I get to my grandparents' house, but maybe I can text you or something.*

*Bailey*

To: baileys@brownehigh.net
From: jennac@brownehigh.net
Re: My New Plans

*Hey, Bail,*

*That sucks about your mom taking the internet away. I'm dealing with that here, and I hate it. I wish I could just respond to your emails right away, but they're pretty strict here on giving everyone the same amount of time. I've had fun and learned a lot here, but I'm ready to get home. And "yes" to the texting!*

*Jenna*

Jenna had to catch a ride home from the airport since her parents were out of town with her brother. It was so strange to be in the house by herself for a few days. She had to cook her own meals, do her own laundry, and start trying to plan her move to school. She figured it was good practice since she'd be living in a dorm with some girl named Mandy. Jenna had found out via her last email exchange with Bailey that she'd left the day before Jenna arrived home, and she couldn't believe she'd missed Bailey by a day. She hadn't seen her in over eight weeks! She'd gone three months without seeing her every summer when school let out, but she knew now their fall breaks didn't line up. That meant they wouldn't see one another until the end of November, for Thanksgiving, and that seemed like a lifetime away.

# CHAPTER 2: THE BREAKS

"You haven't talked to her since you left for school?" Mandy asked.

"We texted a few times when we both first got to school, but we've both been busy. I haven't even talked to her on the phone," Jenna replied as she slid her backpack over her shoulders.

"Are you nervous?" Mandy asked as she sat up on her bed. "Does she know you have the hots for her?" She wiggled her eyebrows.

"I do not have the hots for her," Jenna argued and reached for her roller bag.

"But you like her. You told me she's the only girl you've ever felt that way about."

"I know. I still don't even understand that," Jenna said. "But I do have to go, or I'll miss my flight."

"Good luck. Have lots of sex with the girl you *don't* have the hots for," she joked.

"Mandy!"

When Jenna arrived home, she had dinner with her parents and her brother before going up to her room for her first moment of actual privacy since she'd gone away to school. She liked Mandy, but they had one small room together; Jenna missed having her own room. Upstairs, she grabbed for her phone, ready to text Bailey to try to find a time they could meet up. Since tomorrow was the holiday, and they'd likely both be with their families, she was thinking Friday or Saturday. She had to fly back to school on Sunday and assumed Bailey would be returning the same day. Jenna sent her text and waited anxiously for the reply.

She enjoyed school. She had made friends and would be pledging a sorority during the spring semester. Classes were okay enough, but she was bored taking only the prerequisites. She was ready for a break; she was ready to see Bailey. She hadn't dated anyone, despite her friends trying to get her to go out with a few guys here and there. When Mandy asked her why she seemed so uninterested, she'd made up some story about getting over a bad breakup and not being ready. Then, Mandy caught her staring at an old picture of Bailey on their high school website. Jenna had told her the truth then – or, at least, her version of the truth. She still thought about Bailey in the way she thought of no one else, which made absolutely no sense to her. Except that it did. It did make sense. Bailey was so pretty. She was so nice. She made Jenna laugh when they did talk. She also replied to text messages pretty quickly.

Jenna took a quick look at the screen, saw Bailey's name, and opened the messaging app on her phone. Her face immediately fell: Bailey's family had decided to visit her aunt, uncle, and cousins for Thanksgiving. Bailey was on her way there as Jenna read the message on her phone, and she would be driving back to school on Sunday. They had missed one another again. Jenna typed a message back, asking about Christmas. They made a new plan.

Christmas came and went, though. Bailey's family was incredibly well-off. Her father had planned a trip to Europe for Christmas break and had invited Samantha and her family. Jenna realized then that she might not ever see Bailey again, after all. They had so few breaks from school, and clearly Bailey didn't view a visit to see Jenna as something important. Jenna would make her own plans for spring break, which was her next break from school. She would go to Florida with her friends from school, and she would drink, flirt with boys, and relax. She had done well in school; she had earned this break.

***

"We're under twenty-one. They're not going to let us in." Jenna stood behind Mandy and Mandy's boyfriend, Max, at the entrance to a club.

"Max is twenty-one. He'll go first and get us in," Mandy replied, turning her head back slightly.

It was their last night in Florida before they'd all fly back to campus. Jenna was exhausted. She now needed a vacation from her vacation. She did want one more night of fun, though, before she had to start classes again. Mandy and Max had invited her out. That morning, she had been a little hungover from the previous night, after drinking in their hotel the night before, but she had wanted one more night of fun. She'd powered through, eaten a big dinner, and just after eight, they headed out to the club with a few more friends and hundreds of other people from every college in the country.

"Jenna?"

Jenna turned around at the sound of *that* voice. Then, she smiled when she saw her.

"Hey, Bail," she greeted.

"What are you doing here?"

"Spring break. You too?" Jenna asked.

"Yeah. I'm here with Sam."

"Sam's here?" Jenna asked as she looked around.

"Sam's here with her boyfriend. I'm a third wheel." Bailey shrugged.

She was wearing a pair of dark jeans with a V-neck shirt that matched her vibrant eyes, and she looked good. Jenna knew the reason she still hadn't managed to date anyone, despite the school year being close to over.

"I'm the third wheel, too," Jenna told her. "Do you maybe want to be third wheels together?"

"We could *not* be third wheels together and just go somewhere else?" Bailey suggested.

She seemed more confident somehow. Maybe college had done that to her? Either way, Jenna liked it.

"Mandy?" Jenna turned back to her roommate, who had been talking to Max and not paying attention. "I'm going to go. I'll see you back at the hotel."

"What?" Mandy asked as she glanced at Bailey.

"Hi," Bailey greeted. "I'm Bailey."

"Bailey?" Mandy glanced back at Jenna. "*Really?*"

"We're going to go do something. You two have fun." Jenna pulled on Bailey's arm to get her away from Mandy before the girl had an opportunity to embarrass her.

"I can't believe you're here," Bailey said as they walked along the beach after she had told Samantha she would see her back at Sam's apartment. "I'm sorry about Thanksgiving. And Christmas, too. My family has been nuts ever since I went off to school. I blame it on being an only child. It's like my mom doesn't know what to do without me there."

"It's okay," Jenna replied as she carried her flip-flops in her hand, and they walked along the shore. "I get it. Things came up."

"It's not that I…" Bailey stopped herself, and Jenna wondered why. "Anyway… How's school?"

"Good. You?"

"Good," Bailey answered just as quickly. "Have a major yet?"

"Nope. I'm still figuring that part out. You?"

"I declared English, but I don't know if that's what I'll keep. I'm mainly doing that to keep my mom happy. She wanted me to declare something," Bailey explained.

"I guess I'm lucky my parents don't really care about that stuff."

"My parents are all right. They just care too much; my mom more than my dad. He's so busy with work, I don't think he cares either way. My mom just wants to tell her friends at the country club about me, and she needs something to brag about."

"She *should* brag about you," Jenna said and felt the heat hit her cheeks instantly.

The night was a muggy one. She could feel the moisture in the air just like she could feel it in the water that moved in between her toes as she walked along the water's edge. The moon was bright, but so were the lights in the parking lot nearby. College students were still milling about, but most of them were likely in the bars, leaving the beach less populated than it had been each day they'd been here.

"She should?" Bailey asked as Jenna looked at her toes while they walked.

"Yeah, you're awesome, Bails," Jenna replied, and trying to divert attention away from her comment, she asked, "So, when do you leave?"

"Tomorrow morning. I have an early flight. You?"

"Tomorrow afternoon." Jenna looked out at the water, which was barely visible in the dark.

"It sucks that I didn't run into you sooner. We could have hung out."

"We're hanging out now, though," Jenna replied, turned to Bailey, and smiled at her. "So, tell me more about school."

They walked and talked for a long time before they turned back around and walked over their steps the water had erased. When both of them were too exhausted to walk anymore, they put on their shoes and had a car take them back to Samantha's apartment, which was closer than the hotel Jenna was staying at. They sat on Sam's sofa and ate popcorn while they talked. They hadn't spent this much time together in such a long time. Hell, they'd never spent this much time together, and they'd never been alone for this long before. Jenna liked it.

"It's, like, three in the morning," Bailey finally said.

"I should go. Sam will probably be back soon."

"She's staying at her boyfriend's tonight. She told me earlier. And her roommates are gone for break. I have the place to myself for my last night here."

"She's staying with him when it's your last night?" Jenna asked.

"She's spent a lot of time with him this week even though I'm here. I get it, I guess; they just started going out a few weeks ago. It's all new."

"But you came all this way to visit her."

"I came all this way to get a break from school and some other stuff."

"Other stuff?" Jenna leaned in.

"There's just this girl..." Bailey faded out and moved the popcorn bowl from between them to the coffee table.

"Hey, I'm home," Sam yelled after opening the front door.

"I thought you weren't going to be here tonight," Bailey turned to deliver.

"I changed my mind. Jack wanted to stay out later, and I was ready to crash. It was closer to come back here." Sam moved to the sofa and sat between them. "Jenna?"

"Hey, Sam," Jenna greeted reluctantly. "I should probably go. You have an early flight, and I have to get back to the hotel."

"You can stay here," Sam suggested as she rested her head on Bailey's shoulder. "There are two bedrooms." She pointed down the hall. "I'm going to bed. Night, Bails." Samantha stood up and wobbled a little.

"Night, Sammy," Bailey replied as Sam waved at both of them and headed toward her own bedroom.

"I really should go," Jenna said once Sam closed the door behind her.

"You could stay. Like she said, there's room." Bailey turned back to her.

"Are you sure?"

"I have stuff you can wear."

She could be wearing Bailey's clothes, Jenna thought to herself and smiled.

"I guess I could stay," she said after a moment.

Bailey headed into her bedroom and returned moments later with a t-shirt and some shorts for Jenna. She then walked Jenna down the hall to the other bedroom, where she passed her the clothes and smiled at her.

"Sleep well," she said.

"Hey, Bail?"

"Yeah?"

"I know we're leaving tomorrow, but maybe we can keep talking after we get back to school? Maybe we could hang out this summer once we're both home."

"I'm not going home for the summer."

"You're not?"

"No, I got this internship... It's an awesome opportunity for me. They normally don't give it to students entering their sophomore year, but my professor recommended me, and I just found out last week that I got it."

"Wow." Jenna's throat was suddenly dry. "So, you're not going home at all then?"

"No. Well, for like a weekend maybe. I have to grab stuff to pack and things like that. Then, I'm off." Bailey shrugged one shoulder.

"Got it." Jenna glanced down at the floor. "And you'll be up early tomorrow? I probably won't see you before you go?"

"Not unless you want to wake up at six, which is in about three hours."

"I'll wake up at six." Jenna met her eyes again. "I'll see you off or something," she added.

"Jen, you don't have–"

"I'll set my alarm." Jenna held up her phone and

noticed it wasn't responding to her touch. "Shit. It's dead. What did people do before cell phones to wake up on time?"

"I think they're called alarm clocks, Jen." Bailey laughed at her.

"Well, I need one if I'm waking up at six in the morning."

Bailey considered something for a moment before she said, "I'd let you borrow my charger, but my phone's almost dead, too. How about I charge mine right now and set the alarm? I'll wake you up, and you can charge your phone while I get ready. You'll have enough charge to get you back to the hotel."

"Right. Sure. That's good." Jenna turned to head to her bedroom before she turned around. "Hey, Bail?"

"Yeah?" Bailey stopped walking into her room for the night.

"Can I just crash with you instead?"

"In my room?" Bailey asked as she stared back at Jenna.

"Yeah. Would that be okay?"

"Sure, Jen."

When they climbed into the full-sized bed, Jenna stared up at the dark ceiling. The room was only illuminated by the light from the table lamp on Bailey's side of the bed... Bailey's side of the bed! They were sharing a bed. Jenna was sharing a bed with Bailey Sayers.

"Good night, Jen."

"Night, Bail."

Bailey flipped the switch, and they both settled in for the few hours of sleep they'd be able to get before Bailey had to wake up for her flight. Jenna wasn't sure when she fell asleep, but she knew she hadn't been touching Bailey when she did. Now, she had woken up suddenly with the feel of Bailey pressed against her back as Jenna faced the wall. Bailey's arm was around her waist, and her breath was beating down on the back of Jenna's neck. Jenna smiled, breathed in and out deeply, and fell back to sleep. When she woke again, Bailey was already gone. Jenna's phone was charged to twenty-four percent, and there was a text message awaiting her.

"I couldn't wake you; you looked so peaceful. I charged your phone a little before I had to go. Sam's probably still asleep, so you can stay as long as you want; get some more sleep. Text me when you can."

# CHAPTER 3: BEST AND WORST OF TIMES

Junior year of college had started off all wrong. Jenna had started to date Paul, a senior she'd met in one of her classes, almost immediately after school had started back up. Everything seemed to be going well, until Paul wanted to take things further and further. Jenna hadn't been ready. She knew it was stupid; she was twenty years old, about to turn twenty-one, and she was still a virgin. Paul, however, was not. They'd been dating over a month, and they had only kissed. Jenna had slept over a few times, but that had been the extent of it. He hadn't pressured her, but she'd known he was tired of the wait. He'd ended things around the time of their fall break. That was *perfect* because she hadn't planned on going home for fall break while everyone else in her sorority had, so she was pretty much alone and missing home desperately.

"Hey, mom." Jenna waved to her mom through the screen of her laptop.

"Hey, sweetie," her mom replied.

Her mom didn't look right. Her eyes were red as if she'd been crying. Her hair was slightly mussed, which was also unlike her. And while it was late afternoon back home, her mom was still in her flannel pajama shirt from what Jenna could see through the video chat.

"Is everything okay?" Jenna asked.

"Honey, I need to talk to you about something," she said.

That was how Jenna found out her mother had been diagnosed with breast cancer. By the end of their conversation, Jenna's mom had actually thanked her.

Jenna's sorority was participating in a run for breast cancer awareness month in late October as their philanthropy event for the semester, and when Jenna had casually mentioned that to her mom back in August, it had reminded her mom that she needed to schedule her mammogram. Because of that, they'd caught it early, but she would still need treatment.

Jenna's mind went into a fog for the next few days. Her father had called her to tell her about the treatment plan, what her mom would be going through, and how Jenna could help by staying focused on school, calling her mom to talk about anything other than her illness, and coming home for Thanksgiving. Of course, Jenna would go home for Thanksgiving. That wasn't even an option anymore. When Bailey had called for their weekly conversation, Jenna had gone through the motions.

They'd been talking like this ever since spring break freshman year. It ebbed and flowed with how busy they both were. Sometimes, it was every week for a month, other times, they wouldn't talk for two months. Then, they'd text one another and somehow get back on track. Jenna had yet to fully figure out her feelings toward Bailey, and being apart like this didn't make things any easier. She would be on the phone with Bailey, and she'd fall into her voice. She would hear Bailey laugh, and it would make Jenna smile because she had caused it. She'd thought of telling Bailey a hundred times, but what was the point? They still had nearly two years of school in different states left.

When Bailey had told her about her first girlfriend, Sasha, Jenna about lost it. Bailey had requested a video chat to come out to Jenna, and Jenna had watched her face as she spoke about Sasha and how much she liked her. Jenna had kept her mouth shut then because Bailey was happy. Then, Jenna met Ben. She'd dated him for a few weeks, but she'd never been able to get Bailey out of her mind. When Bailey told her she and Sasha had ended,

Jenna thought she would finally get her chance. It was the distance that prevented her from being honest with Bailey then. She just kept thinking about how she wasn't sure if she was gay, like Bailey was, and she didn't know if she was bisexual, either, because Bailey had been the only girl she had ever been attracted to like that.

"Listen, my parents are going to my aunt and uncle's place again this year, but I can come back home for Thanksgiving," Bailey offered.

"I can't ask you to be away from your family for a holiday, Bails," Jenna replied as she walked to class, holding her phone to her ear.

"Are you kidding? I'd love a chance to be at home without them there. I love my parents, but going to school this close to home was clearly a mistake. My mom visited me last week and complained about the state of my apartment. She's the one who picked out the place! Now, suddenly, it's in an unsafe neighborhood, and it needs everything fixed," Bailey said. "Besides, I'd like to see you. It's been so long, Jen."

"Since spring break freshman year," Jenna said. "I can't believe I talk to you all the time, but I haven't seen you since then."

"You had to go and stay there for the summer," Bailey replied.

"And you got that internship again. I mean, did you not learn enough the first time? Did they have you repeat it because you need a remedial internship?" she teased.

Bailey laughed and answered, "Yes, that was it."

"So, you'll really be there? Home, I mean?" Jenna asked.

"I can even pick you up at the airport when you fly in," Bailey offered. "We can hang out as much or as little as you like; I know you want to spend time with your mom."

"And you're sure you don't want to spend Thanksgiving with your parents?"

"Jen, I promise you, I'm not missing much." Bailey laughed again. "I have to go, though. I'm meeting Viv for coffee."

"Oh, okay. I have class in, like, five anyway. I'll talk to you later," Jenna replied.

Viv was Vivian. She and Bailey weren't officially dating, but the way Bailey described it, they were trying to figure out if there was something between them after meeting at a campus event. Bailey was the vice-president of her class; she had a lot of events she had to attend or help run. Viv was a sophomore she met while at an LGBTQ event. They'd been meeting up every few days for the past several weeks, but, according to Bailey, she still wasn't sure she wanted to date Viv. Jenna usually gritted her teeth when Bailey talked about Viv or any other girl she was interested in. When she'd been dating Paul, Bailey had listened to Jenna as she complained about him or even talked about how sweet he had been in the beginning. That was another reason Jenna hadn't told Bailey about her feelings: Bailey seemed unphased by the idea of Jenna dating someone. That had to mean something, right?

\*\*\*

"Hey, Bail," Jenna greeted the moment Bailey appeared in her doorway.

"Hey," Bailey greeted back with a wide smile.

"I know I've seen you on video and in pictures, but you look really good, Bails," Jenna said before she could stop herself.

"So do you." Bailey pointed at her. "Are you ready?"

"Hi, Bailey. How are you? I haven't seen you in a long time." Jenna's mom approached from behind Jenna. "Jenna talks about you all the time, though."

"Mom!"

"She does?" Bailey asked and glanced back at Jenna.

"Let's see… You are the vice-president of your class;

you'd made the dean's list the past two semesters; you have a girlfriend named Sasha; you–"

"Mom, stop." Jenna turned back to her mom and gave her a warning glare.

"Actually, Sasha and I broke up a while ago," Bailey said. "I don't have a girlfriend these days."

"What about Viv?" Jenna turned back to Bailey, who still stood in the open doorway.

"Just friends," Bailey replied.

"Mom, we're going to Bailey's house, okay?"

"Bailey, Jenna said your family is out of town. Why don't you join us tomorrow?"

"For Thanksgiving?" Bailey asked. "I can't do that. It's a family thing."

"Of course, you can. We'd love to have you. We have way more food than we can eat, and Jenna will be making her famous stuffing."

"You have famous stuffing?" Bailey lifted an eyebrow at Jenna.

"Famous within these walls," Jenna replied and stepped on the stoop to join Bailey. "You should come, Bail."

Bailey smiled wider and said, "Okay."

Jenna had never been to Bailey's house. How was that possible? They were juniors in college, had known one another since grammar school, and had become friends officially, she'd say, at the beginning of high school – it had been close to seven years, and she had never been to Bailey's house. Bailey's house was larger than her own, and when Jenna saw the basement, she realized that was an understatement. Bailey's father had not only finished the basement but also included a game room and a theater along with a living area and a small kitchen area. Bailey's room was even downstairs; she basically had an entire apartment in the basement of her parents' house. Jenna had a small bedroom in her parents' house.

"This is amazing, Bail," Jenna said as she sat on the

sofa in the living space of the basement.

"It's been pretty great, yeah. I like having privacy when I'm here. My mom used to come down here all the time when I was home, but my dad put a lock on the door upstairs for me." Bailey laughed. "It was so funny the one day she tried to come down but couldn't get in; she had to call me."

Jenna smiled at Bailey, who sat down next to her.

"So, what happened with Viv?"

"Just diving right in there, aren't you, Jen?" Bailey winked to indicate she was joking. "I think it just boils down to the fact that I was spending a lot of time trying to convince myself I was attracted to her. She's gorgeous; it's not a physical thing."

"Then, what was it?" Jenna leaned her head on her hand and placed her elbow on the back of the sofa as she turned to Bailey. "If you were physically attracted to her." Jenna's mouth went dry.

"When we kissed, it didn't feel right," Bailey said. "Like, I didn't want to be kissing her. I wanted to grab coffee with her and hang out, but I don't want to sleep with her."

Bailey had just brought up sex. Bailey had obviously had sex. Why was Jenna blushing right now?

"I get it."

"I guess I just thought that if I was going to finally do that with someone, it should be someone I really want to do that with," Bailey offered.

Jenna found herself looking away from Bailey then. Her eyes darted around the room, looking for something else to stare at, because looking into Bailey's eyes after hearing what she'd just heard, seemed wrong somehow.

"You and Sasha didn't? I mean, you guys–" she tried to ask without really asking.

"We did stuff, but not that." Bailey shrugged. "I was her first girlfriend; she was mine. We were taking our time, and then we broke up." Bailey leaned over toward Jenna.

"Don't get me wrong, we both wanted to; I just don't think we were ready."

"I get that. It was like that for me with the couple of guys I've dated."

Bailey leaned back and said, "You didn't..."

"I haven't, no." Jenna shrugged this time. "I guess I've been waiting for the right person."

"Me too," Bailey replied. "I liked Sasha, but I never really thought she was the *one* for me. I guess it's silly to assume you'd find the right person for you in college, huh? I mean, it happens, but it's more likely not to happen like that, right?" Bailey stood. "I have a sweater in my room."

"Huh?" Jenna said at the sudden change in topic.

"You're cold. Come on." Bailey smiled as she motioned for Jenna to follow. "You have goosebumps, Jen."

"Oh."

Jenna wasn't cold. The goosebumps weren't from the temperature in the room; they were from the conversation she was having with Bailey right now. She had assumed Bailey and Sasha had slept together but that Bailey had also likely slept with other girls. Jenna stood, followed Bailey into her bedroom, and watched Bailey pull a sweater out of her closet and toss it to Jenna.

"Thanks," she told Bailey.

"Is it weird for you to come back to your old room when you're used to living on your own? It's weird for me." Bailey sat on the edge of her bed.

Jenna realized she was in Bailey's bedroom for the first time then. Bailey was sitting on her own bed, staring up at Jenna, and she was beautiful. Her eyes looked at Jenna expectantly. Jenna was trying to cover up whatever her eyes might be saying because, in that moment, she knew more than ever that if she kissed Bailey, she *would* like it. She would *really* like it. God, she really liked Bailey. She might even more than liked Bailey.

"It's weird, yeah," Jenna said softly as Bailey leaned

back on her hands and seemed to be taking Jenna in. "What?" Jenna asked.

"Your eyes just–" Bailey started and stopped. "Is everything okay? You look, like, really intense right now."

"I'm okay."

"Is it about your mom?" Bailey asked.

At that change in topic, Jenna sat next to her on the bed and flopped backward.

"I wish I had just gone to school here. I'm too far away."

"How's she doing?" Bailey flopped down next to her.

"My parents don't tell me anything. It drives me nuts. All they say is that the treatments are working, but it's a long process. It's like, I'm an adult; I can take it."

Bailey turned on her side, rested her head on her hand, and said, "You're still their kid, though, Jen. They want to protect you."

"I've been thinking about taking a semester off." Jenna turned her head toward Bailey.

"Really?"

"I should be here while she's going through this."

"How would *she* feel about that?" Bailey asked.

"She won't let me. I already told her about it, and she said she wouldn't let me in the house. I know she's kidding, but still."

"I'm sorry, Jen. I wish there was something I could do."

"You're doing it now," Jenna replied with a shy smile. "This helps."

"Just hanging out?"

"Being here with you, Bails; it helps."

"Well, I'm glad then." Bailey chuckled. "I'm here whenever you need me."

"You are, aren't you?" Jenna asked and turned her body to the side.

"What?"

Bailey rolled over until she was on her back. She

stared up at the ceiling for a long moment while Jenna studied her.

"Bails, do you ever wonder how we keep ending up coming back to each other?" Jenna's eyes went big. "Like, the texting and calls and stuff; we keep coming back to it."

"Well, we're friends, Jen." Bailey turned her head to the side.

"Right," Jenna replied as she stared at the little bit of skin between Bailey's shirt and her jeans.

Before she could stop herself, her hand reached out. Her fingertips grazed the skin so softly, it was almost as if they weren't there. Bailey's eyes moved to Jenna's. Jenna's eyes continued to stare at her own fingertips as they slid over the soft skin.

"Jen…"

"Sorry," Jenna replied as she pulled back her hand with bright-red cheeks.

"What's going on?" Bailey asked her after she sat up and turned to face Jenna, who was still lying down.

"What *isn't* going on?" Jenna asked.

"Hey, talk to me," Bailey pled.

"Let's see… I'm miserable in school; I can't stand the roommate I'm forced to live with in the house; I got dumped because I wouldn't put out. And, oh, yeah, I have a massive crush on the person who's been my best friend these days. That's saying a lot, too, because I don't even talk to her all that much, and I never get to see her because I decided one day in high school that Michigan was where I wanted to go to college."

Bailey stared down at her, letting Jenna finish and take a deep breath before she replied, "Her?"

Bailey's face went white, and her mouth was slightly open. Her eyes were concerned, sure, but there was something else in them, too. It was something Jenna had only ever seen directed at her with the guys she'd dated, and that was always during very specific times in their relationships.

"Oh," Jenna said out loud as she realized the common theme of those moments. "Bails?"

"She's a girl, Jenna? Your crush is a girl?"

Jenna ran her hand over to Bailey's on the bed, where she touched Bailey's fingertips with her own.

"She's you, Bailey."

"Me?"

"You." Jenna linked their fingers then. "For a while now."

"Me?" Bailey repeated. "You like *me?*"

"I do." Jenna sat up and moved slightly closer, but not too close so as to not scare Bailey away. The girl looked shell-shocked. No, she wasn't a girl. Bailey Sayers was a woman now. "I never knew how to tell you."

"You like me like that? Like, how I like girls? How I… do things… or want to… how–"

Jenna moved into Bailey's space; Bailey's nerves on display like that turned Jenna on in a way she had never experienced before. She straddled Bailey's hips in one smooth motion, not knowing where this bravado came from, and Bailey looked up at her then, her eyes wide and dark.

"Yes," Jenna answered.

She then leaned down and captured Bailey's soft lips. It took only a moment before Bailey's lips moved with them, Bailey's hands moved to Jenna's hips, and Bailey moaned into Jenna's mouth.

She wanted this, Jenna thought. Bailey wanted this. She wanted her. God, Jenna wanted her back. Bailey's hands moved quickly under her shirt as Jenna took Bailey's face into her hands. When they pulled apart for a moment, it was so that Bailey could help Jenna pull her shirt up and off her body. Then, Bailey's eyes met Jenna's again.

"Are you sure?" Bailey asked.

Jenna nodded, reaching behind her back to unclasp her bra. She removed it and tossed it to the floor. Bailey's eyes went to her chest then. There was this smirk on her face that Jenna could only smile at. She reached back down for Bailey's lips, reconnected her own to them, and tried to take in every single moment of this. Bailey's hands were on her back again, stroking Jenna's skin up and down. They slid down to her hips, where they stilled for only a moment. Once their tongues met, Jenna moaned, and Bailey's hands gripped Jenna's hips, encouraging them to move against Bailey.

Bailey moved her mouth to Jenna's neck, where she let her tongue trace along Jenna's skin. Jenna could barely hold in her excitement. Bailey's lips on her throat were causing a fire to build low in her belly. Jenna needed more than this; and she had waited so long for this moment, she wanted it now. Bailey must have understood because she moved to lay Jenna down onto her bed, lifted off her own shirt, removed her bra, and fell back on top of Jenna, reconnecting their lips. Yes, they were both sure.

"God, Bails," Jenna said as Bailey lowered her lips to her breast and took a nipple into her mouth.

"So long, Jenna." Bailey lifted her head and met Jenna's eyes. "I've wanted this for so long."

Jenna didn't know what to say to that. She thought about saying she felt the same way, but she didn't want to have a long conversation about how long they had both felt this way. She wanted Bailey's mouth back on her body. So, she just nodded as she smiled at Bailey.

Bailey's lips moved to Jenna's other breast, and she wasn't hesitant in her movements. She reached for Jenna's button and undid it before she unzipped Jenna's jeans. Jenna knew she was wet. She wondered, for a moment, if Bailey was, too. Then, Bailey's lips were on her stomach, and they just danced along Jenna's flesh while Bailey's hands grasped her breasts. Bailey played with Jenna's nipples while her lips slid lower and lower still.

"Off, Bails," Jenna said as she reached for her own jeans, trying to pull them off her body.

Bailey sat up, pulled them off, and tossed them aside

before she resumed what she was doing. When her lips moved lower, to the waistband of Jenna's panties, Bailey stopped. It was as if she had just realized what they were about to do. Bailey moved to stand then. At the end of the bed, Bailey looked down at her with a look that Jenna couldn't describe. She only knew enough to know that look was good, though. Bailey stripped off her own pants, leaving her in navy-blue boy shorts and nothing else. She lowered those to the floor, too, and stood in front of Jenna completely naked.

Jenna couldn't believe this was actually happening. Bailey tugged on her legs until she had them hanging over the bed. Then, Bailey knelt and reverently reached for Jenna's panties. Her eyes being on Jenna's the whole time, she pulled them down and off. She then took each of Jenna's legs and, in turn, placed them on her own shoulders, as if she had done this a thousand times.

"I've dreamed of this," Bailey said as she kissed Jenna's thighs.

Jenna could only watch as one of Bailey's hands reached for her breast again while the other rested on the inside of her thigh, so close to where she needed it. God, Bailey was so close. After a few more light kisses, moving ever closer, Jenna's hips bucked in the air, causing Bailey's eyes to meet Jenna's with dark orbs before she let her tongue slide between Jenna's folds.

"Oh," Jenna gasped.

Her hips lifted slightly as Bailey repeated the action. Then, Bailey's fingers spread her wider in order to allow her mouth more access. She took Jenna softly and slowly as if she wanted to make this last as much as Jenna did. Bailey's lips were sucking on her clit right now. Her hands were on the outside of Jenna's thighs, encouraging her wider. God, this was what all the fuss was about, wasn't it? This was why people talked about sex all the time. It felt so good, what Bailey was doing to her. When Bailey started moving faster, Jenna almost lost it. Her hand went to the back of Bailey's head, which caused the woman to moan. Jenna moaned back softly because of that, and then Bailey was moving faster, sucking and licking harder. Jenna watched Bailey's head bob from between her own legs, feeling a fresh pool of wetness and wondering only for an instant if that would bother Bailey, but Bailey lowered her mouth to Jenna's entrance, slid her tongue inside, and pulled it back out several times before moving back to Jenna's clit. When Jenna came, it was with Bailey drawing rapid circles around her clit and with a loud near-scream of Bailey's name.

Bailey didn't move at first. She stayed and continued to kiss Jenna's skin before she finally moved up Jenna's body. She then encouraged Jenna back to the top of the bed, where she cradled Jenna in her arms. Once Jenna had felt the last of the tremors leave her body, she lifted herself up to look at Bailey. She was gorgeous.

"You don't have to–" Bailey started and stopped. "We can just stay like–"

Jenna kissed her gently then. She knew what Bailey was trying to tell her, but she also knew what she wanted. She lifted herself up, climbing on top of Bailey in the process, and felt Bailey's legs spread beneath her. She rested herself between them.

"Oh, Bails," she said as she felt the wetness between Bailey's legs.

"That feels good, what you're doing," Bailey breathed out before Jenna could kiss her.

Jenna wasn't sure what Bailey was talking about until she realized her hips were rocking down into Bailey's core, lighting them both on fire as they kissed. Jenna was finally experiencing what she had only been able to dream about before. She sucked on Bailey's nipples one at a time while Bailey's hands ran up and down her back. One of them gripped the back of Jenna's neck, encouraging her to suck harder. Jenna guessed that Bailey really liked this. She moved to the other breast to continue the movements, earning several gasps and moans. Then, her hand slid down Bailey's stomach and rested between her legs. She cupped Bailey's sex, felt the warmth of it against her hand, and couldn't think of anything else as she allowed one finger to slip between Bailey's folds.

"Jesus, Bails," Jenna said. "This is…"

"Don't stop," Bailey replied.

Jenna didn't stop; she added another finger. She slid them up and down as Bailey's hips responded. Jenna looked down to her own hand and watched it move inside Bailey's folds. She felt her clit, and it was hard. She was slick, and her clit was hard. That meant something. That meant she was ready to come, right? Jenna stroked her harder and faster. Bailey made the sexiest sounds Jenna had ever heard in her life. Then, Bailey's hips lifted so quickly, Jenna hadn't been ready for it. Her fingers slipped down to Bailey's entrance accidentally and almost went inside. When Bailey gasped at the contact, Jenna moved her fingers back to the spot and slid one inside. She waited for Bailey's reaction – which was to buck her hips again – then slid the finger out, and slid two fingers back inside.

Jenna held herself up and kissed Bailey as she stroked her inside. She didn't really know what she was doing; she didn't know if using her fingers like this would actually work. Bailey had made her feel so good; Jenna only wanted to give her the same pleasure. She pulled her mouth away from Bailey's, met her eyes, and noticed they were closed so tightly. Jenna moved down Bailey's body, kissing her skin as she went, and when her mouth met its destination, she stilled her fingers for a moment. She slid her tongue against Bailey's clit, reveled in the taste of her, and slid her fingers in deeper. Bailey's moans grew louder as Jenna worked against and inside her until Bailey stiffened entirely, called out, and trembled. Bailey had trembled at her touch. Jenna waited until the trembling had died down before she moved back up Bailey's body to stare down at her.

"God, Bailey. That was…"

"I know," Bailey interrupted her, kissed her, and pulled Jenna down into her farther.

They continued to explore one another for the next several hours before Jenna had to leave. Her mom had called twice, asking when she would be home. Jenna didn't want to leave Bailey, but she also knew her mom needed her. When they'd said goodbye, it was in Bailey's car, with Jenna leaning over and kissing her sweetly.

"I'll see you tomorrow?" Bailey asked.

"I can't wait," Jenna replied.

"I know it's a holiday and everything, but we should talk. We haven't really talked about this." Bailey pointed between them. "We should talk before you go back to school, right?"

"We should." Jenna kissed her cheek. "This is good, Bails. Whatever this is, this is good."

"I wish you could have stayed," Bailey said as she cupped Jenna's cheek. "I have the house to myself for the rest of the week. I know you're here for your mom, but do you think there's a chance you could stay over just one night? We could do more of what we did before." Bailey blushed, and Jenna thought it was adorable. "And we could talk. We could talk all night, Jen. I love talking to you."

"I love talking to you, too," Jenna said. "And the stuff we did before, that was good, too."

Bailey's blush deepened. Jenna kissed her one more time and opened the car door.

"I'll see you tomorrow," Bailey repeated.

"Tomorrow," Jenna said back, climbed out of the car, and closed the door with a smile on her face.

\*\*\*

When Jenna woke up the following morning, she couldn't keep the smile off her face. She and Bailey were doing this. They'd had sex, they had talked a little, and they would talk more today. She'd find a way to go back to Bailey's place. They would talk more and probably repeat their activities from the day before. Jenna would find a way to stay the night and wake up next to her. Then, they'd plan how it would work while they finished up school.

Jenna was still tossing out the idea of taking a semester off. If she did that, she and Bailey could see one another all the time. She could also see her mom and be here if she needed anything. Jenna dressed for the day. She would normally wear jeans and a nice sweater but, with Bailey coming, she wanted to dress up a little more. She threw on a strapless dress that was a deep plum. She also had matching nail polish, and her dark hair was down, framing her face perfectly. She hadn't put on shoes yet, but she had planned to wear the white strappy heels she liked.

"What are you so dressed up for?" her brother asked when Jenna emerged from her bedroom.

"I'm not *that* dressed up. It's Thanksgiving," she replied and moved past him.

"Whatever," he dismissed and closed his bedroom door behind him.

Jenna smoothed her hands over her dress before she entered the kitchen where her mom would be cooking. They had already made the stuffing, and the turkey was in the oven. Bailey would be here in about an hour, and Jenna couldn't believe she and Bailey would be sitting at the same table as her parents less than twenty-four hours after they'd been one another's first time. They'd been each other's second and third time, too. And, technically, fourth, since they'd done it again out in the living room before Jenna absolutely had to leave. She'd see her again today, though. If Jenna could walk her out after dinner, maybe they could even make out in Bailey's car before Jenna had to get back inside.

"Mom?" Jenna asked when she entered the kitchen and saw her mother lying on the floor.

# CHAPTER 4: IT CHANGED EVERYTHING

When Jenna's mom collapsed that day, Jenna's entire life had changed. They'd rushed her to the hospital when they had been unable to revive her. The doctors later said there were complications with her treatment. She'd been admitted to the hospital, and for several days after, Jenna had forgotten about everything else. When she had finally reached for her phone, it was completely dead. She had no charger, which made her flash back to Bailey charging her phone on spring break. She had smacked her forehead when she realized Bailey had likely been waiting for her at the house and had probably called to find out what had happened.

Jenna had texted her the moment she'd gotten home. Bailey had offered to come over, but Jenna, her father, and brother were going back to the hospital as soon as possible. Jenna hardly left her mother's room until it was time to fly back to campus. It left them no time to talk, and as much as Jenna wanted to see Bailey, she couldn't process anything other than what was happening to her mom.

When Jenna arrived back at campus, she talked to next to no one. She had tried calling Bailey a couple of times, she'd left messages, and Bailey would call back and do the same, but they just kept missing one another. Jenna wanted more than anything to talk to her, to figure out what they were to one another now. They finally arranged the day and time when they could talk. They'd cleared their calendars just so they could talk for an hour or two. Then, Jenna had gotten another phone call.

\*\*\*

"Jenna?"

Jenna turned to see Bailey standing there, dressed in all black.

"Hey, Bail," she said softly.

"I wasn't sure if I should come," Bailey replied as she made her way toward Jenna.

They were standing in Jenna's house. People were walking around them, talking softly and solemnly about her mother. Jenna's father was talking to one of her mother's friends. Her brother was sitting on the sofa, not talking to anyone. He had a plate of food in his hand that looked like it had yet to be touched. Then, there was Bailey Sayers, standing off to the side of Jenna's living room.

"It's fine," Jenna replied as she stared at her brother. "I don't think he's eaten in three days."

"Who?" Bailey followed her eyeline. "Oh."

"My dad hasn't eaten, either. I should make sure they eat some—"

"Have you eaten?" Bailey asked as she tried to take Jenna's hand.

"Bailey!" Jenna pulled her hand back after she whisper-yelled. "Not here. Are you crazy?"

"I'm not—" Bailey paused as she took her hand back. "I didn't mean... Did you think I was... Jen, I was just trying to comfort you. I'm—"

"Comfort me?" Jenna snapped. "My mom just died, Bailey. She was fine one day. Then, she's in the hospital, and now she's dead. You can't comfort me."

"I know. I'm sorry. I don't know what to do, Jen. I just wanted to help."

"You can't help this, Bailey," Jenna said as she tugged on Bailey's arm to escort her to the hallway. They wouldn't be alone. There were people everywhere in the house. "I have to make sure they eat, Bailey. My mom always made sure."

"Okay. Okay, Jen. You can make sure they eat. I'll help you. What can I do?"

"You can't help me. I have to do it. It's my responsibility."

"Jenna, please talk to me. What can I do?"

"You can go. I can't deal with this now."

"Deal with what?" Bailey squinted her eyes at her. "Jenna, I'm not here to talk about us; I came here for you. I came for your mom."

"Bailey, I can't." Jenna's eyes filled with tears. "I can't see you right now."

"Jen, I just told you I don't care about us. I don't care about the fact that you stopped returning my calls or my texts, that we haven't really talked since that day. I don't care about any of that right now. I care about you. I care about being here for you right now."

"I can't look at you, Bails," Jenna replied as tears streaked down her cheeks. "You remind me of what we had. I can't have that right now. It hurts, Bailey." She let her tears fall in earnest.

"Oh, Jen." Bailey went to reach for her but pulled back at the last minute. "I'm sorry. I shouldn't have come. I just—"

"I know. I know." Jenna wiped her eyes and looked up to see the immense hurt in Bailey's. "I'm sorry. This isn't your fault."

"I should go," Bailey replied with tears in her own eyes now. "If there's anything you need – I don't know; I guess I'm just saying that I'm here." She turned to reach for the doorknob. "I'll miss you, Jenna."

\*\*\*

Jenna returned back to school for the summer. She had helped her father and brother deal with packing her mom's things after a reasonable amount of time had passed, but she had missed too much of the semester to pass any of her classes once it was all said and done. Her father had insisted on the summer sessions. Jenna had agreed because she didn't want to argue with the man who'd just lost the love of his life. Jenna's brother had chosen a school nearby. He'd be able to check on their father more regularly and would stay with him through the summer.

Jenna muddled through her classes. She'd garnered some sympathy for her loss and had been able to take two of the finals she had missed, so now she would only be one semester behind if she passed all her summer sessions. The sorority house was nearly empty over the summer. Jenna was so lonely. She had wanted her own room in the house since the moment she'd moved in, but even not having her roommate there for three months couldn't break Jenna's bad mood.

When her senior year started, she opted to move out of the house. She would still be an active sister, but she needed her own space. Her father had sold the home she had grown up in. Jenna had no reason to go back for Thanksgiving or Christmas because her brother had a new girlfriend, and he would spend the holidays with her family. Her father decided to spend the holidays with his sister and brother-in-law. Jenna was alone again. She moved into a cheap off-campus apartment, got a part-time job to pay for it, and continued in a fog until graduation, which was a semester later than everyone else she had gone to school with, including Bailey.

\*\*\*

"Congratulations, Jenna and Joel!" Andrea yelled to the rest of the partygoers. "Who would have thought that just two years ago, when Jenna joined my company, I would find my best friend, who I would then drag to a bar one night where she would meet her future husband. As you all can see, I am taking full responsibility for these two finding each other."

"Of course, you are," Jenna joked as Joel's arm snaked around her waist.

"Seriously, though, I am so happy for you guys." Andrea raised her champagne glass high in the air. "Happy engagement, you two."

The crowd echoed the sentiment as Joel kissed Jenna's cheek, and Jenna smiled at her friends and her father and brother, who had made the trip to New Mexico for the engagement party. Jenna was twenty-four years old. Actually, she was nearly twenty-five now; her birthday was only a month away. Joel had just turned twenty-eight and had popped the question three weeks ago at his birthday dinner. Jenna had said yes.

She did want to marry Joel, but there was just something in the back of her mind that felt wrong about the whole situation. She wondered if all future brides felt this way upon seeing that ring on their finger. Did they all think back to every relationship they had ever had to consider if any of those people should have been the one? Did they think about all the relationships they wouldn't have because they'd chosen to get married, and wonder if they'd be missing out?

Jenna smiled and hugged everyone who attended their engagement party. It had been important to Joel to host everyone at their house. Well, it was still technically his house. She had moved in about six months prior, but her name wasn't on it; she wanted to buy somewhere else. Preferably, somewhere that wasn't New Mexico.

Joel was set on staying since he had grown up there. His whole family still lived close by, his job was there, and he loved the place. Jenna had ended up there by accident. When she finally managed to graduate school with barely a passing GPA, she had applied to any company that had a role similar to what she would want to do long-term. That's how she ended up interviewing for the office in New Mexico, not expecting to get the job. When she got the offer, she had considered turning it down at first, but she had no other prospects and no money saved up. She had moved, started work, and met Andrea. They became best friends. Then, she met Joel one night at a bar.

When she first started dating Joel, she knew he was a great guy that she could fall in love with. That had happened; Jenna had fallen in love with him. The only problem was that she still had someone else in the back of her mind; there was something that had gone unresolved for years now.

Every year, when Thanksgiving came around, Jenna thought of exactly two things: she thought about her mom, and she thought about Bailey Sayers. She thought about how much she missed her mother, and she thought about how much she missed Bailey, and how she had made her feel.

\*\*\*

"I know. I'll miss you, too," Jenna said to Joel as she meandered her way through the airport to get to her gate. "Oh, sorry," she said to the person she bumped into while not paying attention.

"It's okay," the woman replied.

"Joel, I've got to go. Yeah, me too," she replied and hung up the phone.

"Sorry, again." Jenna turned to the woman who was trying to untangle their roller bags.

"It happens. Are you running to catch your flight?"

"Trying to get there, yeah. It's boarding now."

"Oh, well, we're good to go here." The woman managed to get her roller free.

"Jen?"

Jenna snapped her head at the sound of the voice coming from her right.

"Bail?" Jenna said mostly to herself as Bailey came into view.

"You two know each other?" the woman asked.

"*You two* know each other?" Jenna asked the woman.

"Jenna, this is Callie," Bailey introduced.

"How do you two know each other?" Callie asked both of them.

"We went to high school together," Bailey replied.

Then, Jenna watched Bailey snake her arm around Callie's waist in the same way Joel always did to her. Her mouth went dry at the sight of Bailey touching another woman, claiming that woman as her own in the way that she had once claimed Jenna's mind, body, and soul.

"What are the odds?" Callie said. "Jenna and I bumped bags. We were untangling them so she could run and not miss her flight."

"You've got to go?" Bailey asked, eyes not leaving Jenna's since she spotted her.

Jenna checked her watch and answered, "My flight's boarding now. It's a work thing, and I'm presenting; I can't miss the flight."

"We're going on vacation ourselves." Callie kissed Bailey's cheek. "Anniversary trip for us."

"How long?" Jenna asked Bailey.

"We met in school, but we didn't date back then. This one was still trying to get over some ex-girlfriend." Callie pressed her hand to Bailey's chest, and Jenna remembered what it felt like to touch Bailey there. "Anyway, we ran into each other a little over a year ago, and we've been dating ever since."

"Congratulations," Jenna said softly.

"To you too, I see." Bailey pointed at Jenna's hand gripping her roller.

"Oh." Jenna followed Bailey's eyes to her ring. "Thanks."

"How long?" Bailey asked.

"Together about a year and a half; just got engaged last month," Jenna answered as her heart raced in her chest.

"Congrats, Jen."

"Thanks."

Jenna wanted nothing more than to talk to Bailey. She hadn't seen her since her mother's funeral, and she hadn't spoken to her since then, either. She'd felt so terrible about how she had treated Bailey that even the idea of texting or calling her seemed like it would do more harm than good to both of them.

"Too bad we can't all grab some coffee or something," Callie said. "I'd love to hear embarrassing stories about Bailey from high school."

"Right." Jenna snapped back to attention. "I've got to go. I'm sorry. I really can't miss–"

"Your flight." Bailey nodded. "I get it."

"Hey, Bail?"

"Yeah?"

"It was really good to see you," Jenna said.

"You too, Jen."

Jenna gripped her roller hard, nodded at the two of them, and walked past them to get to her gate.

# CHAPTER 5: BEST LAID PLANS

"You have been putting this off for months," Joel told her as he tossed the magazine on the coffee table. "Andrea has been passing you these magazines to try to get things started, and I keep finding them in the trash. Do you not like the magazines, or do you not want to plan our wedding?" He sighed as he stood. "Should we hire a wedding planner? Would that help? Maybe it's just stressful for you. I haven't been around a lot. I can maybe take a few days off work, and we could plan it together."

"We've only been engaged for six months, Joel. What's the problem with waiting a while before we start planning?" she asked.

"Because I want to marry you, Jen!" he exclaimed as he stood over her in their living room. "That's the whole point of getting engaged. I proposed so we could get married, and you haven't even allowed us to set a date yet."

"There's a lot to consider, Joel. It's not like I can just pick a random date. Your parents, my dad and brother, Andrea, and everyone else all have to be available."

"It's *our* wedding, Jenna. They will be there no matter what day we pick. They just want us to pick one," he said as he sat back down next to her.

Jenna took a deep breath and replied, "You're right. When I get back from this stupid convention, we can sit down and pick a date."

"Why can't we do it now?" he asked.

"Because I have to pack now, Joel. I have an early flight, and I'll be in meetings, networking events, dinners, and whatever else they throw at me for a full week. Can we just do it when I get back? We'll pick a date and move on already."

"Wow, Jen." Joel stood up again and didn't bother turning back to her as he said, "I love how excited you sound about planning the most important day of our life."

Jenna dropped her head to the back of the sofa and closed her eyes. Joel was right: she had been putting this off. He had asked her at least ten times to pick a date or, at minimum, start working on the details. She kept telling him she would. Then, she wouldn't. Andrea had been buying her bridal magazines and either leaving them here or at the office on Jenna's desk. She'd been trying to get Jenna to take the hint. And Jenna got the hint. She knew they had gotten engaged in order to get married; she understood the path. Seeing Bailey that day at the airport had caught her completely off guard, though. And seeing Bailey with a girlfriend at the airport had caught her completely off guard, too. Jenna hadn't slept the entire work trip and had been sleeping irregularly ever since. Sex with Joel had been regular, at best, since the beginning of their relationship, but ever since she'd gotten back from that trip, she had withdrawn from him. It had become something he had to press her for, and, sometimes, she'd still turn him down. She wasn't being fair to him, and she knew it. She should want to marry Joel. She did want to marry him, right?

\*\*\*

Jenna had decided to have dinner in her hotel room that first night since she had no desire to network at the company's welcome event. There were over sixty offices in the country and two in Canada. Of all the fifteen thousand employees, only one thousand were selected to attend the convention. Jenna had been one of them. It had come at a really good time, though, because she'd needed a break from Joel and, to a certain extent, her life. Andrea hadn't been selected to attend, and truthfully, Jenna was glad for a break from her maid of honor, too.

"Jen? What are you doing here?" Bailey asked her at the buffet breakfast the following morning.

"What are *you* doing here?" Jenna walked toward Bailey, who had been piling bacon on her plate but left the line when she had seen Jenna.

"Convention, obviously. Are you one of the guest speakers or something?"

"I work here, Bails. New Mexico office. You?"

"Same place I went to school, Jen. You live in New Mexico?" Bailey asked as she touched Jenna's elbow and dropped her plate on an empty table. "How long?"

"I got the job after school, and I moved there for it," Jenna explained.

"I didn't know," Bailey replied.

"I didn't know you worked here, too."

"How would you? It's not like you ever bothered to call me back."

Jenna stared at the floor for a moment before lifting her eyes to meet Bailey's.

"My mom died, Bails." Jenna shrugged. "After you and I…" She stopped herself and looked away again. "I didn't call you back, that's true, but I didn't know what to say to you, Bailey. The phone worked both ways, though, you know?" Jenna suggested as she plopped down onto a chair, suddenly needing the support for her wobbling legs.

"You made it clear that day, Jen: you didn't want to hear from me. You didn't want me there."

"I needed to focus on my family, and I didn't handle things well; I know that. It doesn't matter, though. We still had school to get back to. I was miserable without you, but I couldn't be with you, either. I should've had the courage to tell you that. I didn't, and I'm sorry. I spent the whole summer at school trying to get caught up from all my terrible grades. I stopped going back home after that. Then, I got the job, and I just assumed you'd moved on." She paused as Bailey's eyes bore into her. "I was right; you met Callie."

"Jen, we should talk," Bailey said.

"I can't. I have a meeting with my team. They're over there." Jenna pointed at a table about twenty feet away, where her team was waiting for her with their own breakfasts. "I was just grabbing food."

"But you're here all week, right?" Bailey asked.

"I leave Saturday morning," Jenna replied. "You?"

"Same." Bailey smiled.

"We should grab dinner," Jenna suggested, not knowing what else to do.

"Tonight?"

"I can't tonight," Jenna said as she recalled a dinner thing she had already agreed to attend. "Tomorrow?"

"I have a drinks thing. Night after?"

"I think I'm free. I have a meeting until six, but I can do seven."

"Seven, it is."

"It'll be nice to catch up, Bails," Jenna said.

"I still can't believe you're here," Bailey replied as she shook her head in disbelief.

"I can't believe *you're* here. Let's talk at dinner. I'll make a reservation," Jenna offered. "I have to get going," she added reluctantly.

***

"We broke up," Bailey began. "Callie and I."

"When?" Jenna asked, suddenly uninterested in her wine and very interested in what Bailey was saying.

"Not long after we got back from our trip," Bailey explained.

"What happened?"

172

"I ended things. We're just at different points in our lives, I think. You and I are almost twenty-six; she's younger and in a different place. I was ready to start settling down, and she's not."

"So, it was a circumstance thing but you still love each other?"

Bailey considered for a moment before she said, "Not exactly."

"Not exactly, Bails?" Jenna sipped her wine.

"You wouldn't understand, Jen." Bailey finished her own wine.

"Why not?"

"Can we just move on, please? How's New Mexico? Do you like it there?"

"Don't do that. Don't change the subject, Bail."

"Because of you, Jenna," Bailey answered loudly. "I broke up with Callie because I am stupid. I let seeing you at that airport get to me. When she asked what was going on, I told her about us. I told her that I'd loved you back then, that we'd slept together, and that you didn't want anything to do with me after that; that's why I wasn't ready to date her when I first met her at school." Bailey's eyes flitted around the small restaurant. "She didn't take that news well, but she understood because she and I both had our histories. Then, I basically stopped having sex with her because I'm a horrible person, and she put two and two together. I ended it because it wasn't fair to her that I was still hung up on my lifelong crush. There. Are you happy now?"

"Lifelong crush?"

"Jenna, I told you that day at my house that I'd wanted that with you for so long. Did you think I was kidding?"

"I'd wanted that with you, too, Bails." Jenna finished her wine. "I didn't know how to tell you back then."

"Well, it doesn't matter now, does it?"

"Why not?"

"You're wearing someone else's ring, Jenna." She pointed to Jenna's left hand.

"I'm sorry, Bails." Jenna rested her hand on top of the small table they shared.

"Why? You had every right to get engaged. I don't own you. I never did."

"Yes, you do," Jenna replied softly. "You always have."

Bailey stared at her, and Jenna thought of the girl she had touched for the first time while in Bailey's bedroom. Bailey looked older now. Jenna was wearing a business suit, and Bailey was wearing a business suit. They were business suit people now. But they were still also just Jenna and Bailey.

"Jen…"

"I am sorry, Bails."

Their eyes were still connected. Jenna always felt so unbelievably close to Bailey just by looking at her eyes. No matter what changed between them, Bailey's eyes would always be her touchstone.

"We should probably turn in soon. It's getting late, and we have that all-company meeting tomorrow morning in the main hall," Bailey suggested.

"Right," Jenna agreed.

The following morning, Jenna sat in the main hall and listened to a few speeches. There was a brief HR meeting where they reviewed sexual harassment. Lunch was a buffet, and she had meetings with her team right after. Bailey was in a completely different department, in a totally different office, but, somehow, they'd ended up at the same company, and now – at the same convention. At the end of her very long day, where she hadn't seen Bailey once, Jenna went to her room and dressed for bed. Then, there was a knock on her door.

"Hey, Bail," Jenna greeted.

"I had a long day with about fifteen meetings, I think." She moved into Jenna's room without waiting for

Jenna to invite her inside. "I had a couple of drinks; I should probably tell you that in advance." She turned around as Jenna closed the door and pointed at her. "I don't remember anything that happened to me today."

"God, what did you drink, Bailey?" Jenna was in front of her in an instant, feeling Bailey's forehead as if she could feel for something there.

"No, not because of the alcohol; because of what you said."

"What did I say?" Jenna lowered her hand and crossed her arms over her chest. "Do you want to sit down?" She motioned to the bed. "Or, lie down, I guess."

Bailey flopped down on Jenna's bed unceremoniously and said, "Do you have a mini-bar? I don't in my room, but maybe you do."

"I don't think you need anything else to drink, Bails. Let me get you some water. I can make you some crappy coffee in this in-room coffee maker." Jenna smiled and nodded toward the machine next to the TV.

Bailey lifted her head up and smiled at her, causing Jenna's own smile to widen.

"You said I had you," Bailey reminded. "Last night, you said I had you. But I've never had you, Jenna. I wanted you. I loved you; but I never had you."

Jenna moved to lie next to her on the bed and replied, "You loved me?"

They weren't touching at all, but Jenna could feel Bailey everywhere.

"Forever, Jenna." Bailey rolled onto her side, facing Jenna. "That day in my room was the best day of my life."

"Mine too," Jenna replied and rolled to face Bailey. "I am sorry for how I acted after I lost my mom."

"I know," Bailey said as she scooted slightly closer.

"Did you love Callie?" Jenna asked.

"I did in the beginning, yes," Bailey answered, and Jenna nodded, lowering her eyes. "Callie's not you, though, Jen. No one was ever you."

"He isn't you, either, Bails," Jenna replied and reached out to touch Bailey's cheek softly. "No one has ever been you."

"Who is *he*?" Bailey asked.

"Joel." Jenna shrugged one shoulder as she scooted closer to Bailey.

"The fiancé," Bailey said softly.

"Yes." Jenna scooted ever so closer. She wanted to touch her. She wanted to touch Bailey more than she had ever wanted to touch anyone in her life. "We're supposed to be planning our wedding."

"How's that going?"

"It's not," Jenna answered.

"Why?"

"Because I saw you at that airport."

"Jen, this is a bad idea. We shouldn't be close like this," Bailey said.

"I know," Jenna sighed out. "I don't know what I'm doing."

"You're getting married, Jenna." Bailey rolled onto her back.

"And you're drunk and live about a thousand miles away," Jenna added.

"Jen, we don't even know each other anymore."

"*We* will *always* know each other," Jenna offered.

"You didn't even call me." Bailey sat up, removing herself from the bed entirely a moment later.

"What?"

"Jen, we had sex. We talked for hours. We said we'd keep talking, but you never called me."

"I told you—"

"You told me about your mom, and I am sorry about that, but you still didn't call me. I think I just now realized how upset I still am about that. Maybe it's the alcohol; I don't know."

"Bailey, come on." Jenna held out her hand for Bailey to take.

"Jenna, I loved you. And you wrecked me; what happened between us, and then losing you completely – it wrecked me."

"It wrecked me, too. I wasn't ready for what this is between us back then." Jenna stood.

"You didn't call me, Jen. God, for weeks, I waited. Months, years, I waited. I've gotten three new phones since then, and your number is always the first one I make sure to put in the new one just in case you ever decided to call me or text me, or even just let me know you're okay. You could have called."

"No, I couldn't have. I'd already let you down once, Bails. I had to see your face when I said those things to you, and I couldn't do it again." Jenna's eyes filled with tears.

"I can't do this." Bailey moved toward the door of Jenna's room. "I'm going back to my room to sleep it off."

"We should talk, Bailey. We should talk more and–"

"And what? You live in freaking New Mexico, with your fiancé. There's no–"

"Go, then!" Jenna motioned toward the door as she raised her voice. "If you want to leave, just leave. You're clearly still pissed at me. Fine, be pissed. You don't want me, so just go."

"Of course, I want you. I've always wanted you," Bailey fired back.

"Even when you were with Callie?"

"That's not fair." Bailey pointed at her. "You're with someone, too."

"I loved you, too, you know?" Jenna said.

"Don't, Jenna... I don't want to hurt over you anymore, Jenna Cabot. I let myself think I could have forever with you, and you let me go. I understand why, but you let me go. I waited for you. I waited so long... And I did fall in love with Callie. She wasn't you, but I fell in love with her, and I don't regret that. I waited for you, Jen; which was stupid because you and I were never actually together. I can't do this anymore." Bailey wiped her eyes. "I'm going back to my room. We should just leave each other alone. We only hurt each other."

"Bails, that's not true," Jenna said softly as she moved to Bailey. "We don't only hurt each other. I understand that I've hurt you, and I hate myself for doing that, but we have had some good times, too. We were good together."

"One day; we were good together for *one* day. That was all we had."

"I know," Jenna agreed. "I know."

"Let's just call this what it is: we're friends who slept together once and ran into each other at a convention, got a little caught up in the nostalgia, and said goodbye again."

"If that's what you want," Jenna said.

"It's what I need," Bailey replied.

Then, she was gone.

# CHAPTER 6: THE OFFICE

Bailey loved her job. It was, sadly, the best part of her day. She had been given a promotion after her successful kiss-up and performance at the convention, where she had delivered two presentations on improving efficiencies that would also save the company money. Both projects were currently underway, and Bailey had been enjoying the increase in responsibility and the office that came along with it; it afforded her the privacy to work, and it also afforded her the privacy to sulk over the other part of the convention that hadn't been successful.

She'd thought of Jenna nearly every day since the convention. After about a month of lying around, thinking about calling her, Bailey had finally decided she would move on for the first time in her life. She had dated two women since running into Jenna. It was really just a few dates with each woman; none of her attempts actually went anywhere because she still couldn't get Jenna Cabot out of her damn mind.

It had taken Bailey another two months to create her online dating profile. She had given up trying to find a woman in her everyday life; she just didn't go that many places. Samantha had already tried to set her up with the three other lesbians she knew; Bailey was out of options. She used the best picture she could find of herself to put on her profile, answered all their questions, and clicked "create." She had gotten four responses from women within the first eight hours. Three of them Bailey wasn't interested in for varying reasons, but one of them caught her attention. She replied to the woman via the platform's messaging system and waited.

The woman's name was Alyson, and she was an attorney. She was attractive and funny in their messages. They'd waited a few weeks before they exchanged phone numbers and called one another. Their first few phone calls were enjoyable. Alyson had to go out of town for a case but would call Bailey when she returned. Bailey had asked Alyson out, and they'd arranged a date and time in advance, which made Bailey feel like Alyson wasn't blowing her off. The texts Alyson sent her the first couple of days she was gone also helped Bailey think this was actually happening. She was smiling as she read one such message when her boss entered her office.

"Hey, can I borrow you for a minute? We've got a newbie in the office today. She's on Frost's team, but he's out today."

"Sure. What do you need?" Bailey asked.

"Just show her around. She's a transfer, so she's not a novice. She just needs to know where the breakroom is, bathrooms, printer, et cetera."

"Transfer from where?"

"Albuquerque, I think. New Mexico, at least. Thanks, Bails." The woman slapped the side of the open doorframe before she left.

Bailey had heard that correctly, right? There were two offices in New Mexico. She'd looked up Jenna after the convention and found out which office she worked in. Those offices each had over two hundred people in them, including their warehouse employees. What are the odds that Jenna Cabot had transferred to her office?

"Hey, Bail," Jenna said with an offered wave.

One hundred percent. The odds were one hundred percent. Bailey swallowed hard as she scrutinized Jenna Cabot. Jenna was wearing a gray business suit with a white shirt under the blazer. She had on black heels and diamond stud earrings. It was while thinking of jewelry that Bailey lowered her eyes to Jenna's left hand.

"Hey, Jen," Bailey replied. "I guess you're the transfer."

"I start today," Jenna said. "I thought about calling you, but I didn't know what to say."

Jenna moved toward her. She was carrying a leather case in front of her, gripping it with both hands.

"How about telling me you're coming to work in my office, Jen?" Bailey offered.

"What would you have done? Told me not to come?"

"I don't know. Maybe."

"Really?" Jenna's expression showed hurt. "Well, I did just move back, but if this is going to be a problem, I guess I'll just keep my head down, pretend I don't know you, and start looking for a different job. Sorry, I thought we could be civil about–"

"Jenna, stop." Bailey held up her hand in supplication. "Just let me show you around the office. You can meet your team and get to work."

"Are you going to ask me why I'm here?" Jenna asked as they started walking.

"Should I?" Bailey turned her head toward Jenna.

"I applied for this job, Bails. I specifically applied for this office."

"Okay." Bailey motioned with her hand. "Bathrooms are there. Breakroom is down the hall to the right. We have pizza brought in on Tuesdays at noon, if you're interested. The printer for your department is over there." Bailey pointed to the left. "And you can pick up your badge and parking pass with the office manager sometime today."

"Are you mad at me?" Jenna grasped Bailey's forearm. "Can you talk to me?" she asked more softly.

"About what, Jen? I haven't seen you in months. When I did, it's not like it ended well."

"You avoided me for the rest of the convention, Bailey," Jenna said.

"This isn't the time, Jen. I have to get back to work. I

have a meeting in like three minutes, and you need to find your desk."

"Later?"

"Maybe. I don't know, Jen."

Bailey backed away, leaving Jenna where she stood, and headed back to her office. She picked up her desk phone and dialed the extension for their HR department. She wanted to ask what Jenna was doing there. Had Jenna really requested this office? Had she actually applied for a position here? Bailey hung up her phone in frustration when she realized it didn't matter; Jenna was there. Jenna would be working at her office from now on. Bailey was especially happy she had an office now. An office had a door. She stood and closed that door, trying to push all thoughts of Jenna Cabot out of her mind while she got back to work.

***

"Hold on." Sam held out her hands. "Jenna works at your office now?"

"She does. She started on Monday." Bailey took a drink of her margarita.

"What the hell? She didn't give you a heads-up?"

"Nope."

"What a bitch."

"She's not a bitch, Sam. We just have a weird history," Bailey said.

"She slept with you and didn't call you, Bails. She's a bitch," Sam replied and dipped a tortilla chip in the salsa bowl.

"It wasn't exactly like that. Her mom collapsed the next day and got sicker. I understood."

"Why are you defending her right now? You were pissed at her before." Sam bit into her chip. "I'm the best friend; I'm supposed to be pissed when you're pissed. But if you've suddenly changed your mood regarding Jenna

Cabot, let me know."

"I haven't changed my mood." Bailey dipped her own chip. "She just works with me now. I don't have much of a choice; I have to at least be professional with her."

"Professional? With the woman you once told me was the love of your life?"

"That was right after, Sam. It was a text message."

"That you sent me the night you two finally hooked up."

"We did not hook up," Bailey objected. "We–"

"What? Made love?" Sam asked.

"Yes, that's exactly what it was," Bailey asserted. "Sam, I loved her."

"I know, Bails. Do you still? You haven't exactly put a lot of effort into dating since you two ran into one another."

"Which time?" Bailey lifted an eyebrow.

"Every time," Samantha replied earnestly. "Do you still love her?"

"She wasn't wearing a ring, Sam."

\*\*\*

"Bailey?" Alyson greeted her when she walked into the coffee shop.

"Yeah, hey," Bailey replied.

She approached when she recognized Alyson from her picture. They exchanged a somewhat awkward hug, pulled back, and stared at one another.

"Do you want to sit?" Alyson asked and motioned toward the empty chair.

"Yes. Right."

"First time online dating… It's weird meeting in person, right?"

Bailey sat. Alyson sat. They continued to stare at one another. Alyson was even more attractive in person. She had bright green eyes, light blonde hair, and a few well-placed freckles that made her look adorable while also appearing sexy at the same time.

"It is. Why is that?" Bailey asked.

Their waiter approached and took Bailey's coffee order. Alyson already had a cup in front of her. They opted to share a dessert as well, and once the order was placed, their waiter left them alone again.

"I have no idea. This is the first time I'm meeting someone in person, too. It's different than just meeting in a bar, though, right?"

"I've talked to you already. I know your bio. So, yes." Bailey smiled at her.

"We get to skip some of the basic stuff then. That's kind of nice."

"Like this is already a second date?" Bailey lifted an eyebrow at her.

"I'll take that." Alyson took a sip of her coffee and winked at her.

\*\*\*

"I can't wait. I'll see you Friday," Bailey said into the phone before she disconnected from Alyson.

"Bails, can I grab you for a sec?" Jenna stood in the open door of her office. "I need your help with the projector in the conference room; it's not recognizing my laptop."

"You can call IT. They're one floor down; they'll be up in like two minutes."

Jenna had been in the office for over a month now. They'd hardly spoken since she had arrived, and Jenna had been trying; Bailey knew that much. She just hadn't been interested. Well, that wasn't right. She was interested. She wished she could be nice to Jenna. She wished she could just talk to her, tell her how she feels so she could really move on. She'd thought she had forgiven Jenna, but seeing her at that convention and then again in her office only proved to her that she still had some work to do on that front.

"Bails, please."

Bailey glared at her, stood up, and said, "Fine."

They headed into the conference room, and Jenna closed the door behind them. Bailey looked around for Jenna's laptop, but the table only had one cupcake with a candle. She turned to see Jenna smiling at her.

"Happy birthday, Bails."

"My birthday is on Friday," Bailey replied.

Jenna moved to the table, where she used a lighter to light the candle on top of the cupcake.

"You're twenty-six years old on Friday, yes, but I'm out of the office on Thursday and Friday. I wanted to do this before I had to go." Jenna stood upright again. "Happy birthday, Bails."

"Thanks, Jen."

"Blow out the candle."

"I guess I should. I don't want the sprinklers to go off. Did you get the largest candle they had in store?" Bailey blew out the candle that was in the form of the number twenty-six. "It's bigger than the cupcake, Jen."

Jenna laughed and replied, "I know. I wanted the numbered one, though."

"Why?" Bailey laughed, too, as she removed the candle from the cupcake and licked the bit of the icing off the bottom.

"I don't know. I just like them better than the little stick ones."

Bailey smiled at her adoringly. Jenna was adorable. Her face had scrunched as she made a gesture with her fingers to indicate the thin candles.

"Well, thanks."

"It's vanilla. That's your favorite, right?"

"How did you know that?"

"Did you forget?" Jenna asked. "Your eighteenth

birthday."

"Right, I did forget." Bailey dipped her finger into the icing and licked it.

Jenna's eyes got big as she said, "You didn't have a birthday party that year."

"I did, but I didn't invite you. I thought you were too good for me."

"Wait. What?" Jenna asked, seemingly surprised at the comment.

"I had a birthday party every year; my mom made me. It was usually just Samantha and I, with a couple of friends I had in my neighborhood."

"I guess I just assumed that, if you had a party, you'd invite me."

"I honestly didn't think you would come." Bailey shrugged.

"Why not?" Jenna sat in one of the conference table chairs.

"We didn't hang out, Jen. I never got invited to your parties." Bailey sat in the chair next to Jenna.

"I didn't think *you'd* come," Jenna replied.

"What? Why?"

"You just seemed so much cooler than me back then, Bails."

"I'm sorry, what?" Bailey couldn't help but laugh. "You had a million friends and participated in everything; I had four people at my birthday parties."

"You were always so okay with who you were, Bailey. You owned who you were as a teenager. You were good with the friends you had, and you never tried; you never worried about being popular or missing out on a game or dance."

"You did?"

"I did, yeah."

"Were you not okay with that?" Bailey asked.

"I guess I was. I liked high school. I don't have any regrets. Well, one regret, maybe."

"What's that?" Bailey asked.

"That I chose to go to school in Michigan. Do you have any?"

"One, maybe," Bailey offered.

"Share, please." Jenna smiled.

"That I didn't tell you how I felt on graduation day like I'd planned," Bailey replied honestly.

"You were going to tell me?" Jenna leaned forward.

"I wanted to ask you out, at least," Bailey said as she slid the cupcake toward Jenna on the table. "I didn't. I was terrified of how you'd react."

"Really?"

"Little did I know, you and I would…" Bailey lifted both eyebrows.

"I didn't know back then," Jenna said. "I mean, I don't know how I would have reacted. As much as I liked you, I was also very confused about it. I don't know what I would have said."

"I guess we'll never know then. Why do you regret going to school in Michigan? Your mom?" Bailey asked.

"No. I wish I had more time with her, of course, but that's about you."

"Me?"

"Yeah. I used to think about you and I getting together." Jenna leaned back in the chair. "I don't know… I think, in my mind, if I had gone to school closer to home, you and I would have stayed in touch more. Maybe we would have seen one another. I kind of pictured things progressing further than that."

"You thought about that?" Bailey leaned forward this time. "Us?"

"Yes, Bails." Jenna slid the cupcake back toward her. "I still do."

"Is that why you're here, Jen?" Bailey asked.

"In the office?"

"That's what I'm asking."

"Yes, Bail; I came back for you."

"What about Joel?" Bailey asked.

"I broke up with Joel." Jenna held up her hand. "Did you not notice this hand is empty?"

"No, I noticed." Bailey nodded toward the hand. "But why, Jen? Why now?"

"Because I want us to try, Bailey."

"We did try."

"No, we didn't," Jenna said as she leaned forward again. "We didn't even really get started, Bailey."

"I got started. Did you not get started? I was pretty sure you finished." Bailey met Jenna's eyes. "Four times."

Jenna chuckled and said, "I did. I definitely did."

"Hey, do you two need the conference room? We had it reserved." Barry, the Manager of Marketing, opened the door without knocking.

"Oh, no." Bailey stood suddenly. "Sorry, guys."

They both stepped out of the conference room, with Bailey still holding her cupcake in her hand. They stood in the hall for a moment and stared at one another.

"I brought you a cupcake the morning of your eighteenth birthday. We shared it because you insisted I have some," Jenna reminded her.

"I remember now."

"Bails, what are you doing on Friday night? I'll be back from the other office around dinner time. Can I pick you up? We could go to dinner to celebrate and just talk." Jenna paused for a moment. "I've been waiting, Bails. I knew you were still upset with me. I waited. I came home because I wanted to be close to my father and my brother, and I wanted to be near the place I grew up; that's all true. But I also wanted to be near you. I want to go out with you, Bailey. I'd like to take you on our first official date this Friday night." She smiled hopefully.

"Jen, I can't." Bailey looked away from Jenna's captivating eyes only for a moment before peering into them again. "I already have a date."

"Oh," Jenna replied.

\*\*\*

"So, is she your girlfriend yet?" Samantha asked as she sat on the sofa in Bailey's apartment the following Saturday morning.

"We've been on three dates," Bailey replied and dipped her hand into the popcorn bowl.

"And how was it?" Sam turned to her and looked excited.

"The date? It was fine. We went to dinner. She told them it was my birthday, and they brought out chocolate cake with a candle. Then, she dropped me off."

"Wait. That was it?" Sam glared at her. "You two didn't do anything?"

"She kissed me good night." Bailey shrugged and snacked on more popcorn.

"And how was it? I ask because I want to know, but I'm also a little upset that you two didn't have sex. I mean, it's birthday sex, Bails. Plus, it would have been your first time. So, it would have been doubly amazing," Sam surmised.

"The kiss was good, and we did not have sex. I think we were both pretty tired from our work weeks. She works, like, eighty hours a week minimum, it seems. I did invite her in, but she said she had to go home to do more work."

"Would you have done something with her had she stayed?" Sam asked.

"I don't know. Why?"

"You like this woman, right?"

"Yes, I like her. She's nice. She works a lot, so it's not always easy to get a hold of her, but I like her," Bailey replied.

"But not enough to sleep with her?"

"Not on a third date just because it's my birthday, Samantha."

"Fine. Fine." Sam turned back to face the TV.

"What's going on with you?" Bailey asked. "Why are you so concerned about me sleeping with someone I just started dating?"

"Have you been with anyone since Callie?"

"No, but–"

"So, definitely not since Jenna Cabot just showed up one day?"

"No, but–"

"And there's no correlation between those two things?" Samantha interrupted again.

"Sam, come on." Bailey set the popcorn on the coffee table in front of them.

"What? I can't ask if something's going on there?"

"She did confirm something for me on Wednesday," Bailey told her.

"What's that?"

"That she is single, and she came back here for me. Well, she mentioned other things, but I'm included."

"She told you that?" Sam turned to face her again.

"Pretty much."

"And then you said…" she moved her hand in a circular motion, encouraging Bailey to continue.

"She asked me out for my birthday, and I told her I had a date with Alyson."

"She asked you out?"

"She said she wanted to try." Bailey lowered her head to stare at her hands. "I just started seeing Aly, though. I really like her, Sam."

"And you *love* Jenna Cabot."

"It's not–"

"Do you, Bails? Do you love her?"

"I don't even really know her anymore, Sam. We've been apart so long."

"Why can't you date her to find out if there is something between you two?"

"Because it hurts too much to be hurt by her."

"So, Alyson?"

"Yes, Alyson." Bailey nodded.

\*\*\*

"Start over?" Bailey asked.

"Yes, I would like us to start over," Jenna suggested.

"So, pretend like we don't have, like, eight years of history? More, if you add the four years during high school."

Bailey sipped on her iced tea while staring at Jenna across the table.

"No, we couldn't do that even if we wanted to," Jenna replied. "But we can try to get to know one another again."

"What's the endgame, Jen?"

"The endgame?" Jenna asked and looked a little confused. "There is no endgame, Bails. I thought we could just hang out and become friends again, like we used to be."

"Friends?" Bailey asked.

"It's all you'll give me these days," Jenna said almost too quickly. "Sorry, that's not what I meant."

"No, it is. But I get it." Bailey sighed. She considered Jenna's offer while she stared into Jenna's hazel eyes. "I'm free this Friday."

"Yeah?" Jenna brightened. "After work?"

"Sure."

"We could grab dinner or something," Jenna suggested.

"Sounds good, Jen."

\*\*\*

"What happened to Alyson?" Sam asked her at lunch on Friday.

"Nothing. Why?"

"Nothing… like nothing is happening between you two because you're no longer seeing one another, or nothing because nothing has changed?"

"I don't know that I understand that question." Bailey laughed at her best friend as she signed the credit card receipt.

"Are you two still seeing each other?"

"Yes, we're still seeing each other. I told you she works a lot, though. She's busy this weekend, prepping a case for her boss or something."

"But you still like her?"

"Yes, Samantha." Bailey stood from her chair and slid her jacket over her shoulders.

"But you're going out with Jenna tonight?"

"I'm *hanging* out with Jenna tonight," Bailey countered.

"Right. Sure, you are." Samantha slid her own jacket on. "What are you two doing?"

"Dinner."

"And a movie?" Samantha lifted her eyebrow. "Like, maybe a standard date? She'll drop you off after, you'll stare longingly into her eyes, and end up making out on your front porch?"

"I don't have a front porch." Bailey pointed at the door. "And we're just hanging out. She wants to see if we can be friends again."

"And then she'll make out with you?"

"Sam, stop." Bailey chuckled at her friend as they made their way out of the restaurant and to their respective offices.

*\*\*\**

"Where are we going?" Bailey asked after climbing into Jenna's car.

"Do you remember that old drive-in next to MacArthur Park?" Jenna asked.

"Yeah, it closed down, like, five years ago, right?"

"It re-opened about a month ago. My brother owns it now. He and my dad do, technically, since my dad lent him the start-up money."

"Your little brother owns a drive-in?" Bailey turned and asked.

"He's twenty-five, married, and his wife is expecting. He's not so little anymore." Jenna turned the car left, down a two-lane street. "We used to go as kids. My mom loved it. My baby brother bought it right before he got his MBA. Can you believe what an overachiever he turned out to be?"

"I don't really know him." Bailey shrugged as she looked out the window. "I only met him a couple of times, and it's not like we spent a lot of time talking."

"Oh," Jenna began. "I always forget that part."

"What part?" Bailey looked at her.

"The part where you're such an important piece of my life, but I forget you didn't know my family. We didn't hang out in high school, and you only went to my house once." Jenna paused. "Twice, if I'm counting the funeral."

"It is weird," Bailey agreed. "I feel like I talk about you all the time, but I don't know much about your family or you these days."

"That's what tonight is all about, Bails," Jenna replied.

She pulled them into the drive-in, but Bailey wondered what was going on when she saw the concession stand with dimmed lights, the black screen in front of them, and no other cars save one next to the only building on the property.

"Jen? Where is everyone?"

"The place is dark tonight," Jenna explained. "He only has it open on Saturday nights and Sunday matinées right now while he staffs up. I asked him if I could borrow it tonight."

"You asked your brother if we could *borrow* his

drive-in movie theater?" Bailey turned to her.

"I did." Jenna parked the car front and center, giving them the perfect view. "I'll be right back."

She climbed out of the car without waiting for a response. Bailey turned around to watch Jenna as she jogged toward the concession stand, where she met a figure in the dark that Bailey guessed was her brother. He passed her something Bailey couldn't make out. Then, Jenna returned to the car but didn't get inside. She dropped a box onto the ground in front of them and moved to Bailey's side of the car, where she opened the door for her.

"What's going on?"

"We're going to sit outside. It's such a nice night. Is that okay?" Jenna asked.

"I guess." Bailey got out of the car and walked around to the front.

The big screen in front of them lit up white.

"I brought a blanket." Jenna moved to the backseat, where she pulled out a blanket. "And concession stand treats are in the box. I got one of everything."

"That was your brother, right?" Bailey asked as they laid the blanket out together.

"He's heading home now. He was just stocking tonight. See? There he goes." Jenna waved at her brother, who drove off.

"Jen, you didn't have to do all this."

Bailey sat on the blanket. Jenna joined her and pulled the box in front of them.

"I wanted to. I thought it would be fun. I haven't been here since he opened, and I wanted to experience it without the crowd. I thought you'd like it."

"I do, Jen. This is pretty cool." Bailey took the popcorn Jenna passed her. "What are we watching?"

"*Clueless*," Jenna shared, turned to her, and smiled. "Is that okay?"

Bailey swallowed at how gorgeous Jenna looked right

now. The white screen turned to start up the movie, and the flickering lights hit Jenna's hazel eyes, making Bailey warm inside. She lowered her eyes to the popcorn and popped a few kernels into her mouth to distract herself as she nodded at Jenna's movie choice.

"I love that movie," she said after a moment.

"I remember," Jenna said.

They'd watched *Clueless* that day at Bailey's house. After they had shared the most intimate of experiences in Bailey's bedroom, they talked and made their way to the living room in the basement. They would have gone to the theater to watch it, but Bailey had meant to turn on the music so it would surround them with sound while they played some games or sat around and talked. She had hit the button for TV instead, and *Clueless* had been on. Jenna had made fun of Bailey's outburst at her father's ridiculous programming of all the buttons on the remote. They'd sat in the living room and watched it for a while, until Jenna's light touches grew more insistent, and they tore at one another's clothing again.

This time, they sat in relative silence save their shared laughter at the funny moments in the movie. When it was nearly over, the junk food box had been pushed aside. Jenna was leaning back on her hands, watching the movie, while Bailey was sitting cross-legged, leaning forward. Just before the end wedding scene, Jenna's fingers made an appearance in Bailey's hair; she was playing with the ends that had fallen over Bailey's back. Bailey didn't move. Jenna hadn't touched her like this in years. Bailey sat in that position – letting Jenna play with her hair – until the credits started to roll. Then, Jenna stood without a word, grabbed their garbage, and walked in the direction of the concession stand. Minutes later, she returned and sat down next to Bailey. The screen was dark now. The only light came from the street lamps that illuminated the path to the theater. Jenna stared at her without saying anything for a moment before she lay down. Bailey followed suit because she didn't know what else to do.

"I miss you, Bailey," Jenna said into the night.

"I'm right here, Jen." Bailey turned her head to Jenna.

"No, you're not," Jenna replied without turning to face her.

"What's that mean?"

"You used to be so open with me, Bails. Even if you didn't say something, I could tell how you felt. I could see it on your face because you let me in. You don't let me in anymore."

"Because I've been hurt, Jenna. I don't–"

Jenna turned her head to Bailey and said, "I will never stop apologizing for what happened back then. I won't. I just need to know that, someday, there's a chance you'll forgive me."

Bailey stared into those eyes again and replied, "I forgive you for that, Jenna. I already have. I guess I'm still holding onto what happened after the funeral."

"Because I didn't call?"

"Because we slept together. You were my first, Jenna. God, I waited so long. It felt like a lifetime back then. I don't think I knew what I was waiting for, though. It wasn't like I thought I had a chance with you in high school or even in college until it actually happened. Each time there was a chance I could lose my virginity, though, I didn't. I just couldn't go through with it." Bailey sighed. "Then, you kissed me, and I knew."

"You'd been waiting for me." Jenna smiled shyly. "And I'd been waiting for you."

"Why didn't you call me, Jen? I could have been there after your mom died. I could have just been a shoulder to cry on or someone to distract you. I understand why you needed time at first, but then weeks turned to months and months to years. You couldn't even email me to let me know I should move on? I mean, the things we said to each other that day…" Bailey paused. "They meant something to me."

"They meant *everything* to me, Bailey Sayers," Jenna returned and cupped Bailey's cheek with her hand.

Bailey felt the touch and lost her train of thought. She was brought back to that day in her bedroom, where Jenna touched her for the first time. She closed her eyes at the sensation of Jenna's thumb dragging over her bottom lip. When she opened her eyes, she saw Jenna's dark eyes staring back at her.

"This was supposed to be us getting to know each other again," Bailey said back.

"We are." Jenna leaned into her and pressed their foreheads together. "But, when I'm with you, it takes everything in me not to kiss you, Bails. You can imagine how hard it's been for me at work."

"Jen, we should–"

Jenna's lips were on her own, and they were just as soft as Bailey remembered. Jenna's hand was on the back of Bailey's neck, pulling her closer. Bailey did not object. She kissed Jenna back until Jenna rolled her onto her back and climbed on top of her. Jenna's lips connected with Bailey's neck, and she kissed her slowly, hovering over each spot of the skin, nibbling at it, kissing it, and then blowing cool air over it before moving onto the next spot.

"I didn't plan this, if that's what you're thinking," Jenna whispered into her ear. "But I want it, Bails."

"Are we really alone?" Bailey asked.

"Yes."

Bailey reached for the hem of Jenna's shirt and tugged until Jenna lifted up. Once it was removed, Jenna wasted no time with her bra. Bailey worked the button and zipper on Jenna's jeans and tugged them down while her lips moved across Jenna's stomach. When she sucked a nipple into her mouth, Jenna gasped and held Bailey's head to her body. Jenna pulled at her own jeans then as she moved back to remove them. Bailey lifted her own shirt off, peeled her bra hastily away from her skin, and unbuttoned her jeans in the time it took Jenna to strip down to black panties. Jenna was on her then. She kissed Bailey while she pulled at Bailey's jeans until their lips were forced to disconnect in order to remove them. She then climbed back on top, pressed their breasts together, and reconnected their lips. The first touch of Bailey's tongue to Jenna's skin had Bailey on fire, sliding her hands into Jenna's panties and grasping her ass. When she slid one hand around to the front and cupped her, Jenna's hips bucked into her.

Bailey slid her fingers through Jenna's sex, coating them with Jenna's desire for her. It had been so long. Bailey felt Jenna jerk when she began stroking her clit. Jenna's kisses turned sloppy while Bailey coaxed her orgasm out of her. Jenna sat up and rocked her hips against Bailey. She was close; Bailey could tell. She slid two fingers inside her, pressed her palm to Jenna's needy clit, and let Jenna take her pleasure from her hand. When Jenna's hips began jerking frantically, Bailey sat up and sucked a nipple into her mouth. Jenna came then. Her hips rocked wildly against Bailey's hand. Her own hands were in Bailey's hair, pressing Bailey closer to her body.

"Yes, Bailey," she whispered as she came down from her high. "God, Bails."

"I want you again," Bailey said against Jenna's chest. "Roll over."

Bailey pulled out of her and sat back, allowing Jenna to lie on the blanket next to her. Bailey pulled hard at Jenna's panties until they were dangling from one ankle. Then, she took Jenna with her mouth. *God, the taste of her!* She had missed having Jenna this way. Jenna said her name a few more times while Bailey stroked her with her tongue. When Jenna finished, Bailey moved up her body and kissed her everywhere. She wanted to leave her mark somewhere on Jenna; she wanted to claim her.

Jenna rolled them over, once she'd been able to take no more, and completed the same action on Bailey's skin, as if trying to claim her in the same way. When Jenna's fingers entered her, Bailey felt whole for the first time since they'd been together like this. Jenna moved slowly, but only for a moment, before she picked up speed and took her. She took Bailey. That was the only way Bailey could describe it. Jenna's lips were gentle against her neck; they were loving. Her fingers inside Bailey, though, were thrusting hard. They were claiming, too. Jenna's thumb stroked Bailey's clit, brought her to a fast orgasm, and then her lips joined her thrusting fingers. She took Bailey again, and then once more, until Bailey was doing everything she could to avoid screaming Jenna's name.

They were naked, having sex next to a public park. She whispered Jenna's name instead as Jenna bought her back down, paying attention to the sensitive skin on the inside of Bailey's thighs before she lay her head tiredly against Bailey's stomach. They didn't say anything as they stayed in that position and Bailey stroked Jenna's hair. When Jenna finally moved, it was to allow Bailey to cradle her against her chest. They stayed that way then while Jenna ran her fingers along Bailey's skin until it grew too cold. They dressed in silence, packed up the car the same way, and drove back toward Bailey's apartment.

"I'll see you on Monday?" Bailey asked after she opened the car door.

"Are you serious?" Jenna questioned, putting the car in park. "Bailey…"

"I need some time, Jenna." Bailey slid out of the seat and stood next to the car.

"Time for what?" Jenna asked. "We just made love, Bailey. That wasn't just sex between two people who had done that before; that was making love."

"I'm seeing someone, Jen; you know that."

Jenna climbed out of the car and walked around to Bailey's side.

"No, I didn't. You mentioned you had a date on your birthday, but I didn't know you were with someone. I couldn't, because you never talk to me, Bailey," she said, frustration clear in her tone.

"I'm not *with* someone; we're just dating. I want to see where it goes."

"You want to see where it goes? We just slept together, Bailey!" Jenna's voice grew louder as they stood in Bailey's apartment parking lot. "You want to see where it goes with some other woman now that we've done that?"

"You just came back here, Jenna. You showed up out of nowhere after we ran into each other at that convention."

"After we bumped into each other at spring break, and after we bumped into each other at the airport." Jenna groaned. "Do you really not get it?"

"Get what?"

"We're supposed to be together, Bailey. How else can you explain that I saw you at some random bar in Florida, that I bumped into your girlfriend at the airport, and that we ended up working at the same company? How many airports are there in the world? How many flights at how many different times? I saw you there, and it hit me that you had someone."

"You had someone, too, Jen; someone you'd gotten engaged to. You had moved on. I had to move on, too," Bailey argued.

"I never moved on," Jenna retorted. "How could I? How could I move on, Bailey, when I know what it's like to be loved by you?" Her voice cracked as tears filled her eyes. "I said yes to Joel, but I shouldn't have. That's one of many mistakes I have made in my life, but I broke up with them. I came here for you."

"That's just it, Jenna. This isn't some romantic comedy. You don't get credit for the grand romantic gesture when it involves moving across the country and showing up to work at my office."

"What do I get credit for?" Jenna asked as she wiped at her cheek. "Do I get credit for loving you?"

"You don't even know me anymore, Jenna," Bailey argued.

"That's bullshit, and you know it. I do know you, Bailey Anne Sayers. I know how you look when you're concentrating hard because you don't understand something. I know how you look when you're sad, how you look when you're happy, and how you look when you're turned on." Jenna paused. "I know your favorite color is green; your favorite book is *Little Women*, but you secretly also love *The Hunger Games*. I know your mom annoys the crap out of you and has probably asked you about grandkids at least ten times this year. I know you love your father like crazy and that you two have a special relationship. I know you don't like sports, but you put that aside when your dad wants to take you to a baseball game. You hate beer, drink red wine only, and shy away from hard alcohol; unless you're at a work convention where the booze is flowing and the girl you once loved shows up and scares the crap out of you because you might just still love her. And you're terrified because you know she loves you back." Jenna looked around to see that they were still alone, while Bailey stood completely shell-shocked. "She does, you know? We're not teenagers anymore, Bails. We're not at two different colleges. We're not living in two different states. There's nothing to stop us this time; and that scares the shit out of you, because you might actually get what you've wanted all along."

Bailey didn't say anything for a moment as one of the other tenants dropped their garbage into the dumpster, stared at them for a second, and then went back inside his apartment.

"I need time, Jen."

"Time for what?" Jenna's voice softened.

"To think."

"Fine." Jenna held up her hands in defense. "Take your time, Bailey. And, yes, I guess I'll see you on Monday." She turned to walk back to the driver's seat.

"Oh, I forgot something. I know what you look like when you come; I know what your face does when you reach that point and know it's me doing that to you because I don't want to do that to anyone but you ever again. Until you really get that, I guess I'll see you at work."

Bailey stood there as Jenna drove away, leaving her there in her parking lot alone with her fear and worry that this time, losing Jenna was her own fault. She had no one else to blame.

***

"Bailey, can I talk to you for a second?" her boss asked, entering her office and closing the door behind her.

"Sure."

"Can it be off the record?" the woman asked as she sat in one of Bailey's two guest chairs.

"Off the record? Am I a reporter now?" Bailey smiled at her.

"It's sensitive. I'd like to know this will stay between us," her boss offered.

"Oh, of course. Is everything okay?" Bailey leaned forward in her chair, clasping her hands together on her desk.

"I'm starting my own company. The paperwork's been filed already. I have a business partner, great financials and business plan, office space, and just about everything else ready to go."

"You're leaving?" Bailey asked. In that moment, she realized part of what she loved about her job was working for this woman. "When?"

"I'll give standard notice, so it won't be tomorrow; but no one else knows, either."

"I won't say anything," Bailey said.

"Thank you, but that's not the sensitive part." Her boss leaned forward, too. "I'd like to take you with me."

"Me?"

"I can pay you twenty-five grand more, to start, than what you make here. We don't have the benefits sorted out yet, but we're working on it. There will be full medical, vision, and dental. It's a start-up. You'd have equity as well."

"Hold on. Wait." Bailey leaned back in her chair as if that would help her process all this information. "You want to—"

"Steal you from here. Yes, I would. Bailey, you're great at your job, but I think you have more to offer. I'd like to make you a VP, give you your own department. In time, you can build out your own team."

"I'm only a manager here."

"Exactly," the woman said. "You can wait for me to give my notice, interview for my Senior Manager position, and they'll give it to you. You can do that, Bails, but you won't move any higher than that here until someone retires. When that happens, you'd probably have to move, because Dave is the Director here, and he's only forty-two; he's not going anywhere anytime soon. You could come with me, make more money, have stake in the company, and build a team of people to work for you," she explained.

"Wow."

"I know it's a lot. I don't need an answer now. I'll email the files and job information to your personal email account. You can think it over. I do need to know soon, though. I'm hoping to put my notice in next Monday."

"It's Wednesday," Bailey said.

"Is that not enough time?"

"No, it is. I just…"

"Think it over, Bailey. Let me know by Sunday if you can. Call me if you have any questions I can answer. This is a good deal, Bailey. We have investors and a great plan. We just need the right team to make it all happen."

"Okay. I'll let you know by Sunday," Bailey replied, still a little in shock.

\*\*\*

"Nice place," Sam said as she entered Bailey's new office.

"Thanks. I still have to set everything up, but I like it." Bailey stood and looked around the space.

So far, she had a desk, her laptop, and three chairs. The office had a wall of windows and a glass wall with the door. She still had decorating to do, but she'd been here for three days so far and had spent most of her time conducting interviews with candidates who would, hopefully, fill out her small team of three to get started. She had given her professional notice along with her boss after reviewing their plan and their financials. Her father helped her on Saturday by taking a look at everything to make sure it was on the up and up. Aly even reviewed her paperwork to make sure she wasn't signing her life away. That had been the first time she'd seen the woman in over two weeks, thanks to her workload. Bailey understood. Aly was trying to get on a partner track, and billable hours were key. Bailey only wondered how they'd find any time together now that Bailey had taken on this new job. It came with longer hours and a lot of extra responsibility.

Alyson hadn't seemed bothered by Bailey's decision to take it on. She had slept over after reviewing the paperwork for her but had been so exhausted after a ninety-hour work week that that was all they did. She and Alyson still hadn't slept together yet. Bailey considered that to be a bit strange, considering how far along they were in this thing time-wise, but it also made total sense when she thought about how often she actually saw Alyson.

"So, how's it going?" Sam asked as she sat on the edge of Bailey's desk. "And this better not interfere with your other responsibilities."

"Oh, the wedding?"

"Yes, the wedding, Bailey. *My* wedding. You're my maid of honor. That's a lot of responsibility."

"I know, Sam. I will be the best maid of honor in history as soon as I get settled here."

"The wedding is in less than a year."

"Exactly; plenty of time," Bailey teased.

"I hate you," Sam lied.

"Which is why I'm your maid of honor." Bailey winked at her friend.

"What did Jenna say when you told her you were leaving?" Sam asked, changing the subject.

"She hasn't been in the office," Bailey replied with a shrug.

"Where has she been?"

"They had her traveling around to a few places. I pulled up her calendar before I told HR about my decision. She's giving presentations to five different offices this month, and she doesn't come back until next week."

"So, she doesn't know?"

"I emailed her," Bailey admitted.

"You emailed the woman you clearly love – who also happens to love you back – that you left the company you both work for?"

"Hey!"

"What? I'm right to ask because that's a dick move, Bails."

"When did you suddenly join Team Jenna?"

"I didn't suddenly join any team; I've always been on the team that makes you the happiest. You are frustrating as hell, Bails."

"How is this my fault? She's out of town."

"The phone works, right? Do you need a new one that dials out? I can ask them to put one in here right now. I'll call your cell provider and make sure your phone's still on."

"I can't call her, Sam."

"Why not?" Sam stood.

"Because I'm a coward."

"You just took a job at a brand-new company, and

you have no idea if this is going to take off or not. How does that make you a coward?"

"With her, Sam. With her, I'm a coward."

"That's because it matters, Bailey." Samantha moved to the door of Bailey's office. "One of these days, you'll stop pretending you don't know that and actually go for it."

# CHAPTER 7: THE WEDDING

Jenna's email back to Bailey had been brief. It contained five words. *"I'm taking the hint, Bail."* That was it. Bailey dove into her work. It was all new, exciting, and it kept her busy and distracted. She had meetings, interviews, processes to create, systems to analyze, and people to coordinate with. She didn't bother replying to Jenna's email because she knew she had nothing to say that would make it better. She'd messed up. Jenna had every right to be upset with her now in the same way Bailey had been upset with her back then.

"I get that this is important, Bails, but we've hardly had an hour to ourselves since you took this job," Alyson told her.

"I know, babe. I'm sorry. This meeting is a big deal. If we get this client, it'll bring in more revenue than three combined. They're located in Texas. I have to go," Bailey replied as she rolled her suitcase toward the front door of the apartment. "When I get back, we can start planning that vacation we keep talking about."

"I don't want a vacation, Bailey. God, you just show up and say you need some stuff you left at my place so you can go on a work trip. I haven't seen you since last Saturday. We went shopping for shoes. That's the last date we went on, Bailey: shoe-shopping," Alyson said and moved to the front door to open it.

"Aly, I'm sorry. What do you want me to say? I can't not go, but when I get back, we can–"

"What? Talk about the vacation you know we'll never take? Bailey, we haven't had sex in over a month. Did you even realize that?"

"I've–"

"You've been busy and so tired; I know. You say that every time. I'm just done hearing it."

"So, we're breaking up, Aly? You can work eighty hours a week, and it's fine, but I work the same or go on some trip I *have* to go on and, suddenly, it's my fault we don't have enough time together?"

"I'm trying to make partner."

"And I'm a VP."

"Of a start-up with fourteen employees; it's hardly the same thing. Half the company is VPs, Bailey."

"Is that what you think? That I'm not really a VP because the company is small?"

"No, I didn't mean that. I'm sorry." Alyson let go of the doorknob. "I'm sorry," she repeated.

"We've been together for over a year, Aly."

"And you still won't move in here or even consider getting a place together. When we first started dating, we talked about this stuff. I told you I wanted to settle down. I wanted to get married, become partner, have kids with my wife. You've turned my apartment into your extra storage space."

"So, it's just over because I work too much and don't want to move in yet?" Bailey asked.

"Do you think you'll ever want to move in?" Alyson asked softly. "I mean it, Bailey. Answer me honestly."

"I don't know," she replied.

"Bailey, you're almost twenty-seven, but I'm thirty years old; I'm at that point. Are you at that point? Do you want the things we used to talk about?"

"Yes," Bailey said.

"Do you want them with me?" Alyson asked. When Bailey didn't say anything right away, she added, "You can pick up the rest of your stuff when you get back."

Bailey didn't bother trying to change Alyson's mind. If there was one thing she'd learned over the course of their relationship, there was no changing Aly's mind once it was set. The only thing Bailey could do was leave. So, she did. She went on her work trip, made her pitch, came home, and found a box of her things on the welcome mat in front of the door to her apartment. Her relationship with Alyson was over.

*** 

"Can you believe I'm getting married today?" Samantha asked as she smoothed her dress in front of the floor-to-ceiling mirror in the dressing room of the church.

"I can't, actually, but that has more to do with how boy-crazy you used to be." Bailey laughed at her joke.

"Never tell him that." Sam pointed at Bailey through the mirror. "Bails, I have to tell you something."

"Okay, what?" Bailey asked as she clasped a necklace behind Samantha's neck.

"Well, two things, actually." Samantha paused. "One is that I invited Jenna to the wedding, and she RSVPed that she'd be here," she said that very quickly. "Also, I'm pregnant. I'm only eleven weeks, and no one else knows. So, congratulations to me, right?"

Bailey felt the sweat form on her skin at the mention of Jenna's name before she looked at Sam's concerned expression.

"Congratulations, Sammy."

"Are you mad?"

"No, I'm not mad; I'm curious since you and Jenna hardly know one another."

"I got the idea when you and Alyson broke up. My

aunt ended up declining her initial RSVP, and I had an extra seat. I thought maybe if I got the two of you in the same room together—"

"Sam, I haven't seen her in a long time, and clearly this is not meant to be."

"Why not?"

"Because it's never worked. Something has always come up."

"No, something has always gotten in the way; there's a difference." Sam turned to face her. "You don't have to talk to her, but I wanted you to know she said she was coming."

"Thanks for the somewhat heads-up. I could have used one *before* you invited her, but that would not have been your way."

"Also, I'm pregnant. Did you get that part?"

"I did." Bailey hugged her best friend, careful not to mess up Samantha's hair. "Congratulations, Sammy. I'm going to be an awesome aunt."

"I know you are. I just can't wait until you find this little one its other aunt."

"What?" Bailey lifted an eyebrow.

"Oh, my God, Bailey. I meant, I couldn't wait until you find your damn wife. It's taking you forever for no reason."

"Sam, it's not Je—"

"We're ready for you." Samantha's mother walked into the room all smiles.

\*\*\*

When Bailey's eyes darted around the church while the reverend spoke the words that would unite Sam with her husband, she didn't see Jenna. There were only about a hundred and fifty people; none of them were Jenna. She made the rounds at the reception, catching people up on her life, but still, there was no Jenna. When she sat down at the table, reserved for the bridal party, Bailey sipped on the champagne and wished she had something more to talk about than just her job.

"So, how are you?" Sam asked as she flopped down next to her and stole her champagne.

"Shouldn't I be asking you that? You're the one that just got married today. Are you drinking that?"

"No, I just don't want you to have glass anywhere near you when I tell you what I'm about to tell you," Sam said as she pushed the glass aside. "I didn't invite her, Bailey."

"What?" Bailey turned to her and tried to pretend she didn't know what Sam was talking about. "Who?"

"Oh, please." Sam squinted at her. "I didn't invite Jenna to my wedding. I just wanted to see how you'd react if I told you I did."

"Yeah? Nice, Sam," Bailey said sarcastically. "What was the point of that?"

"You've been looking for her all day, haven't you? At the church, you scanned the crowd. You've been doing the same thing tonight, Bails."

"I haven't," she lied.

"Bailey, what do you think that means?"

"It means, I didn't want to see her, so I was trying to make sure I avoided her."

"You don't even believe that," Sam replied and stood. "I have to go dance with my husband. Why don't you try being real with yourself?"

***

When Bailey got home from Samantha's wedding, she sat at her desk in her apartment, pulled out a sheet of paper and a pen, and got to work. It had been a long time since she had written by hand and slid a letter into an envelope. Once done, Bailey did her best to try to sleep, but it didn't come until well into the early morning.

Monday morning, she dropped the letter into her outgoing mailbox and went to work, knowing that by choosing that medium, she'd have to wait. It took over two weeks for a response to come. When Bailey saw it, she rushed into her apartment, tossed her bag on the couch, and sat down next to it. Then, she read.

> *Dear Bailey,*
>
> *A letter? Really? What is this, the 1900s? I'm kidding, of course. I haven't received a letter in a very long time. It was nice getting something in my mailbox that isn't a bill. It's been forever, Bails. I guess it feels like that whenever I go any period of time without seeing you. It's weird, though, Bailey. You made it pretty clear when I left on my work trip and came back to find out you'd left, that you wanted nothing to do with me. Well, you said you needed time. But then time passed, and I didn't hear from you. Now, you say you want to get to know each other again. We've done this before. What's different now? We live about twenty minutes away from each other, but you mailed me a letter. Why? Answer those questions, and I'll let you know if I want to continue whatever this is.*
>
> *Jenna*

Bailey went straight to work on her response, slapped a stamp on the envelope, and rushed down the street to the post office drop box that had the latest pick-up time. Her response read:

> *Jenna,*
>
> *Why did I send you a letter? Why not just see you in person? Because I did see you in person. I was at the mall, helping Sam with her wedding registry, and I saw you in the department store. You were wearing this green shirt and jeans. I knew that if I walked up and started talking to you, it would be a mistake; we would end up right back where we started. I can't take my eyes off you; you can't keep your hands off me.*

*Then, I say I need time, or you say you need space. I didn't want that this time. There's something nice about receiving a letter. Instead of sending an email, I thought this would be better. I don't think I can promise anything. I just know that I miss you. I miss everything about you, Jenna. I was hoping we could try to get to know one another this way and see if something comes out of it. Even if it's just that I get my friend back because you've moved on, that's okay. Oh, and you made one mistake when you told me how you knew me that day. You said my favorite color was green. My favorite color is somewhere between green and brown; it's hazel.*

*Bails*

Another two weeks went by. Bailey bounced when she saw Jenna's handwriting on the envelope. She sat on her sofa, poured herself a glass of red wine, and opened it.

*Bailey,*

*So, we're just going to write letters back and forth for a while? Forever? Like a month? Until you think you're ready to see me in person and not jump my bones? Maybe that's unfair. Maybe I'm still a little mad at you. But I don't want to not reply to these letters because I don't want to risk losing whatever this is. So, if you want us to get to know one another like this, let's do it. Where do we start?*

*Jenna*

Bailey reread the part about Jenna still being upset with her. She understood, but it still hurt to see that in Jenna's handwriting.

*Jen,*

*Tell me about work. What's happened since I left? Are you happy there? Do you hate it? It's been so long; I bet a lot has changed. I am sorry for how I left. It all happened so quickly. One day, I'm okay with the job I have, and the next, I get an offer to be a VP. I couldn't pass it up. You were gone,* and I had to put in my notice. I sent an email because I didn't know how to talk to you then. I'd messed up that night at the drive-in, and I didn't know how to talk to you after that. What we did that night was perfect, Jenna; I hope you know that. I just wasn't ready to deal with the possibility of being hurt again.

If you're curious, my job is good. I really like what I'm doing. I travel some, but not too often. We've gotten a couple of big clients recently and will be expanding our office space soon. I have five people that report to me now, which is crazy; I never thought I'd be managing people. I'm making good money. I'm actually starting to look at houses since I can afford a down payment and a mortgage now. That's crazy, right? I'm about to have a mortgage. Sam has one. She has a husband, too. I don't know if you heard. She got married recently, and they have a baby on the way. That's nuts, right? Anyway, I guess I'll just wait for your letter.

Bailey

Bailey got worried when two weeks passed with no response from Jenna. It was another three weeks before the response finally came. She had checked her mail two times a day in some cases and considered just emailing Jenna to find out if she had replied. Maybe it had gotten lost in the mail. Maybe Jenna had been out of town. When it finally came, she opened it while sitting at her desk at work.

Bailey,

Tell Sam congratulations for me; that's great news. As for work, I'm not there anymore. I quit about six months ago. I'm at this little firm on Peach Street now. It's nothing fancy, but it pays the bills. To be honest, it was just too hard to be at the office and know you weren't there. I'd walk past where your office used to be, and there was someone else in it. It just made me sad. I started looking for something right after you left. I know, pathetic, isn't it... I like my new job, though. I don't have to travel as much, which is nice. It's not as high-stress, either. I don't think I'll end up staying here forever, but it's good until I figure out my next move.

I guess I can understand why you didn't call about leaving. I don't even know how that conversation would go. I was happy when I heard about the opportunity for you. I want you to be happy, Bails. I want you to have the best job in the world for you, and the house that you want, and everything that comes with it. Do you still want all those same things you used to want? Like the wife, the kids, and everything else? What happens if you pick out your house, find someone, and they hate it? Would you move? And, yes, that night was perfect, Bails. Can I ask something else? Are you still with Alyson?

Jenna

Bailey had to wait another three weeks for the next response. By then, she was growing tired of waiting and considered just emailing or texting Jenna. She knew, though, that if she did any those things, she would lose what restraint she did have. Bailey was enjoying this back and forth, and she wanted to learn more about Jenna; this was a good way of doing it.

Hey, Bail,

Yes, I'm single. I haven't been with anyone since you. I'm sorry to hear about you and Alyson. I mean, I'm not. I'm actually happy to hear about that. But if I just said that, that would be mean. Like I said, I want you to be happy. If Alyson was the person to do that, then I'd want it to work out for you. My brother's drive-in is doing really well. I help him out sometimes on the weekends, but not too often. It's a little weird for me. I can't exactly tell him why, though. I don't think he wants to know that his sister had sex in the grass of his place of business.

I meant what I said that night, Bailey: I can't do it forever; I get lonely a lot. Andrea, my best friend, has come out *to visit a few times, and I'm going back to New Mexico to see her. She wants me to meet her new boyfriend. Outside of Andy, though, it's lonely waiting for you, Bailey. I don't know how much longer I can have hope that this is going to work out.*

*Jen*

Bailey wiped tears from her eyes when she read Jenna's letter, and she didn't have the heart to reply right away. After a few days had passed, Bailey sent Jenna a lighthearted letter where she updated her on a few new favorites in her life. While hazel was still Bailey's favorite color and *Little Women* was still her favorite book, she had a new favorite book series, a new favorite author, a new favorite movie, and a new favorite hobby. Bailey had started working out to relieve stress, and her runs had become one of the best parts of her days. Jenna replied and filled Bailey in on all her favorites, including a new favorite sport; she had taken to watching golf with her father and brother on the weekends. They continued to exchange letters like that for the next couple of months before Bailey got a text message that changed everything.

# CHAPTER 8: THE MESSAGE

<u>Jenna Cabot</u>: I'm thinking about you.

It was the first text Jenna had sent Bailey in years. Bailey stared at it, checked Jenna's name at least five times to make sure she wasn't crazy, and then went to reply.

<u>Bailey Sayers</u>: What are you thinking?

She made her way to the kitchen, grabbed the popcorn she'd just finished preparing, picked out a bottle of water, and went to the sofa, balancing all of it as she held her phone up to see if Jenna would reply.

<u>Jenna Cabot</u>: That I miss you, and I don't want to wait for another letter.

<u>Bailey Sayers</u>: What are you doing?

Bailey grabbed a few pieces of popcorn while she stared at her phone.

<u>Jenna Cabot</u>: I already told you. I'm thinking about you, Bail.

<u>Bailey Sayers</u>: You can only think about me? You can't do anything else while you're doing that?

Bailey had added an emoticon she hoped would tell Jenna she was teasing.

<u>Jenna Cabot</u>: No.

Jenna didn't add an emoticon.

<u>Bailey Sayers</u>: I miss you, Jen.

<u>Jenna Cabot</u>: Why can't we talk, Bails?

<u>Bailey Sayers</u>: We're talking right now.

Jenna Cabot: You know what I mean.

Bailey Sayers: Where are you?

Jenna Cabot: In New Mexico, at Andrea's. If I was at home right now, would that change anything?

Bailey Sayers: I don't know.

Bailey answered honestly as she ate more popcorn and took the cap off her bottle of water. She took a long drink while she waited for Jenna's response.

Jenna Cabot: Then, I guess I should go.

Bailey swallowed wrong, nearly choked, and had to take in more water to try to recover. By the time she replied to Jenna, asking her to talk more, Jenna was either asleep or had decided not to reply.

\*\*\*

Bailey wasn't about to make the same mistake again. She texted Jenna at least once a day for over a week. She would just type "hello" or tell Jenna she was hoping Jenna was having a good day. Sometimes, she'd tell Jenna a little about her day. Jenna didn't reply until day eight; Bailey knew that because she was keeping track.

Jenna Cabot: What are you doing right now?

Bailey Sayers: Just worrying I screwed up.

Jenna Cabot: Are you still scared?

Bailey Sayers: I'm terrified, Jen.

Jenna Cabot: Can I call you?

Bailey stared at her phone for a moment. It had been a long time since she heard Jenna's voice. Her voice, like her eyes, had always done things to Bailey.

Bailey Sayers: Yes.

Another minute passed before her phone rang.

"Hello?"

"Hey, Bail," Jenna greeted, and Bailey closed her eyes at the sweet sound.

\*\*\*

"When are you back?" Jenna asked.

"Not until next Friday. They need a little more handholding than most of our other clients. I'm here to help them implement. Well, I'm here because they like to yell at my people. At least this way, they'll yell at me, and my people will be able to do their jobs," Bailey replied from her hotel room in Sacramento.

"Your people," Jenna replied and laughed. "You're so grown up now, Bails."

"God, I know," Bailey said. "What are you up to?"

"I am looking at a real estate site. My dad saw this house on Parker Street. He's been on this kick about me buying a place; even said he would help me with the down payment."

"You're thinking about buying a house?" Bailey asked.

"Not this one; it's way too close to my dad. It's literally a block away. I love my father, but no, thank you."

Bailey laughed and replied, "But you do want to buy?"

Jenna sighed and said, "Bail, I want to buy a place *with* someone. I'd like to buy a house because it's a place I can share with the person I'm spending my life with. *That's* what I want. I'm just looking at this one to appease my father, who thinks I'm throwing money away every month on rent. Oh, and I have this younger brother, who's super successful in all things, too. So, that's always fun."

"Jen, you're super successful," Bailey defended.

"How, exactly? I have a regular job that pays me a regular wage; I have a couple of friends that I hardly ever see; I'm single and in love with a woman who only allows phone calls between us because she's still scared I'm going to hurt her, when all I want to do is to hold her. I don't even think I can handle having a cat in my life, and my dad wants me to buy a house."

"Jen…" Bailey stared down at the half-eaten food she had ordered from room service.

"No, it's fine. I didn't mean to say all that."

"Yes, you did," Bailey replied. "We should talk about it."

"Can we do that another time? It's late. I need to get some sleep."

"Okay. If that's what you want."

"It is." Jenna paused. "Night, Bail."

"Good night, Jenna."

Bailey hated to admit how she loved that Jenna continued to speak so openly about her feelings for Bailey. They had shared several phone calls now, and in nearly every call, they talked about how they used to feel about one another. They would reminisce about something that happened in high school or something that happened while they were talking in college. They'd also gotten to some of the tough stuff when Jenna talked about her mom's death and how it completely changed her life and her trajectory. She had felt behind in her life ever since, and that included with Bailey. Bailey could only listen as Jenna sobbed lightly over the phone.

They talked about how they kept reconnecting somehow in the most random of places, how Bailey's relationships had all ended, and how Jenna had tried with Joel but knew it wasn't right the moment he proposed. They'd talked for hours since Jenna's first phone call. Bailey was wondering why they were still just talking, but then Jenna would say something like that, and she knew they still had stuff they needed to work on.

\*\*\*

"No one since Alyson?" Sam asked.

"No," Bailey replied as she helped her best friend put together the crib in Sam's nursery.

"Aren't you, like, hard-up or something?"

"Aren't you, like, pregnant and super horny or something?" Bailey teased.

"Yes, I am. But I also have a husband; he puts out whenever I want," Sam said with a playful wink. "You, however, have a strange phone relationship with Jenna Cabot and are, therefore, not getting any."

"I don't need *any*. I'm doing just fine, Sam. I appreciate your concern, though."

"Bails, how long are you going to keep doing this to yourself? I mean, I'm proud of you for reaching back out to her and trying to get to know one another, but this has been going on for months now. Do you realize that our ten-year high school reunion is coming up? I got the invite the other day."

"I got one, too." Bailey sighed and leaned back after finishing with a screw. "I don't think I'm going to go, though."

"Is Jenna going?"

"I don't know. I didn't ask."

Samantha threw one of the small pillows they had bought earlier that day at Bailey and grunted at her in frustration.

"You annoy the shit out of me," she said.

"Sammy, you're about to be someone's mom," Bailey replied as she chuckled.

"Then, my kid will know how frustrating his or her aunt is, because you are the only person I have to use this language with."

"I'll ask her if she's going. Would that make you feel better?"

"Yes, it would make me feel better. Whether Jenna Cabot will be in attendance or not, you're going to that reunion with me."

"Won't you be going with your husband that always puts out?" Bailey asked as she wiggled her eyebrows.

"He, sadly, is out of town that night; some work retreat he can't miss. I'm secure enough in my life to show up stag and just explain how hot he is to all the petty people who judge. I plan to show them pictures."

\*\*\*

"Hey, Bail," Jenna greeted. "I'm sorry, I don't have a lot of time to talk. My dad's picking me up for dinner."

"Oh, I thought we were talking tonight."

"I know. I'm sorry. He just sprung this on me. I'm actually trying to get ready right now. He literally called me when I was driving home from work, and I am not going to a dinner with my father, brother, and sister-in-law in the damn business suit and heels I've been in all day."

"You're changing right now?"

"Yeah, trying to, but I never do laundry, so it's proving kind of difficult. Do you think *Miguel's* will let me in wearing fuzzy socks, sweatpants, and an old t-shirt I got at an airport once because I needed a shirt after I spilled food all over myself?"

"Wow, Jen." Bailey laughed at her. "I should probably let you go. It sounds like you've got a lot going on."

"I do. I'm out of clean bras, too. I'm going with a sports bra, damn it."

Bailey closed her eyes at the thought of Jenna running around her apartment half-naked, trying to find something to wear.

"Okay." She exhaled deeply, trying to cover up her thoughts. "I'll let you go then. We can talk more later."

Jenna didn't say anything for a moment, and Bailey heard the ruffling of what she guessed was clothing. Then, there was silence.

"I'll call you when I get home, Bailey."

"Oh, okay. You don't–"

"I'll call you when I get home. Wait up for me, okay?" Jenna sounded certain about something.

"Okay."

When Bailey's phone rang hours later, she was already in bed. She had been watching something on TV while doing paperwork but had put that aside moments earlier when her eyes started re-reading the same sentence over and over.

"Hey," Bailey said.

"Hi," Jenna replied, but her voice sounded strange. "You waited up for me."

"You told me to wait up. Is everything okay?"

"Why?"

"Your voice sounds different," Bailey said as she put the phone on speaker.

"Where are you?" Jenna asked.

"In my bed. It's after midnight, Jenna. Where did you think I'd be?"

"You're not in bed, Bails. You're lying on the grass with me. We're staring at the stars."

"Jen, what—"

"Bailey, close your eyes and picture it with me."

"Okay." Bailey closed her eyes hesitantly. "Why are we lying in the grass staring at stars?"

"Because I wanted to, and you wanted to make me happy," Jenna replied. "We've been lying there for a while now, though. It's chilly now. We've covered ourselves with a thin blanket, and I'm lying on your chest, running my hand down your stomach."

"Jen…" Bailey's breath came fast when she realized why Jenna's voice sounded so strange. "Are you…"

"Yes," Jenna said softly. "I know what happened earlier today, Bails. When you heard I was getting dressed, something changed. What were you thinking then?"

"That I wished I could see you," Bailey answered immediately.

"Why?"

"Because you're gorgeous, Jenna; because I wanted to see your skin again. I wanted to touch it."

"Touch it now," Jenna suggested.

"It's not the same." Bailey's hand stilled on her own stomach.

"You wanted baby steps. I think this is the next baby

step, don't you? Bails, I'm serious; I'm touching myself right now."

"Jesus," Bailey gasped out. "Really?"

"Yes."

"What are you doing?" Bailey asked.

"Picturing us in that grass with my hand sliding inside your pants."

"What would you do then?" Bailey asked as she allowed her hand to move down slowly, imitating Jenna's imagined actions.

"Slide between your legs." Jenna gasped. "I'd want to touch your clit. It's always so hard for me, Bailey. Do you want me to do that?"

"Yes." Bailey gasped as her own index finger moved over the suddenly wet area between her legs.

"Soft and slow or hard and fast?"

"How close are you?"

"Close, but I can stop," Jenna said.

"No, don't stop," Bailey objected.

"Fuck, Bails," Jenna grunted. "Say that again."

"Don't stop, Jenna."

"I won't." Jenna paused. "You always feel so good. I want to touch you."

"You are, Jen."

"Are you touching yourself?"

"Yes. I'm close already. God, Jen!"

"Come for me, Bail. Please, I want to hear you."

When Bailey came, it was with her own fingers touching her skin, but it was to Jenna's words as Jenna continued to create the fantasy of them lying on a blanket, staring up at the stars while they made love. When Jenna came, it was with her own fingers but to the sounds of Bailey's orgasm ringing through the phone.

"What did we just do?" Bailey asked after a long moment of shared silence.

"Took another step," Jenna replied. "Any chance you want to take another one?"

"Already?"

"We can talk for a while first," Jenna suggested. "Tell me about your day."

Bailey laughed wildly and replied, "We just did *that*, and you want me to tell you about my day?"

"If I'm ever going to get you naked and do that to you for real, I believe you'd like us to get to know one another again. Those are the rules, right?"

Bailey realized then that while she had enjoyed talking to Jenna via their letters, their texts, and their phone calls, she also didn't need them anymore.

"Jen, do you forgive me?"

"Huh?" Jenna asked.

"For what I did that night and after, do you forgive me?"

"For the drive-in?" Jenna got serious.

"And then leaving without talking to you," Bailey added.

"Tell me why. Be honest with me, Bails."

"Because I was scared."

"Of what, Bailey?"

"Of losing you again," Bailey said.

"I'm right here, Bailey. I'm still here. Doesn't that mean anything?"

"It does."

"And I'm not going anywhere," Jenna added. "I will always be here. You just have to take the leap with me, Bails."

"It's a scary leap," Bailey replied.

"I'm taking it with you."

Bailey sighed and said, "Jen, do you forgive me?"

"Yes, Bailey. I forgive you. Do you forgive me?"

"For what happened after your mom died?"

"For pushing you away at the funeral and not talking to you, yes," Jenna supplied. "Do you forgive me?"

"Yes," Bailey said. "I forgive you, Jen."

"Then, why aren't we together, babe?"

"Did you just call me 'babe'?" Bailey laughed.

"Yes, I did. Bailey, focus; this is big. I need you to answer the question."

"I don't know, Jenna. That's the answer."

"Do you love me, Bailey Sayers?"

"Like crazy," Bailey said. "I always have."

"I love you," Jenna replied. "Always have."

Bailey smiled at that revelation and said, "And we're…"

"Going to take the next baby step," Jenna suggested.

"Which is?"

"We're going to go on our first date," Jenna revealed.

# CHAPTER 9: THE REUNION

"Well, where is she?" Samantha asked.

She and Bailey were sitting at one of the round tables in the Camden Hotel's ballroom. Terrible pop music was playing over the huge speakers as the DJ leaned over his tables, likely queueing up another bad song from her teenage years. Bailey was almost twenty-eight years old, and she was at her ten-year high school reunion. She was sitting in a very uncomfortable metal chair, awaiting her date for the night but, hopefully, also her date for forever. Jenna and her had arranged to meet at the event because Bailey had a last-minute work trip take her out of town until that afternoon. She had rushed home from the airport, readied herself quickly, and made it just in time to pick up Samantha, who was now as big as a house and ready to pop.

"I don't know. She's late, I guess," Bailey replied.

"I'm catching an Uber home so you two can finally have a damn date; she better show up," Sam said.

"She did," Bailey said as she patted Sam's forearm. "Look."

She said that last part more to herself than Sam. Jenna was standing in the doorway of the ballroom. She was dressed beautifully, in a navy-blue over-the-shoulder dress and white heels. Jenna's hair was down around her shoulders, and her eyes were scanning the room, likely looking for Bailey. Bailey stood and, without thinking, walked toward her.

"Fine, don't say goodbye or anything," Samantha said jokingly.

Bailey was a woman on a mission, and her mission was Jenna Cabot, the most beautiful woman in the room. Jenna's eyes connected to Bailey's when Bailey was only about five feet away. When she Jenna her, she made a beeline for Bailey, and before Bailey knew it, Jenna's arms were around her neck, pulling Bailey into her.

"I missed you," Jenna said and pulled her closer.

"I missed you, too," Bailey said.

They embraced for several moments before Jenna pulled back, and Bailey saw the tears well up in Jenna's eyes. She leaned forward and went to kiss her but pulled back at the last moment when she realized where they were. They were in the middle of their high school reunion. They'd never discussed this stuff before, but all their moments in the past had been in private. Bailey didn't know how Jenna would feel about any kind of public display.

"Jesus, Bailey. Just kiss me already," she said.

Jenna tugged Bailey forward, and her lips connected with Bailey's seconds later. Bailey opened her mouth to invite Jenna in and celebrated when Jenna's tongue met her own for the first time in way too long.

"Damn, I did not see that coming," a voice from behind Jenna said.

They pulled apart for a moment, and Bailey looked over Jenna's shoulder to see Stephanie, one of the girls that Jenna used to hang out with.

"Shut up, Steph," Jenna said.

She pulled Bailey back in and kissed her again. Stephanie probably walked off, but Bailey didn't notice. When they finally broke apart, Jenna hugged Bailey once more, as if she couldn't get enough of her. Bailey would never get enough of holding Jenna like this. When they finally pulled apart again, Bailey saw that those tears had fallen over Jenna's cheeks. She used her thumbs to wipe them away.

"How would you feel about going for a walk?"

"I'd like that," Jenna said.

They walked side by side for over an hour, and they held hands as they walked. They were both completely content being with the other person for the first time in a long time. Around midnight, they finally made their way back to the hotel. The party was just breaking up, and their former classmates were on the street either saying their goodbyes or smoking cigarettes. Jenna and Bailey said goodbye to a few people they'd known back then. Bailey leaned into Jenna. They didn't acknowledge what they were to anyone else; they just held onto one another and withstood all the curious glances from their former classmates. Jenna turned to face Bailey, and, without a word, she nodded toward the hotel. Bailey smiled and nodded, too.

"I got a room," Bailey said once they were in the lobby. "I know, it's silly; we live about fifteen minutes away. I just thought it would be nice if we were on neutral territory tonight."

"I'm in," Jenna replied.

Then, Bailey had a thought.

"Is there any chance I could convince you to go somewhere with me? It's close by."

"I'll go anywhere you want, Bailey Sayers," Jenna replied and kissed her cheek.

Bailey smiled at her and tugged on Jenna's hand. A few moments later, they were in Bailey's car, heading toward their destination. When she pulled into the parking lot, Bailey turned off the car. She climbed out and waited for Jenna to do the same. Then, she took Jenna by the hand and walked them to the spot.

"It was here," Bailey said.

"What was here?" Jenna looked around. "Oh," she said. "It *was* here."

"When I stopped you that day after graduation, it was to ask you out on a date," Bailey shared. "I chickened out, obviously."

"I can't believe that was ten years ago," Jenna said as she looked around at their old high school campus. "I knew back then. I mean, I *suspected* what I felt for you was more than friendship, and I didn't say anything either, Bails." She took both of Bailey's hands in her own. "We're here now, though."

"I'm in, Jenna. I'm in this. I want everything with you. It's always been you for me. You know that, right?"

"I know." Jenna smiled widely. "It's always been you for me."

"We're together now. This is it." Bailey nodded. "No more chickening out or being so scared we push the other person away, okay?"

"Okay." Jenna's tears welled up in her eyes again. "I missed you so much, Bailey." She wrapped her arms around Bailey's neck. "When we get back to the hotel, I need you to hold me, okay? I need to feel you."

Bailey squeezed her tightly and replied, "I'll hold you forever, Jenna Cabot."

\*\*\*

Later, at the hotel, Bailey had every intention of only holding Jenna through the night. She had gotten them a room only because it meant that if they needed a private place to talk, they could do so there. They had waited to have this date for so long. While it was an odd first date, to say the least, it seemed like a perfect opportunity for the two of them to finally see one another again at the reunion celebrating high school.

The room wasn't fancy, but it had a minibar. Bailey took two bottles of red wine and poured them each a glass. It was almost two in the morning. They were both tired but running high on being together again. Bailey presented Jenna with the glass. She took it from her position sitting on the side of the bed, tipped it to her lips to take a sip, and set the glass down on the table next to the bed. Then, she just stared up at Bailey, who, in turn, stared down at her.

"I guess we didn't really talk about what happens next," Bailey said, took a drink herself, and rested her glass next to Jenna's on the table.

"You mean sex?" Jenna asked directly as her eyes roamed Bailey's body. "Because I would like that to happen next, Bails."

"Jenna!" Bailey chuckled lightly.

"What?" Jenna laughed and grabbed Bailey's hips. Her expression grew serious then, and she said, "Take off your clothes, Bail."

"You don't want to wait?"

"For another ten years?" Jenna asked seriously. "No, I don't want to wait anymore. You spent all of high school and beyond waiting for me, and I've spent, like, the past five years waiting for you. We are done waiting for each other," she said. "Now, take off your clothes, Bailey."

"You got bossy," Bailey replied and offered her a wink.

Jenna's expression did not change. She wanted Bailey; she wanted Bailey naked, and she wanted Bailey naked now. Bailey didn't want to disappoint Jenna. She loved how dark Jenna's eyes got when she was turned on. She loved the expression on Jenna's face. It was the same one she saw that day in her bedroom all those years ago. Bailey complied. Slowly, while Jenna watched her closely, she disrobed until she was left only in a pair of white boy shorts. Jenna licked her lips, causing Bailey to soak her boy shorts all the way through. Then, Jenna pointed, and Bailey pulled them down her legs and kicked them off.

Jenna continued to stare at her. As she sat there, in her dress, Bailey was stark naked and being scrutinized. Jenna smirked that sexy smirk, reached for Bailey's hands, and pulled her toward herself. She spread her own legs to allow Bailey to stand between them. Then, Jenna's lips were on Bailey's skin. They kissed between her breasts, moved higher to Bailey's collarbone, and then lower again to Bailey's breasts. When Jenna looked up at her, Bailey's hands went to Jenna's hair.

"I love you," Bailey offered.

"I love you," Jenna said.

She stood then, moving Bailey back a little as she did. She lifted her own arms, giving Bailey the signal, and Bailey reached around and unzipped Jenna's dress. With a few strategic movements, Jenna's dress was on the floor. Bailey turned Jenna around in her arms before she unclasped her bra, ran her hands up the straps, and slid them off Jenna's shoulders. Jenna let it fall to the floor while Bailey kissed her back and neck, bringing her hands up Jenna's abdomen before clasping her breasts in her hands. Jenna turned her head slightly. Bailey kissed her neck, nibbled on her earlobe, and repeated the action on the other side. She reached down, with Jenna still facing away from her, and pulled at the waistband of her panties. Then, Bailey lowered them, going along with them to the floor. She kissed the back of Jenna's thighs, her ass, and turned Jenna around.

She breathed Jenna in, kissed the inside of her thighs, her abdomen, and stood in front of her. They stared at one another without touching, somehow knowing this was an important moment for them. Maybe it was the most important moment they'd ever had or would ever have. Bailey stepped into Jenna, placed her arms on Jenna's hips, and kissed her. She kissed her slowly, while her arms snaked around Jenna's waist and rubbed up and down her back. Bailey kissed her slowly as Jenna's tongue met her own, and they danced together. She kissed Jenna slowly because she had wanted to kiss this woman every single day for as long as she could remember.

When she pushed Jenna back slightly, and Jenna's legs hit the side of the bed, she let go of Jenna's waist and allowed her to fall back. They settled into the bed together, with Bailey lying on top. Jenna's arms moved to Bailey's neck and pulled her down into herself. Bailey could tell Jenna wanted it fast, but Bailey only wanted slow right now. She planned to savor Jenna Cabot. She knew they had forever this time. They were going to make it work now, because they had tried everything else, and being apart hadn't worked for either of them. They were better together. They were supposed to be together.

Bailey covered Jenna's body with her own, and she kissed her slowly again. Jenna tried to move the kiss at a faster pace, but Bailey held firm to the slow style of getting to know one another in this way again. Her lips moved to Jenna's neck, and it didn't take long for Jenna's hips to begin to move up, attempting to locate the friction she craved. Bailey smirked against Jenna's skin but continued at her pace. Her lips moved to the other side of Jenna's neck. Then, she moved lower. Her mouth covered Jenna's breast, pulling the nipple into her mouth and sucking softly and slowly until she let it go with a pop. She also felt a corresponding hip lift off the bed.

"Bails…" Jenna let out.

"Let me, please," Bailey begged as she took Jenna's other nipple into her mouth.

Jenna stopped moving her hips, which caused Bailey to smile as she moved her mouth down Jenna's stomach to circle her navel with her tongue. Jenna gasped when it jutted inside quickly before repeating its circle.

"Bailey?" Jenna asked softly.

Bailey lifted her head to meet Jenna's eyes.

"This is all I've ever wanted; *you* are all I've ever wanted," Jenna stated.

With that, Bailey moved lower. She took Jenna into her mouth, enjoying the slow pace and making Jenna squirm beneath her until she came with Bailey's name on her tongue. When Bailey went to slide back up Jenna's body, Jenna held on to Bailey's hips, shook her head, and gave her that sexy smirk. She pulled Bailey's hips up and up farther, until Bailey understood her meaning. She positioned herself over Jenna's face, spread her palms on the wall behind the bed, and lowered her center over Jenna's mouth. When Jenna's tongue slowly raked up her clit, Bailey nearly came that very moment.

\*\*\*

Bailey rolled over in her sleep. She wiped her eyes as she tried to open them, reaching to her right just to feel an empty bed. Her eyes shot open, and she turned her head to see that Jenna wasn't next to her.

"Relax, Bails. I'm right here," Jenna said.

Bailey turned her head toward the bathroom to see Jenna coming out of it, still wearing the t-shirt and underwear from the night before. She then moved to sit on the side of the bed next to Bailey.

"Morning," Jenna said and placed her hand on top of Bailey's.

"Good morning," Bailey replied. "You're so cute sometimes," Bailey smiled up at Jenna in her borrowed shirt, and then her face turned serious again, "I want us to do things right this time."

"Me too," Jenna agreed.

"I love you," Bailey said.

Jenna slid back into bed next to her and replied, "I love you, too."

Bailey's fingers moved into Jenna's hair, toying with the loose ends. She kissed Jenna softly while Jenna's hands slowly roamed Bailey's naked back. Jenna moaned into Bailey's mouth, and Bailey felt Jenna's leg lift, spreading herself for Bailey's hand. Bailey put her thigh between Jenna's and slid her hand into Jenna's panties. Jenna was already wet, as if she'd been waiting for Bailey to wake up and touch her again. As Bailey stroked her, Jenna kissed her. Bailey brought her to orgasm once before sliding her hand lower and entering Jenna just as she was coming down. Jenna stopped kissing her then and rolled onto her back. Bailey took a hint and climbed on top, and without removing Jenna's underwear, she moved in and out of her with ease. She was now staring down at Jenna in wonder. How had they managed to get this lucky? They'd gone through so much alone and so much together, but they were finally here.

"Do you realize we've never done this?" Jenna said moments after she lay her head on Bailey's chest.

"I'm pretty sure we did this last night and a few more times before that," Bailey replied while sliding her hand up and down Jenna's back.

Jenna chuckled against her chest and said, "I meant the waking up with each other part; we've never done that before."

"I guess we haven't," Bailey agreed. "It's nice."

"Yes, it is. I want to do it all the time, Bails."

"Okay," Bailey said.

Jenna lifted her head up to stare down at Bailey, gave her a wink, and climbed on top of her.

"I mean it, Bailey. Ten years, we've waited. I want every day with you," Jenna said as her fingertips grazed the skin of Bailey's stomach.

"I'm in, Jenna. No arguments here," Bailey said as she held onto Jenna's hips.

"Bails, I'm asking you to look at houses with me," Jenna said as she smiled down.

"Houses?" Bailey lifted an eyebrow.

"You want one; I want one." Jenna paused and grasped Bailey's breasts in her hands. "Let's get one together."

"Are you getting me turned on just so you can convince me to buy a house with you?"

"Were you not already turned on? If not, I was doing something wrong a minute ago. I thought me saying your name when I came would do something to you," Jenna teased.

"Oh, it did." Bailey lifted her hips once before

lowering them down just as quickly, causing Jenna to laugh. "We've never lived together, Jen. Are you sure?"

"I'm sure I don't want to be without you again." Jenna reached down between Bailey's legs and cupped her sex. "It'll take us time to find a place." She slid a finger between Bailey's folds, causing Bailey to lift her hips slightly again. "And I plan to spend every night with you before that; my place or your place, it doesn't matter." She lowered her fingers to Bailey's entrance. Her hips were still situated against Bailey's. "Bails, this is it. This is us," Jenna said as she entered her.

Bailey responded by gripping Jenna's hips and encouraging her farther inside.

"It's only ever felt this good with you," Bailey said as Jenna filled her completely.

"Because it's supposed to be this way," Jenna replied.

They rocked together like that until Bailey writhed beneath her near orgasm, watching Jenna rub herself on Bailey's skin. Somehow, even though Jenna still had her panties on, it was the sexiest thing in the world. Bailey stared up into Jenna's eyes and held on to them as she came.

"I missed those eyes when we're like this," Bailey said after she came down.

"They missed what they're seeing right now."

\*\*\*

"Sam has a daughter; that's so crazy to me," Bailey said.

"She does, Bails. That's what happens when a woman gets pregnant – about nine months later, a baby pops out." Jenna laughed at her own teasing.

"You're hilarious," Bailey said as she climbed on top of Jenna to straddle her. "Did you do it?" she asked.

"I did." Jenna gripped Bailey's hips. "I called the bank. We have an appointment for early next week."

"So, we're really going to buy a house? You and me?"

"We're just getting the process started, babe." Jenna ran her hands up Bailey's back under her shirt. "It'll take a while, but yes, I want a house with you. I want a home for us and for whatever little ones we have one day."

They were on the sofa in Bailey's apartment. Jenna had been staying over fairly regularly since the night of the reunion. When she wasn't at Bailey's place, Bailey was at her place. Jenna had meant it when she said she didn't want to spend another night apart. Bailey didn't want another night alone, either. Lying next to the love of her life, falling asleep next to her, waking up the same way, and having talks like this where they discuss their future, made everything they'd been through worth it.

"How many little ones are we having? I'm thinking we should babysit Sam's first to see how much we can actually handle before we commit to any particular number," Bailey offered.

Jenna placed one hand on Bailey's stomach and used her other hand to lift Bailey's t-shirt. She looked at her hand before her hazel eyes met Bailey's.

"When I was with Joel, he used to talk about having kids one day," Jenna began. "Every time he would bring it up, I couldn't imagine doing that with him." She paused. "It's terrible, I know. I just knew it wasn't his kids I wanted to have someday."

"Mine?" Bailey asked and placed her hand on top of the one Jenna had on her stomach.

Jenna nodded silently.

"That night," Bailey continued, "after our first time together, I remember thinking about what it would be like to be with you. I was a kid back then, but I'd picture moments like this. We'd just be lying around, watching TV, or even working side by side. I didn't even know what we were working on; it was just us with laptops." She laughed, and Jenna joined in as she rubbed Bailey's stomach. "I thought about this stuff back then; but even with Callie and Alyson, I never got that far. I was in a relationship with both of them, but when I saw those future steps, they were always with you."

"We're in the future now, I think," Jenna said, leaned forward, and kissed Bailey's stomach. "I love just sitting around the house with you. I loved going to meet Sam's new baby with you. I loved watching you with her and how you looked up at me in that moment where you held her for the first time. I could picture you and I doing that with our own daughter. And it wasn't just one day, Bails; it was one day soon."

"We should probably find that house first, Jen. This apartment is not big enough for all of us," Bailey replied.

"Hey, Bail?" Jenna said, suddenly serious.

"Yeah?"

Jenna shook her head as if trying to convince herself not to say something and, instead, said, "Never mind. Let's pull up some listings and take a look."

\*\*\*

"We're very good, yes," Jenna said into her phone.

She had been on the phone with her best friend, Andrea, for the past hour. Bailey had unpacked half the stuff in the bathroom, taken a shower, and re-entered the bedroom to find her girlfriend still on the phone. She shook her head and laughed silently. Jenna and Andrea hadn't been able to talk all that much lately with Jenna's promotion at work and the two of them finally moving into their new house. Jenna smiled at Bailey, who was wearing a towel and nothing else.

"Like a miracle," Jenna said and winked at Bailey.

Bailey wasn't sure to what Jenna was referring, but Jenna's wink had the exhaustion from the move dissipating very quickly. Jenna was lying on their bed in a pair of very short shorts and a tank top. It was *their* bed. It wasn't Bailey's bed that Jenna sometimes slept in or Jenna's bed that Bailey hated because it was way too firm. It was the bed they'd gone to the store to pick out together. Bailey knelt in front of Jenna on the bed, released the towel from the front, and let it fall. She then rubbed her hands up and down Jenna's bare legs.

"Bails." Jenna laughed as Bailey tickled the underside of her knees. Then, Jenna said, "What? No."

Bailey assumed Andrea had picked up on what Bailey was doing to Jenna. She lifted an eyebrow at Jenna before reaching for Jenna's tank top to pull it back up and over her head while Jenna attempted to balance the phone call with Bailey's touches. She laughed a little more as Bailey slid shorts off her body, followed quickly by Jenna's panties.

"Yeah, can't wait." Jenna watched Bailey's lips touch her skin on the inside of her thigh. "Bailey," she whispered as she covered the phone with her hand. "Babe, stop it," she repeated before moving her hand out of the way. "I can't wait to see you," she said that to Andrea and then followed it with, "Oh, she's treating me right." Bailey's head moved to Jenna's center, and she kissed her there softly before she nuzzled her, causing ripples of pleasure to shoot through Jenna. "Okay. Sorry, Andy. I've got to go."

Jenna hung up the phone. Then, Bailey lifted up to straddle her. She had managed to get Jenna naked for the first time in their bed, in their new home. They'd done the back and forth with their apartments until they found their dream starter home. They'd done it right this time. They didn't speed through everything to make up for what they had missed. They didn't go so slow that they'd never see their dreams become a reality. They didn't run when it got hard. Tonight would be their first official night of living together, despite the fact that they'd basically been living together since the reunion. They'd had all the standard arguments a new couple living together would have, in their apartments, and they had a good routine between them now. Bailey couldn't be happier than she was in this moment. She was staring deeply into Jenna's eyes; and while there was desire there, there was also love. There was *always* love. Bailey smiled and hoped her own love for Jenna was reflected in her eyes.

"Hey, let's go outside," Jenna said suddenly.

"We're naked, Jenna. I just got you completely naked, and I plan to do things with that nakedness now," Bailey replied.

"Outside, Bails. We have a fenced backyard now." Jenna winked, shifted Bailey off her body, and moved to stand. "Come on, be naked outside with me."

"If that's what you want, babe, I'm in," Bailey replied as she laughed.

"Do me a favor – grab two blankets: one for under and one for us to share." Jenna held up two fingers and wiggled her eyebrows.

"You're lucky I've already unpacked the linens," Bailey replied and went to the linen closet just outside their bedroom.

Jenna rushed past her down the stairs and out to the backyard. Bailey made a stop in the kitchen where she'd left something on the counter, grabbed it, and headed out to join her. She put her item on the grass and laid out the blanket. Jenna turned to her side as if blocking something from view after she sat on top of it. Bailey sat in front of her for a moment, picked up her item, and handed it to her girlfriend.

"Happy anniversary, Jen," Bailey said.

"We said no gifts, Bails. We just bought a house, babe."

"Just open it, Jen."

Jenna took the thin dark-green velvety box from Bailey's hand and opened it to reveal the diamond-heart necklace Bailey had bought her. It had been the best anniversary Bailey had ever celebrated. They had eaten takeout on top of boxes, continued unpacking their things together, and then moved to their bedroom where Andrea had called Jenna, and Bailey had unpacked the bathroom and taken a shower. Now, she was sitting naked on the blanket with the woman she knew she would one day marry and raise children with.

"Bails, this is beautiful," Jenna said. "Put it on me."

She held it up and moved the box to the grass. Then, she passed Bailey the necklace and turned around in her spot. Bailey clasped the necklace around her neck, kissed her shoulder, and Jenna turned back around to face her. Jenna then reached for the heart around her neck, looked up at Bailey, and smiled with tears welling in her eyes.

"I love you, Jen." Bailey leaned over Jenna and kissed her, causing Jenna to lower her body onto the blanket. "And I have every intention of taking advantage of you being naked right now." She kissed Jenna again.

"Can you wait for just a second?" Jenna asked softly. "I have a gift for you, too," she added.

Bailey pulled up and straddled her. She *could* wait; Bailey was lying in the backyard with her soulmate. They would soon be making love and staring up at the stars. Jenna placed a ring box on her own stomach and looked into Bailey's eyes.

"Jen…"

"Hey, Bail?" she said with a hopeful smile.

# PATH I & II: EPILOGUE

When Bailey made her vows, this is what they sounded like:

*"Jen, you are my best friend. I have loved you since that first day, freshman year, when you hung that mirror in your locker."* Bailey laughed, and Jenna laughed, too. *"You are the only person I ever wanted to have this with, and I still can't believe I get to have it with you. I promise to laugh with you, cry with you, and grow with you. I will love you when we are together and when we are apart. I promise to support your dreams and respect our differences. I promise to love you and be by your side through all the days and nights of our lives because there's no one else I want to wake up next to, Jenna Cabot."*

When Jenna made her vows, this is what they sounded like:

*"I choose you, Bails. I have chosen you over and over in this life. You were my first love, and you're my forever love. I can't wait to discover new things with you, go on new adventures together, and build our family. I am yours. I marry you with no hesitation or doubt, and my commitment to you*

*is absolute. You are the love of my life, the other half of me, and I love how you make me a better person just because you're in my life. I love you, Bailey Sayers."*

When Andrea gave her maid of honor speech, it sounded like this:

*"I'll keep this short because I know Sam, here, is chomping at the bit to deliver her speech,"* Andrea began. *"They say that a successful marriage requires falling in love many times, always with the same person. Well, these two really did that, didn't they?"* She took a pause for laughter, which she received. *"Many of us have been lucky to fall in love before. Real love, though, is when you are able to fall in love with that same person over and over again. It's when you're willing to work through all the hard times and the even more difficult times to get back to the happy times. It's when you continue to come back to one another for over a decade – like these two, because they just couldn't see their lives with anyone else. That's love. That's what we're celebrating today. To Bailey and Jenna!"*

When Samantha gave her maid of honor speech, it sounded like this:

*"You may all know, I am fiercely protective of Bailey. I would do anything for her. She is one of the most important people in my life. We have known one another since grade school, and she's been the one constant in my life as we've gone through all the changes life brings. Over the years, we have laughed together, cried together, and had so many amazing memories. I am truly blessed to have Bails in my life. She's been a sister to me, a sister-in-law to my husband, and now, the best aunt in the world for my daughter. Since I am so protective of her, though, you can imagine how skeptical of Jenna Cabot I was when Bailey first told me how she felt about her. Now, keep in mind, this was all the way back in college.*

*While we'd all gone to school together, I didn't know Jenna the way Bailey did. When Bails told me that they just kept missing one another because of one circumstance or another, I both wanted Jenna to disappear forever and never leave Bails at the same time, because, as the best friend, the most important thing to me is that Bailey is happy. No matter what they had to go through to get here, though, Bailey is happy now. Jenna makes her happy. So, when I heard Bailey say in her vows today that Jenna is actually her best friend, I was not offended in the slightest."* Samantha paused for laughter from the crowd, including Bailey and Jenna. *"Okay, I was a little offended... But I will forgive her because Jenna should be that person to her now. Your wife should be your best friend, Bails. I am so happy you two found a way to one another."*

When Bailey and Jenna danced at their reception, it was to the first song they ever danced to while alone in their new house. It had been slow and romantic, and the song played in their kitchen while they'd been cooking dinner. Bailey had stopped Jenna's hand from stirring and took her in her arms. They'd danced pressed together like that in their kitchen, and they danced pressed together in the same way in front of their friends and family, celebrating their love.

When they made love for the first time after becoming wives, it was slow and deliberate. They touched one another everywhere and repeatedly. When they woke up together for the first time after their wedding, Bailey made breakfast, and Jenna made them coffee. They ate at their kitchen table in relative silence while they both enjoyed the sounds of their rings clanging against their mugs.

When they went on their honeymoon, it was to a place they could explore together, each for the first time. They backpacked, they relaxed, they ate food they'd never likely eat again, and managed to make a couple of vacation friends. They made love both indoors and out, and both fast and slow. When they returned from their honeymoon, they showed their friends and families their pictures and regaled them with their stories.

When Bailey decided to start her own company, Jenna was there to help her with the business plan. She gave her the encouragement when Bailey wanted to back down; she gave her wife the shoulder massages when Bailey got stressed. When Jenna got a promotion at work that required her to travel more, it was an adjustment for the both of them. Jenna did her part by trying to make her trips as short as possible whenever she could, and Bailey did her part by going along with Jenna when she could, just so she wouldn't have to go the extra days without seeing her wife.

When they fought for the first time, *really* fought, they both cried. They both yelled. They both got quiet. They both wondered how they would get through it when neither of them seemed to be able to come up with a solution. When they fought for the first time, they had to remind themselves of what it was like to be without the other. They had to remember that they would always be better together. They had to remember those vows they made that day in front of everyone they loved, and they had to be willing to talk it out; even when it hurt, even when they cried.

When they held their child in their arms for the first time, neither of them ever thought it would get better than that moment. Bailey and Jenna cried in that moment. They laughed in that moment. They loved more than they ever thought possible in that moment.

Life is all about the *moments*, moments that add up. Sometimes, we live in them. We stop to make a mental note that this is something we'll want to remember forever. Maybe it was that moment you became a parent for the first time and you held the baby in your arms.

There are so many moments in our lives. There went one just now. You just lived a moment. Did you stop to think about what happened next? Have you ever wondered if you had one moment in your life back to change, what that moment might be? Would you really change it? Would you be too scared to take that chance? What if you could know how it would all work out ahead of time? Would you take the chance then? And if that were possible, would any of us?